NO
perfect
COUPLE

IMPERFECTION SERIES BOOK 3

Award-winning Author
DD LORENZO

Chapter 1

Carter

Sang Run Cemetery
McHenry, MD

I've never liked cemeteries. There is an illusion of peace and tranquility, but it's just that—an illusion. I don't feel anything resembling peace when I come here, only anger. They say that death is a void, but I think the only one who feels nothing is the one who's in the grave. I feel sick. The headache I've had for the last hour is mixing with an upset stomach. Today is the last time I'm planning to come here and I feel like I owe Lacey an explanation.

. . .

I'VE ONLY BEEN HERE ONCE BEFORE, Lace, but you know that. I didn't talk to you then. I just sat down on the mound of dirt covering you. I know it doesn't make sense, but I was pissed at you for leaving me.

While I was driving here today, memories messed with my head. I've done a lot of driving over the past few months. You know I do that when I need to think about things. I've always tried to be the person who steps up to the plate when they're needed. Now Declan needs me. I think you would be proud of me. I packed everything and am taking Cody with me. I'm leaving the mountains for the beach. I don't know when I'll be back, Lace.

You don't need me anymore, and I can't figure out what to do with myself since you left. This thing with Declan, well, I could be there with him for a while, and maybe it's a good thing, because I hate it here. The Band-Aid rips off my heart every time I think of how I lost you. I've left my job, closed up the house, and am headed down there now. The change of scenery is as much to help him as it is for my sanity. Just remember; I love you, sweetheart. I always will.

Chapter 2

Carter

T*he ripple effect.* I rotated a silver-dollar-sized stone in the palm of my hand as I mulled the term over in my mind. Sitting at the edge of the pier, my long legs dangled over the end of the weathered wood. The tips of my worn Katahdin boots barely grazed the surface of the water, while the breeze messed with my hair. I stared at my reflection in the lake, knowing one thing was for sure—I'd never be a pretty-boy like my brother, and that suited me just fine.

There were only two of us. Declan was the good-looking one; I was the rough and dirty one. The differences between us meant we weren't competitive in any area. I think that's the reason we always got along so well.

Now, life as I knew it was about to change again.

After living in Ocean City for a year, I'd come back to my home on Deep Creek Lake. Though I hated to admit it, my brother's accident had been a distraction from mourning the loss of my wife. At least now I felt like I could manage the grief. Accepting her death hadn't become easier, just easier to bear.

Staring ahead at the water, I mindlessly chucked the handful of rocks I'd grabbed on my way down to the pier. One by one, I pitched them, sometimes skipping a stone across the lake's smooth surface. It was a boyhood habit, something I did when I couldn't think clearly. As I threw them, I listened for the *kerplunk* sound and watched the ripples created by the disruption. Now that I'd finally come home, I welcomed the solitude. Unlike the beach, where I was surrounded by people, there wasn't a soul to disturb me. My place at the lake was secluded and quiet. Sometimes too quiet due to my wife's absence.

When Lacey was alive, I'd slip away from the world, and from her, to wind down. I hadn't realized how many little things made me happy until they no longer did, but happy was the last word I'd use to describe what I felt today. Coming home meant I had to face the remains of my life. It was a good thing, but it didn't feel like it.

Avoidance. Diversion. Ignorance. Whatever you called it, had become my survival technique. It worked when I was at the beach, but now that I was home it was nearly impossible. I couldn't avoid driving on the road where Lacey had been killed—plowed down while riding her bike. Too many scenarios ran through my head. The worst was wondering if she'd been scared or if she called out for me, and I wasn't there. I tortured myself while each day became just another twenty-four hours I survived without her. One thousand, four hundred, and forty minutes. Eighty-six thousand and four hundred seconds of breathing air. I had to take my life back. A life that I no longer shared with Lacey.

I was an introvert; Lacey was the outgoing one. Now that I was no longer busy with the Ocean City crowd, I wondered how much of a hermit I'd become. I would always screw up in the social life department and happily let Lacey take the lead. She was great at reminding me who to talk to or what to say. She made me take off the invisible cop hat, because, when I wore it, I was intimidating. All of that had come to an end when I received the call telling me she was gone.

Grief had many stages and I felt like I was stuck in one. There were times when I felt mutilated and raw. The days were a blur of different tasks and activities, and while living with my brother, I'd become quite an actor. But I didn't want to be the kind of man who lived up to everyone's expectations. Now that I was home, I only wanted to be myself. I lacked a sparkling personality and I didn't know if it would be too much trouble to develop one. It's a hard thing to admit that the only reason people love you is that you pretend to be what they need. Thinking back on my life, I realized I'd never been accepted or loved for just being me. I had even tried to be the man that I thought Lacey wanted me to be. Fast forward to now. There was no one I wanted to impress. I could put away all the different personas I had developed. Now I could just... be.

The hardest part of arriving back home had been walking into the empty house. Memories of Lacey had both consoled and assaulted me. I hadn't changed anything since her death, and impressions of her were everywhere, like the unfinished scrapbook pieces still sitting on her desk. I'd even detected the slightest hint of her perfume. Cody had trudged on massive paws through each of the rooms, making her inspection. She was moving slower than she used to. Could dogs get depressed? Lacey and I had always said, unlike any dog we'd ever known, we could see a smile on Cody's lips. Today she wasn't smiling. She'd followed me to the room I didn't want to enter. The one I dreaded—our bedroom.

I'd paused at the molded pine door and leaned against the frame. Nausea sucker-punched me. Memories had rushed back, and feelings of loss and emptiness shrouded me. I'd quickly backed out of the room, defeated, closed the door, and made my way through the kitchen and out of the house, through the back door.

On my way to the pier, I'd scooped up some rocks, and then I sat, throwing away some mental garbage.

With the toss of the stones, I'd assigned a thought to each one. As the recollections pulled me through the awful muck and mire, I dealt with the pain in my own way. I'd been at it for a while when I felt Cody approach. Her weight had made the old boards bounce. She had a distinct sound and feel as she trotted up to me, nudging my shoulder.

"Hi, girl." Her cold nose touched the skin at my neck, and I sank a hand into her thick coat. "Did you get lonely up there all by yourself?"

Lonely. Such a small word to hold so much meaning. I had to find a new term to focus on, and not concentrate so much on how the ripple effect played into my life. One that would motivate me to locate the man I'd become. A man living without the woman he loved. A man discovering who he really was.

Chapter 3

Manuel

As he neared his destination, Manuel Vallega's beautiful Italian loafers scuffed against the metal nosing on the stairs. He had just one thing on his mind, Marianna.

Already he didn't care for the staff in this establishment. They were pompous and arrogant. The guards masqueraded as medical personnel. Although they were in actuality doctors and nurses, their jurisdiction over what the patients could and could not do reinforced my dislike for people like them. They always appeared to be on ego trips. Marianna deserved better than this.

His friends would call him Manny—if he had friends. He didn't allow himself the luxury of letting people get too close or personal. He did, however, allow a few select ones the honor of addressing him casually. Marianna was most definitely someone he'd allowed to reside within that small circle. Manny was used to having what he wanted, giving orders, not taking them, or having anyone dictate to him. The people at this facility sprinkled his temperament with a dust of agitation. He found himself entertaining thoughts of the pleasure it would give him to snap a few of their necks. He could almost feel them in his hands. It intensified when the staff dared to give him dismissive looks. Knowing how to play their game, he managed his disdain and skillfully reined in his anger so it appeared to be simply a bad attitude, something he was sure the staff had dealt with in abundance.

The guard led him into a gray room. He seated himself at a lackluster table. Confident that both his appearance and aura were intimidating, he leaned across the top of it. One of his biceps was almost the diameter of the guard's head. As he casually flexed, he detected a tic at the corner of the guard's eye. It made him question whether the man was competent to watch over the room. Although Manny had experienced his share of jail time, none of the personnel here would recognize him. Clifton T. Perkins Hospital Center was a place for criminals requiring psychiatric evaluation and treatment. Questions regarding Marianna's mental state raised the possibility of a not criminally responsible (NCR) defense, which worked to his advantage, and hers. If she was deemed incompetent to stand trial, he might be able to put a few doctors and judges in his pocket to have her released into his custody. So far, Manny's dealings hadn't caught the attention of the DEA, so he resided under the radar of the judicial system. He intended to keep it that way until he could get Marianna back to Colombia.

Marianna had been in this place for months. What angered Manny most was that, as he was concentrating on maintaining the family business, no one had notified him of her arrest. He'd seen it on a televised news report, along with the rest of the world. This situation was partially his fault. He had allowed Marianna to run wild, to sow her oats, so to speak. That had been a mistake and two of his men paid for that mistake with their lives. Their job had been to monitor her and report back to him. Apparently, they hadn't thought it necessary to inform him that Marianna considered hit and run to be an acceptable way to dispose of those who inconvenienced her. Marianna, reinvented as Marisol Franzi, had been charged with manslaughter in the death of a Maryland State Trooper's wife. Manny would never understand why his men always reported her trivial incidents of drunkenness and infidelity but had failed to mention this.

Big mistake. Marianna's arrest had been front-page news. Why wouldn't it be? She was an exceptional woman, a media favorite. A supermodel. He had expected her to be in the tabloids for her antics such as catfights, men, or drugs. But a manslaughter charge was careless. Marianna knew better than to place herself in the crosshairs of law enforcement. Now it was time to rein her in because he didn't have time for this type of nonsense. He had a business to run.

Transitions in leadership were never easy. The operation in Colombia required daily attention. After Marianna's father had died, the duty of running the cocaine business fell to Manny. He had also taken responsibility for Carlos's family upon himself. He now controlled Marianna's fate, as well as that of her mother and siblings. With his permission, Marianna had accepted a modeling position and reinvented herself in New York. It served two purposes—making her happy and allowing him the time to assure a smooth transition of leadership. At first, he'd ensured that Marianna was closely monitored, but since it seemed she'd merely established a bitchy reputation and provided fodder for the gossips with regard to her partying ways, he had relaxed and let her have her fun. Unfortunately, for her, she should have taken her family a bit more seriously. The cavalier attitude she'd developed may have been her undoing. He wouldn't allow that. Manny hadn't spoken with Marianna in almost a year. It didn't matter, though, because time did nothing to lessen his commitment to her. Love was a foreign concept to him. If he was capable of such an emotion, he'd feel it for Marianna. Instead, he could define other things that he felt for her. Responsibility. Anger. Lust.

Marianna's father, Carlos, had been good to him, but not in the ways most people would define the word. Hard as nails, he'd taken Manny in and groomed him in ways that would benefit the business. It was a privilege to be favored by the head of the Colombian Cartel. As a kid, Manny had been starving on the streets of Miami. He'd hustled anything of value, including himself. If not for Carlos, Manny might have become a statistic. Instead, Marianna's father had nurtured him, and he now held the position of head of the organization. He had money, power, and women at his disposal. He was the trustee of one of the most profitable, illegal operations in Colombia. He was feared and respected—which, in his opinion, was much better than being loved. He owed everything to the direction Carlos had given him. Manny had no idea who his birth father was, but he was certain the man was worthless. Then, again, to most people, Carlos had been a piece of shit. Manny held a different opinion. One of the first tasks that Carlos had assigned to Manny was following his daughter, Mari. She was young, independent, and headstrong, much like her father. Her twin Marchelle was docile and didn't cause her papi much concern.

Carlos hadn't trusted Mari. He'd said she was too hard-headed for her own good. He'd tried to break her —many times—but she was resilient and defiant. When Carlos had first given Manny the responsibility of watching over Mari, Manny hadn't formed an opinion of her one way or the other. His mindset was that of a soldier, and he'd preferred to think like one—with his head and not with his dick. He disassociated personal feelings from orders. They were to be followed, not questioned, and because Manny was loyal, Carlos had entrusted him with the care of a particular project, Marianna.

Concentrating on survival hadn't allowed Manny to pay much attention to Carlos's daughter, but as he'd matured, so did Marianna. Carlos had entrusted Manny with Marianna's protection. He'd also wanted to know everywhere she went and everything she did. Carlos had planned to use Marianna to secure an alliance with a rival cartel. She was nothing more than a bargaining chip. A tool to be used for acquisition. A pawn. Her beauty could seduce a snake from its skin. The Colombian heat made dressing light a necessity, and Marianna's choice of clothing made remaining indifferent nearly impossible. Her long legs faded into places he could only imagine as they disappeared beneath sheer dresses or short shorts. Manny's thoughts had diverted from protecting her body to taking it. Dangerous ideas for a man whose job was to obey without question. He'd been in the meeting with Carlos and the black-hearted bastard who'd be Marianna's owner. The kingpin of the rival cartel was much older and had a ruthless reputation with women. They were toys to be used, abused, and disposed of when broken. If the rumors were true, Marianna wouldn't live to see her twenty-first birthday, which was unacceptable.

He'd formed a plan to save Marianna. Appearance was everything in a game of trust, and he'd never given Carlos a reason to suspect him. He'd continued to do his job while detaching himself publicly. He allowed Marianna her seductive games while standing as stoic as one of those London guards he'd seen in photographs. He'd decided Marianna would be his. He continually ruminated scenarios that would assure that she would belong to him and no one else. There was only one fail-safe plan and it consumed his thoughts. When that day presented itself, he'd acted with stealth-like precision, executing every detail. Carlos's game had ended as Manny's had begun, and his role in Marianna's life had evolved. No longer was he simply her protector, he was her savior.

Chapter 4

Manuel

Time ticked by slowly. He'd been waiting longer than anticipated, and it was beginning to piss him off. Manny wasn't a man to waste time or resources. The delay tested his patience, but he had no choice in the matter. Soon Marianna would learn new rules. *His.* Her first lesson would be that there were consequences for not contacting him when something went wrong. His cell phone number was the first one programmed into Marianna's phone. She'd been given explicit instructions to communicate with him if she found herself in trouble. She hadn't listened and this angered him because she knew what was at stake. His brow raised as he entertained the thought that Marianna might be better served if he employed her father's methods of discipline. Carlos's beatings had a way of extracting obedience from tougher personalities than hers. Of course, he wouldn't allow anyone to lay a finger on her except himself. The thought of Marianna stripped and at his mercy put a smile on his lips. Perhaps he'd confine her to his bed. He was, after all, the one who'd given her freedom. He could just as easily take it away.

Manny, please!" she'd begged. "*Let me go to New York. Papi is gone. If I stay here, I have nothing. Don't worry. They've promised me a place to live and great money. I want to work for myself, not rely on your generosity. I can even take Marchelle with me. Two fewer people that you have to support.*

He'd liked hearing her beg. The sound of her pleas had painted pleasurable images in his mind, ones that had nothing to do with her travel plans. They had stared at each other for a long time. A test of wills. A child's game, in which the one who blinked first, lost. Finally, he'd given her his answer.

You can go to New York. But there are conditions.

She'd happily agreed to those conditions since it meant she got what she wanted. What Manny wanted was for her to trust him and the only way to get that was to let her go. Carlos's death had meant there was much work to do. Marianna had been barely an adult, but he allowed her to have the freedom she desired. True to her word, she'd taken care of her sister. He hadn't felt any concern for Marchelle, she was the one person who balanced Marianna. They were *yin* and *yang.* Bitter and sweet. Fury and calm. Now Marchelle was dead and Marianna was locked away from him. He had to get her under control before her actions undermined all of his efforts. His plan was to take her back to Colombia. There, she would be under his control. It would happen. He would do whatever was necessary to ensure the success of his intentions.

Manny watched as Marianna's escort directed her to the visitor's lounge. She was led in like a dog. He shifted to gain a better view, and the chair creaked with his movement. Marianna's face was a canvas colored in pride and indignance. Manny had anticipated a repentant, broken woman, so it pleased him to see they hadn't broken her spirit. Her guard encouraged her to move faster by daring to place his hand on her back, giving her a slight push. Manny scowled and clenched his jaw. Fire raged in Marianna's eyes. She was thinner than when he'd last seen her, too thin, in fact. She looked more victim than model. Her long hair hung lifeless around her shoulders, like a shroud. She appeared disheveled and poorly groomed. He understood some of the reason for her anger. Even as a teenager, Marianna would not have allowed someone to see her this way. He made a mental note to remedy her apparent lack of toiletries. All it would take was one phone call.

As Marianna passed through the final barrier separating them, she spotted Manny and their eyes connected. She snapped her arm out of the guard's hand in an act of defiance, then took a seat across from Manny, folded her hands on the table respectfully, and waited for him to speak.

"*Gorda.*" His tone was comforting as he covered her delicate hands with his large rough ones. He met her smile with one of his own.

Her eyes sparkled, dancing with emotion. "Manny, what are you doing here?" A rhythmic lilt filled her tone, making her sound more carefree than she should have been under the circumstances.

"I could ask you the same thing, *chica,*" he answered. "A misunderstanding, perhaps?" His tone held a warning, and, for a moment, worry clouded her face. But Marianna recovered quickly, the smile returning to her lips.

"I'm happy to see you, Manny. I don't get many visitors other than doctors, counselors, and my attorney. She took hold of his fingers, giving them a squeeze. "I missed you. I know you're here to rectify this. You have a talent for fixing things." She leaned in, giving him a perfect view down the vee of her thick cotton shirt.

Manny could tell she was trying to manipulate him, because they'd played this game before. His brow arched inquisitively, and he leaned into the back of the chair. "Chica, tell me why you're here."

"As you said," she quietly answered, "it was a misunderstanding." Marianna fluttered her lashes and gave him a seductive look. Sensing she was in trouble, she pulled her arms to her sides and pressed her breasts up and together to make them appear more voluptuous. Manny kept his eyes on her face. When Marianna received no response, her shoulders slumped, and her expression became resigned and helpless as she cut the act and spoke honestly. "I seem to find myself in the middle of many misunderstandings, don't I, Manny?"

He detected genuine sadness, a rare emotion for Marianna, and felt a speck of pity. "Yes, baby girl. You do." He spoke in a quiet tone. It was evident that she was shaken, and he mentally orchestrated what his next move should be. With Marianna, it was always a game of negotiation. He would make an offer, and she would counteroffer. She'd previously proved to be a worthy opponent. If he applied the same strategy now, it would give him a better ability to gauge her mental state. He reached for her hands. "Marianna—"

"I don't go by that name anymore, Manny," she interrupted. "I'm Marisol now."

If she'd spoken in an arrogant tone, he would have responded in kind, but resignation filled her. His words were spoken gently. "I know what you call yourself now, baby girl. But you'll always be Marianna to me."

Her expression relaxed as she gave a weak smile. "Then Marianna I'll be, but only for you."

Manny steered the conversation back to the matter at hand. "This *misunderstanding*," he emphasized. "You're in some serious trouble with this one."

Marianna dropped her chin. "I am." Her voice was barely a whisper. She was overcome with emotion for a moment, then looked up at him with pleading eyes. "They say I'm sick, Manny." Her eyes darted back and forth as she nervously glanced around the room. Satisfied no one was listening, she pulled as close to him as she could and whispered. "They say I become someone I'm not—especially when I'm angry. They want to give me medicine to control it. I'm not sure if it's true but I have to do what they say." As if she'd morphed into a different persona, her spine stiffened, and she gave him a determined look. "I think it's bullshit!" Her desperation had turned to defiance. This was the Marianna he knew. Her eyes shifted again as she scouted the room; a veil of paranoia came over her. "I don't like to take the pills, so I don't." A self-satisfied smirk twisted her lips. "There are ways to get around it, you know."

Manny analyzed her behavior, trying to sort through the mixture of confusion, sadness, and rebellion. Marianna had always been moody, but was there something more? Could the doctors be correct in their assessment and diagnosis of Bipolar Disorder? The matter warranted further discussion. Continuing his efforts to comfort her and set her mind at ease, he kept hold of her hands and shifted his body to shield her from the eyes of the staff. "They may be right, chica. I think you should take the medicine the doctors offer. If you cooperate with them, it could help my efforts to have you released."

As if she hadn't heard his intention to help with her release, she pinned him with a murderous look and pulled her hands from his grip. "Whose side are you on? I don't want to be peaceful; I want to be me! If people don't like me, screw them—and screw you too! I love myself the way I am!"

"And look where it's gotten you!" Manny's temper seeped through a crack in his composure, he seethed as the words strained through his teeth. "They're talking murder, Marianna. Vehicular homicide, not to mention the charges for the woman you held captive! I came here to get you out of this mess. Your antics have pulled me away from important business matters. You will do as I say, and before you decide to go off on me again, you'd better remember to whom you're speaking. I'll leave your ass in here to rot! At least here I can keep an eye on you."

Marianna's mood and tone morphed from defiant to desperate. "Manny, you can fix this; I know you can. Please get me out of here!"

Manny took the opportunity to remind her of her delinquency. "Why didn't you contact me when this happened? Your actions cost me time, money, and two of my men. I might have a way to get you out of this, but why should I?" His voice adopted a more malevolent tone. "You've gotten yourself in deep this time, Marianna. Perhaps I should just let the courts dictate your fate." He'd expected any response other than the one she gave. She bowed her head and obediently placed her hands in her lap, not saying a word. She maintained that posture for several moments. Knowing their time was nearly exhausted, he lowered his voice and addressed her. "Marianna, look at me."

She refused. "Now!" The order was issued under his breath but was compelling enough for her to respond. She peered up through thick lashes. "I'm going to do what I can to get you out of here. I want you home. In Colombia." He leaned in closer. "As far as I can tell, the authorities have no concrete evidence that you killed anyone. Reasonable doubt can be raised, especially in light of Marchelle's involvement." Surprise shone in her eyes as he continued. She'd been unaware that Manny knew the details of the case. "I'm gathering more information. The trooper's wife was killed by a car rented by Marchelle. Lucky for you, Marchelle was illegal and now she's dead." He narrowed his eyes. "If you behave, it gives me something to work with." He took her chin between his fingers. "The dead don't talk, Marianna. You'd do well to remember that."

Marianna jerked her chin from his hand. "Marchelle was driving the car." She saw the doubt in his eyes and set about convincing him. "It wasn't me, Manny. I was looking down at a magazine when Marchelle hit Lacey Sinclair. I thought it was an animal. If I'd known it was a person, I would have made her stop the car. I would never have left that woman in the road. I would have called for help." He wasn't convinced and she knew it. "You have to believe me," she pleaded. "I think Marchelle knew she'd hit a woman and got scared she would be deported. That's the only reason why she would have kept driving."

Manny tented his hands, joining his fingertips, as she put together pieces of a fabricated story. "*Mm-hmm.*"

Marianna tilted her head and looked at Manny, shocked. "You believe me, don't you?"

The corner of his mouth lifted; she couldn't tell if it was a half-smile or a sneer. Either could mean dangerous things for her. When he spoke, his voice was rough and graveled. "You would have done anything to save that woman? I don't think so, baby girl. I know you too well." His gaze intensified, burning a hole in any remnant of her composure. "I also know about your history with Declan Sinclair. That part of your life is over. From this point forward, you will not involve yourself with anyone but me. It was a mistake to let you have so much freedom. From now on, you do what I say and you will be honest with me, because, if not, I'll wash my hands of you."

Her eyes widened. "Manny," she said, softly. "I didn't think you... I didn't know... It's just, I thought we were, you know, convenient and—"

He glared at her, cutting her off midsentence. "Save it for your doctors, therapists, or even the press—

whomever you need to convince, chica. Do you think I'm a fool?"

"What do you want from me?" she whispered.

"Perfect behavior, nothing less. I need time to sort out the mess you've created. I have the *abogados* looking at the case. Hopefully they'll find something we can work with." He hated that his ability to touch her was limited. If he had his way, he would pull her into him, crushing her until she agreed to everything he said. Instead, he had to settle for taking her hand in feigned comfort, all the while tightening his grip around her delicate fingers. Pain registered on her face, and he saw she understood his hidden message. "The attorneys I've hired are skilled at what they do for me. I don't want you doing anything to compromise their efforts, understand?"

Marianna snapped her hand out of his grip. "I'm not afraid of you," she snarled. "I'm not some little girl you can manage anymore. I'm a grown woman."

"Marianna..." He said her name as a warning.

"I may be Marianna Hernandez to you, but to myself, I am Marisol Franzi! I have a new life—MY life —and I'm not going to let anyone take it away from me, not even you."

In that brief moment, Manny saw her father Carlos in her. She'd taken everything she learned from her father and put a feminine flavor to it. It had made her ruthless—a bitch—and it was evident she relished the role.

"Visit's over," the guard said as he approached.

Marianna raised her eyebrows, a pompous look glazing her expression. She was obviously pleased to have gotten the last word. *Or had she?*

Manny rose from his seat, his stature towering over her and the attendant. Marianna proudly lifted her chin, disguising any intimidation she may have felt behind a forced smile. Manny looked into her beautiful face. There was only a brief opportunity remaining to remind her of her place before she was escorted back to her room. He gave her a dismissive look. "I'll be back soon, Marianna." He then looked over her shoulder, addressing the man who stood behind her. "Thank you for escorting my wife back to her room."

Chapter 5

Marisol

She was angry. Livid, in fact. *Who in the hell does he think he is, dictating what I will or won't do?*

Marisol believed she and Manny were equals. She'd never depended on him, husband or not, and she certainly didn't consider herself to be his property. He didn't own the little girl he once knew. The only reason the marriage had occurred at all was to ensure her entry into the US. There had been very little contact. In fact, she couldn't remember before today the last time they'd spoken. She'd never sought his help. Her success was her own. *Damn him!*

Marisol knew Manny's game. He played puppeteer to her puppet. His conditions were about control. Their marriage was a formality, yet he had played the husband card—no, the owner card—from the moment he'd walked through the door. His parting statement was meant to make her feel intimidated. Did it work?

No!

Marisol refused to be a bug under Manny's microscope, but the truth was she had little choice if she wanted to get out of this situation. Manny was now a powerful man with powerful friends. She was confident judges and politicians were in his pocket, and if they could work the system to her benefit, she needed to do as Manny instructed. His visit had been unexpected, catching her off guard, but with cat-like reflexes, she'd rebounded to spin the event to her advantage. Men were easily manipulated once their ego was stroked, and Marisol had a reputation to protect. She pushed herself across the bed and leaned her back against the wall, pulling her knees up to her chest. The mood of the room was somber and was reflected in the lackluster paint and industrial furnishings. Marisol contemplated her options. Spending years in prison or in this hospital held no appeal; if she wanted to get out, she had to change her approach. Cooperating during therapy was a must, as was swallowing the pills they issued. In time, she'd have them all fooled, and time was a commodity she had in abundant supply. Manny may be the head of the cartel, but she was Carlos's daughter. Some things were inherited. Genetic. Her father's unsavory traits flowed through her veins, infusing her cells with his inventive DNA, including the insanity that ensured he'd been respected and feared. Her skin was as thick as her father's, overlapping muscles and veins that had been blown open by the endless possibilities. Life in the drug world had turned her father's brilliance to madness, changed Manny from victim to victor, and morphed her from a kingpin's pawn into a powerful and wealthy woman in her own right.

Marisol contemplated her escape from Clifton T. Perkins Hospital. She was determined to get out through whatever means were available. The lawyer who'd visited with Mr. Dietz was worthless. Manny's attorneys were of a higher caliber. She'd need to get into his good graces in order to have unlimited access to them. Her current forced seclusion was, hopefully, temporary, and rekindling a relationship with Manny could be fun, now that her father wasn't alive to interfere. She'd forgotten how attractive Manny was: tall, broad, and muscular with a handsome face. His eyes were a smoky gray, not common for a Latino. Perhaps her desire to get away from Colombia had made her overlook how sexy he truly was, but it hadn't escaped her notice today. His stature caused him to look too large in the visiting area, and he'd shifted uncomfortably. When he'd taken her hands, electricity had sparked, sending lusty messages. Her under-exercised libido was begging for release, and she cursed the sons of bitches who'd humiliated her in the press. Declan and his crew would pay for what they'd done to her.

A bloom of self-satisfaction made its way from Marisol's core, slithering through her veins until a smile snaked the corners of her lips. Ideas began to form, one by one. She would not only be restored to her former life, she would reemerge with a new one. A better one. And she would use Manny to do it.

Chapter 6

Aimee

"That's a wrap!"

I was thrilled that the day was over. The photographer appeared confident that the client would be pleased with the final product, and his enthusiasm indicated he'd gotten the shots he needed. Now we could return to the mainland, and, after a small party to celebrate our hard work, I could go home. We boarded the boat and left the island.

The location for the shoot had been beautiful, and I was in a good mood. Fleeting thoughts of my recent luck ran through my mind like effervescent bubbles. Though Marisol's incarceration was unfortunate for her, it had removed me from her shadow and catapulted me as Bella Matrix's newest star. The agency had distanced itself from the negative publicity. None of our clients wanted a connection with her now that she'd been arrested, and they preferred to replace her seductive look with my squeaky clean one.

Months had passed since Marisol's arrest. Although the events had changed some things in our small group of friends, other things remained the same. Declan's brother, Carter, shared a condo with Blake now that Aria and Declan were back together. I hadn't returned to live in New York, instead choosing to take a room in Paige's house while all of the details of replacing Marisol were worked out at Bella Matrix. Declan watched over Aria; his protectiveness with her always touched my heart. It was a side of him I'd never seen. Their wedding had been a magical experience, one I'd never forget. Other changes had occurred as well, and just like the seasons, new opportunities blossomed. Katherine was now Declan's assistant, elevating her from the confines of a receptionist role and freeing Declan from spending so much time at The Studio. Entrusting more of the day-to-day operation to Katherine's capable hands allowed him to spend more time working from home while Aria healed. A man who'd worked with Aria and her father had stepped up in her absence, so she'd decided to make him her partner. Juan Moreno was now a familiar face whenever we all got together, and I'd noticed on more than one occasion his compliments flustered the women.

Marisol's remand to the Perkins facility had happened soon after her arrest, and it didn't appear she'd be released anytime soon. Her attorney had argued she was in need of psychiatric help and thus was not responsible for her actions. *Psychiatric help? For what, bitchiness?* I hoped they'd keep her locked up and throw away the key.

Absentmindedly, I toyed with a sunlit curl. I was a smart girl. A product of the foster care system, I'd learned early lessons on fortune and misfortune. Opportunity hadn't been a regular visitor in my life and I could almost hear my social worker saying *don't look a gift horse in the mouth.*

Modeling had been a way out of a life going nowhere, and Marisol's misfortune was giving me a break in the industry. Since she was gone, I was no longer just one of the girls in the modeling pool. Bella Matrix had done damage control and made me their new poster child. I had a pretty good life for being a kid from the system. Not that I was complaining, but I'd been working at a grueling pace. There was only one drawback—I was tired. Exhausted would be a better description. I'd taken on a full schedule to prove the agency could count on me. The reward for being grateful and dedicated was I was making more money than I'd ever dreamed, however, I needed a break.

When I'd nervously approached Blake with a request for some time off, he could see I'd been over-worked and had pointed out that tiny lines and dark circles were beginning to appear around my eyes. Not exactly what I'd wanted to hear, but he'd also said that since the clients were happy, I could take whatever time I needed.

Finally, the time had come; this was my last job before going away. I looked forward to visiting my friends. In fact, Blake had offered to drive me to Ocean City when this job was over. I'd taken him up on the offer.

The two of us planned to meet Paige for dinner. She was now not only my friend, but my realtor. We'd had several conversations about finding me a place of my own where I could kick back and relax. I'd traveled to a few places in Maryland and found the state to be very versatile. With mountains to the west and the Atlantic Ocean to the east, there were many options. After viewing several properties online, I'd fallen in love with a most unusual house. In between jobs, I'd stolen away to see the property, and, although it would take a bit of work, the possibilities and potential for transforming it into my home excited me.

Also exciting was the opportunity to visit with Declan and Aria. I missed them. Declan was more a big brother than a friend. He'd talked me down from the ledge of fear several times since I'd been thrust into a brighter spotlight. On one occasion, after a bout of anxiety that had lasted almost a week, he'd sent Katherine to surprise me in New York. In true big brother fashion, he completed the surprise with theater tickets and dinner at one of our favorite restaurants. It was exactly what I needed.

Katherine had become a close friend. We had much in common, especially now that she understood the fashion world. I'd developed a tough shell as a result of my childhood. Declan was my first real friend and he was responsible for introducing me to his social circle. Having such good friends had taught me two things: one, it was okay to be myself, and two, not to take myself too seriously. Unlike some of the kids I grew up with, I was lucky. For a girl with no relatives, I had a great family.

Chapter 7

Aimee

As the boat powered closer to the shore, my excitement grew. The thought of escaping to Ocean City made me feel like I was going home. Not only would I be able to catch up with my girlfriends, but I might be able to get a little information out of Declan about his brother. Declan had told me Carter was going home to Deep Creek and that he would be gone by the time I got there. The news made my heart sink, the weight of disappointment more than I cared to admit. I had feelings for Carter, much more than he had for me, I was sure, but I couldn't help it—and I couldn't hide it from my self-appointed big brother. I reflected on our conversation a few months ago.

"Is Aria prepared for lots of hugs? I won't hurt her, will I?"

"Don't worry." Declan's baritone chuckle met my concern. "She misses you, too. She's so proud of you. In her eyes, you're the famous one. I guess that makes me chopped liver," he laughed. "Whenever I remind her that you and I do the same thing, she tells me to take out the trash."

"Oh, my gosh!"

"Yes, and she always tells me you're more beautiful than I am." His voice grew tender. "I have to agree with her, kiddo. You are more beautiful than I could ever be—both inside and out."

My eyes misted with the sentiment. I had called Declan during a work break, so I blinked away the moisture before it had a chance to ruin my makeup. "I can't wait to see you."

"You sound lonely, but don't worry. You'll be here soon enough. I'm sure you girls will spend all night catching up."

I giggled, remembering many sleepless nights spent with Aria, Paige, and Katherine. "Me?" I teased. "What about you? You'll probably have Carter and Blake out until all hours for a boy's night!"

"Nope. I don't stray too far from Aria these days. Besides, Carter isn't here anymore to get me into trouble."

The news about Carter served an emotional sucker punch. "Why isn't Carter there? Did something happen?"

"Nothing happened. We knew that he wasn't going to stay forever. He has his own life in Deep Creek."

I was at a loss for words, the silence lasting so long that Declan finally spoke. *"Aim, you still there?"*

"I'm here." My voice was soft with fringes of melancholy tiptoeing through the tone.

"Something you want to talk about?" His concern was unmistakable.

"No," I answered, barely above a whisper. I doubted I was fooling Declan as I cleared my throat. *I'm just tired."*

"If you say so." He paused. *"I love you, kiddo, ya know?"*

His words and my feelings had mixed to form emotional hooks. Their sharp points had sunk into my heart, and I'd silently swallowed a cry before being engulfed by my unshed tears.

"Love you, too." The sound of my voice was dark and flat. *"I gotta go. See you soon."*

I hadn't heard Declan's voice in weeks. I missed his teasing and our playful bickering, but I was afraid that when I spoke with him again, I'd reveal more about my feelings than I wanted to. He and Aria were family. Everyone associated with them were also like family to me. When one of them was missing, I felt the loss. Most people could never understand, but when you go from house to house as a child, you have no routine. No security. Nothing you can count on. Declan, Aria, and the friends I'd met through them were more than just people; they were home. Little things that most people took for granted, like cookouts and birthday parties, had more meaning to me than they could know. Now one of the fold would be missing—the one for whom I felt a little more than I should. A feeling I'd never felt before.

The boat lurched as it skipped in the water, jogging me from my thoughts. I relished the beauty around me, but even the bluest water and the clearest sky couldn't keep my mind from wandering to what awaited me when I returned. My excitement grew the closer we approached land. It wouldn't be long now. Soon I'd find myself a homeowner; my first real home. I'd fallen in love with it before I was told where it was located. I had so many ideas for the quirky little place. It was a fixer-upper for sure, and soon I'd be ankle deep in sawdust.

One of my foster parents had been a do-it-your-selfer. I'd learned so much from her. A fond memory caressed me as I remembered the first piece of furniture I'd redone all by myself. The small cabinet had been someone's castaway, but I could see the beauty beneath the nicks and scratches. I'd removed the old finish, sanded the warm oak by hand, and cleaned up the hardware until it glowed. My foster mother had been so proud of my work she'd displayed the piece in the foyer. She died from ovarian cancer the following year, and I hadn't been fortunate enough to have another foster parent like her. She'd uncovered a seed of creativity inside of me.

When Paige had sent the picture of the house, I felt the petals unfurl. I knew it would be my home. I wondered how my friends would react to the news I was moving to Deep Creek Lake. It was a place I'd visited for only a few days over a year ago under sad circumstances. While there, I listened to other people, especially Carter, describe how beautiful all of the seasons were at the lake. It had sounded like a perfect place to unwind. When I discovered there were lots of thrift stores and architectural salvage places, I was even more excited about the adventure.

Some people thought it strange, but I loved old furniture. I could always see the potential new life inside worn-down pieces. Declan and Aria's wedding gift was something I'd loved back to life. When Carter saw it, he was impressed. He hadn't suspected I'd have this type of hobby. He'd called me a prissy girl, albeit in a playful way. That may have been the moment I began to think of him as more than a friend. Carter was a handsome guy, and the more I was around him, the more I liked him. His personality was so different from mine. He had a very dry sense of humor; at first, I wasn't sure how to take him. Nonetheless, I wanted to know him better.

I'd never been intimate with a guy, just the opposite, in fact. When you're a girl growing up in foster care, you tend to keep men at a distance. Although I'd heard the horror stories about abuse, I was lucky. No one had ever tried anything with me, but I always guarded myself. When I got into modeling, I was surrounded by handsome men, but none attracted me. Carter was different.

When we were dancing at the wedding, I loved the feel of his arms closed around me. As I rested my head on his shoulder, I felt a secure and relaxed feeling that I hadn't experienced before. The contentment was like a drug, and I craved another fix. Once the music stopped, and I pulled back, the distance between our lips was barely a breath. He was looking into my eyes, shattering my thoughts into stardust. I could tell he felt something as well.

"A penny for your thoughts." As we neared our destination, Jonatan intruded on my daydreams. The driver of the boat ignored our conversation, but I was sure that my photographer could read my mind. He saw more than images through his lenses; he saw my emotions as well. Heat warmed my cheeks with a blush and I tried to veil my thoughts with humor.

"Oh, they're worth much more than one cent."

"Really? Do tell!" His tone indicated his interest was piqued. "Now I really want to know what you were thinking. Spill." His challenge was playful. After several days behind the camera, he was thirsty for gossip.

"I think I'll keep them to myself if you don't mind."

"And why would you do that?" he teased.

I bit my bottom lip as we docked, savoring memories of Carter. "Because a penny won't buy them. They're priceless."

Chapter 8

Carter

Finally, the office was complete. I'd spent the last few months turning Lacey's old craft room into an office. It would serve as a home base for my new endeavor, MarSin Falcon, Inc. The company was the brainchild of two former co-workers and myself. In recent years, Marcus Bainbridge, Falcon Grey, and I had toyed with the idea of establishing a security company, but similar ventures were popping up all over the place. They were flooding the market and there was no guarantee they were any good. Any asshole with a gun permit thought he could get a business license and pass himself off as a security firm. I needed to find a niche, and after living through a tragedy of my own, I saw a need that hadn't been met and decided that the three of us had the collective talent to meet that need. Poor security footage was an issue in the vehicular homicide case against the woman accused of being involved in my wife's death. Marisol Franzi was guilty of the crime; I was certain of it. But all we had as evidence was a bad quality tape from an old security camera. In addition to Lacey suffering at her hands, I also believed that Marisol was responsible for the death of her twin sister, Marchelle. If there had been proper security equipment near and around the business where they'd rented the car, the case would have been open and shut. Facial recognition software would have easily detected the small differences between the two women. The inadequacy of evidence had caused the case to slow to a crawl, and the lack of progress frustrated me to no end.

There were too many *if only* scenarios with this crime and many others. My colleagues and I had analyzed the challenges faced by small businesses and local law enforcement. We then debated the topic over darts and a few beers. Marcus, Falcon, and I were men for whom justice was in our DNA. Before the night was over, we'd laid out our mission statement. We believed that affordable security services should be a right, not an entitlement. The first goal was to address the needs of small business owners, but we were hopeful that, in time, we would grow our company to be a much larger endeavor.

While I was living on the Eastern Shore, I found myself working for my brother, Declan. As private security, my duties were to protect high-profile individuals associated with The Studio and Bella Matrix. Providing bodyguard services was another direction in which I hoped to take our new company. Falcon Gray was ex-elite forces. A real badass. His time in the military had served him well. He was confident in his ability to work with both sides of our new business. He was certain he could discern the safety needs of one person or an entire company. The military had capitalized on his ability to scope potential threats, making him efficient at revealing risks and eliminating them. He had a hawkish personality, rarely joked, and suffered comments that compared him to a machine. He let people believe whatever they wanted. His friendship with Marcus and me was one of the few instances when he let his guard down. Most of the time, our joking amused him, but he'd often warn us, in jest, to back off or face the consequences. Marcus and I both laughed in his face, telling him to bring it on. Falcon was confident with his reputation and assured us the only reason he didn't kick our asses was that we were friends.

Marcus was skilled in other areas. As a red belt Brazilian martial arts master, as well as an eighth-degree Dan in Krav Maga, he not only wanted to provide security to those who could afford it, he also wanted to start a pro-bono program for people in crisis. One of his sister's friends had been in a violent relationship. The woman had been married to an influential businessman. Payoffs and favors to the local police meant she had no protection. While the bastard used his wife as a punching bag, his money blinded the eyes of those who could have saved her. Marcus told us that although she finally gained the courage to leave her husband, she knew she was taking a chance with her life and couldn't afford to pay for protection. The result of that injustice was her death. When Marcus had heard the gruesome details, it inspired him to help women like her. He hoped to grow our business by training women to defend themselves. Our common ground had been Lacey. Fal and Marc had loved her like a sister, and just like a sister, she regularly called them on their bullshit. As law enforcement and military men, they usually saw life in only black and white. She'd always challenged them over dinner and a few beers to see the gray areas. Her death was inexcusable and unacceptable to both men. Before I left to help Declan recover from his accident, the three of us had spoken many times about the deficiencies in her murder investigation. They had taken it upon themselves to become familiar with Marisol Franzi and the case against her. Unfortunately, they had found a flaw in the arrest that could be trouble. I could only hope no one else would discover it.

As I stacked books on the shelves in my new office, the newspaper article about Marisol's arrest fell out of one of them. I took a moment to reread it. There were so many questions and not enough answers. My blood pressure inched up, rising until the inside of my ears pulsated. Although I hoped justice would prevail, I could feel my temples tightening, a sure sign of another impending headache. I hadn't visited Marisol. I didn't trust myself. I'd heard about the possibility her sister was the driver of the car that had killed Lacey. At first, I had trouble believing it, but as I replayed the day over in my mind, uncertainty crept in with icy fingers. I was with Marchelle as she was dying. She had repeated over and over that she was sorry. Was the forgiveness she was seeking due to her role in Lacey's death? There was no doubt that she'd played a part, and according to Marisol, Marchelle was the cruel one. My gut instinct told me that Marisol was lying. At first, anger consumed me. Now that I had time to process everything, I chose to fight back with calm determination. Justice could be a fickle bitch, but having danced with her for most of my adult life, I believed that we would soon tango again.

Chapter 9

Manuel

W hat the hell was with Americans? Did no one value time? Manny stood impatiently in the office of Mari's attorney. He despised waiting. His eyes traveled around the room taking mental note. Proudly displayed in cheap frames were Mr. Dietz's scholastic accomplishments. He was not impressed. Why Marianna would choose this attorney above other, more competent, ones, he'd never understand. Her lawyer specialized in real estate, for God's sake! She needed a criminal defense man. This lack of judgment only served to confirm his belief she needed his care.

Manny intended to meet with Dietz and clarify what his expectations would be from this point forward. Manny's thoughts wandered as he continued scanning the room. The saying about first impressions popped into his head and he wondered if he would find the occupant as disagreeable as he found the décor. Sterile, ordinary, and sparse were the descriptions that came to his mind. A workplace should successfully reflect the caliber of the man who possessed it. Manny's office certainly did. The opposite of this space, his was vast and bright, with furnishings made of high-quality wood and leather. Carlos had taught him the importance of appearances. Before becoming his successor, Manny believed the attitude to be cavalier and superficial, but that was when he had been young and naïve. Now he understood the significance. There was a difference between a man wearing a suit and a suit wearing a man. A good quality suit could be used as a tool to command respect. Much of Carlos's business had been smoke and mirrors. After years of observation, Manny had used this illusion, and others, to smooth the transition of power from his predecessor to himself. He'd already made up his mind that Mr. Dietz would understand and abide by the Vallega way of doing business.

A rush of cold air accompanied the opening of a squeaky door as Mr. Dietz entered the room. Manny watched as the man went directly to his desk without the courtesy of acknowledging he had a guest. He nervously smoothed his jacket before taking a seat in his weathered chair. There were beige marks along the black surface where the leather had split from usage. Mr. Dietz leaned forward, folding his hands and placing them on his desk. Manny sensed the attorney's fear, although he puffed his chest. He still hadn't made eye contact or extended his hand for a friendly shake. That type of behavior was considered disrespectful in Manny's circles.

"Please have a seat, Mr. Vallega." Mr. Dietz gestured to a pair of worn armchairs facing his desk. "What can I do for you today?"

Manny remained standing, using Mr. Dietz's seated position to tower over him. As the attorney looked up, Manny glared down at him, unnerving the smaller man. Manny noted the signs of intimidation: quickened breath, a little tic at the corner of the eye, and a tense grip. Mr. Dietz pulled his hands back, lowering them into his lap. As he retreated further into his chair, Manny narrowed his eyes and scowled. "What you can do for me is educate me. You have business with Marisol Franzi. I want to know exactly what that business is." Manny's tone was flat and deadly, and he watched as Mr. Dietz swallowed the newly formed lump in his throat.

"She's my client." His reply was tentative, not forthcoming, so a game of cat and mouse began.

Manny took a step back and lowered himself into a chair. "Let's not play games, Mr. Dietz." The intensity of his stare sent deathly arrows soaring through the airspace. "You are inept. Your association with Ms. Franzi is the only reason I have allowed you this one transgression. People answer my questions, Mr. Dietz.

I can assure you that those who choose not to, regret their decision. Manny cocked his head toward a photo in a fake gold frame on the credenza. "I've found that bad decisions can be so hard on a family. Wouldn't you agree?"

The attorney's eyes widened with fear. He opened his mouth to speak, but before he could, Manny held up a hand to silence him. "Let me tell you what I know so that redundancy isn't an issue. I'm well aware you provided legal assistance to Marisol for the procurement of property. I'm also mindful of the fact that you sent one of your friends to Marisol, representing him to her as a competent criminal attorney. I know that you falsified information so she would believe it. What I don't know, is why? Was it for the money? Was it because she is beautiful, and you thought she would favor you? Were you hoping to gain clients because of her affluent social circle? There could be many motives for your actions, Mr. Dietz, so I suggest you carefully consider your answer. The wrong one could mean that you won't leave this office."

The room thickened with tension. Manny patiently waited for an answer, but none came. The beads of sweat that appeared on Mr. Dietz's forehead led him to believe that the man had something to hide. Manny rose from his seat and walked the space.

"Let me make this easy for you. I want to know how you and Marisol came to be acquainted. She trusted you with a great deal of money. Were the two of you intimate?"

"What? No!" The question widened Mr. Dietz's eyes and the declaration rushed out.

"Let me assure you, if you're lying to me, I will find out." Manny paused before regaining focus. Once he had, he curled his fingers over the back of one of the chairs in front of the desk, gripping it tightly. "I've done my homework, Mr. Dietz; but there are a few missing pieces concerning the relationship between you and my wife. Before we leave this room, you will fill in the gaps."

Chapter 10

Aimee

I hadn't allowed myself much time to pack once I returned to New York from the shoot. There wasn't much need for fancy clothes at my new place, and before heading there I was going to connect with friends in Rehoboth Beach.

Paige and Blake were meeting me for lunch, and I was running behind. I rushed to get myself out the door so that I wouldn't be late. It was nearly impossible to not over pack. *When did I accumulate so much stuff?*

The plan was to take six months to be by myself, far away from the prying eyes of the public. I wasn't ungrateful, but I was burned out. My career had proved to be very rewarding, but having the downtime was a welcome change. Once I got my luggage into the car, I reached the beach in record time.

When I entered Dos Locos, I spied them right away. As I closed the distance between us, Blake stood up to greet me as Paige returned my smile from her seat. Paige and I had been together a few days ago at the closing on the house. We hadn't been able to socialize then, so she was celebrating with me today.

I was ecstatic about the house, even though I'd only seen it in pictures. I'd trusted Blake and Paige to inspect it. Although both thought I was crazy to buy such an unusually shaped building, they'd gone through the property with an expert and assured me that it was structurally sound.

My new house was unique, shaped like a boat. I fell in love with it because it was different. I'd always felt like the oddball, the girl on the outside of everyone's circle. This house was like no other, also an oddball of sorts. I couldn't wait to apply the vision in my head to the actual building. When Paige initially showed me the photos, she warned it was a handyman's special. I wasn't intimidated in the least. I lived for projects like this. What was even more exciting was the fact it would be mine. For a girl who had grown up with nothing, ownership meant more to me than for most people. I would be leaving my footprint on the world. As far as the décor, I wasn't concerned about finding things that would reflect my personality. It would be my own little getaway, something I'd worked for and paid for by myself, unlike the condo in New

York. That space, while beautiful, was owned by Bella Matrix.

Blake kissed me on the cheek as he greeted me, and then I slid into the booth to sit beside Paige. The first thing she did was dangle a set of keys in front of me with one hand, giving me a large envelope with the other. Using quick precision, I playfully snatched the keys away from her and pressed them against my chest. "Mine!" A playful laugh escaped, and Paige smiled at me.

"It's definitely yours. Nobody else would want that monstrosity." She shook her head from side to side. "I hope you know what you're doing."

I rolled my eyes. "Of course I don't. I have no idea what I'm in for, but I'm up for the challenge." She was right about one thing; no one else wanted it. The house had sat empty on the market for over two years. Who would want a miniature replica of Noah's Ark to live in? But I had a vision that encompassed more than fixing up an old house. Just because something was dated and different didn't mean it should be ignored or thrown away. Once it was loved back to life, its individuality would make it shine. Kind of like what had happened to me.

"How have you been? I haven't seen you in a while." Blake was my agent, but we rarely saw each other. Our communication was mostly by phone.

I shrugged my shoulders. "I'm fine. Other than working, eating, and sleeping, I haven't done much of anything. Stepping into Marisol's shoes... you have no idea!"

He quirked up an eyebrow. "Paige may have no idea; but remember, I'm the one who had to replace her name with yours on the contracts."

"I'm glad we get to see you today. We didn't get a chance to talk much after the settlement and now you're leaving again." Paige's bottom lip formed a pout.

"You know you can come with me."

"Hell no." Her reply was quick. "Unless it's at least four stars, I'm not venturing in." Her dramatics made me laugh.

"Then you can come up in a few months."

"Well, aren't you optimistic!" Paige's mocking tone was more lighthearted than convincing.

"I mean let me spruce up the place a bit!"

"Spruce up?" Blake looked at the menu, avoiding eye contact. "Overhaul is more like it!"

His comment gave me pause and I had a moment of buyer's remorse. My mood grew serious. "You said the house was in good shape—both of you did. Are you telling me I made a mistake?"

"Don't pay attention to him!" Paige threw eye darts at Blake. She then turned toward me. "The inspector had an eagle eye. I promise."

"The house is kind of neat, but it's not a challenge I'd want to take on," Blake said.

"Because you aren't as talented as Aimee." Paige defended my decision. "It just needs your touch, sweetheart, that's all. The house has good bones. I have no doubt it will be beautiful once you get your hands on it."

With Paige's reassurance, I once more looked forward to the challenge. As the waiter brought our drinks, I began to detail to both of my friends my plans for the renovation.

Chapter 11

Aimee

One more stop. It was good to see Declan and Aria. At their insistence, I agreed to stay the night at their house. Indeed, it hadn't taken much to convince me. I felt at home as Aria and I relaxed on the front porch, talking about anything and everything. It was a perfect, calm night with a full moon. After giving us a little time for girl talk, Declan joined us outside carrying a bottle of wine and three glasses.

"So, what are your plans? Are you going straight to your house once you get to Deep Creek or will you stay in a hotel while you renovate?" Aria asked.

"No, no hotel for me." I reclined back into my chair and propped my feet up on the railing. "Paige assures me that the house is fine to live in, and the pictures back that up. It's not falling apart. It's just worn out.

The owner left some furniture there: a cast iron bed with a decent mattress, some chairs, and a table and chairs in the kitchen. I brought two sets of clean sheets with me. There's no reason to stay in a hotel."

"How about the other stuff, like the appliances?" Declan asked. "Are they working well enough to use them?"

"The washer and dryer are older, but they work, and the refrigerator is pretty much the same. I guess I'll see for myself when I get there. You're looking at the dishwasher!" Exhaustion began to set in. It rolled over me as I gazed at my wine glass. I struggled to keep my eyes open, I didn't want to go to sleep until I'd broached the subject of Carter. "I was thinking about asking Carter if he'd like to come over for lunch or dinner sometime." Declan and Aria exchanged a glance. "What?" I asked, looking at them both.

"Nothing," Aria answered.

"Yeah, right. You looked at Declan the minute I said Carter's name." Aria did it again. This time the glance was accompanied by a questioning look. Like she wanted to say something but was awaiting some direction from him. "See?" I popped up, my sleepiness now replaced with an energetic shot of curiosity. "You're doing it again! What aren't you telling me?"

Declan sighed. "It's just... he's different since he went back to Deep Creek."

"Different? How so?" My stomach began to twist, a knot of unasked questions at the center.

"I can't put my finger on it." Declan leaned his shoulder against the thick post in front of me. "When Carter was here—when he was helping me—he was serious like he always is. But once he went home he became more intense. I don't know. Maybe it was because he had to face everything again, all the memories."

"And justifiably so!" I blurted out. I felt I had to defend Carter in his absence. "Think about it. His wife died, his brother almost lost a leg, and his sister-in-law was almost killed! How can he not be serious?"

"We're not saying it's a bad thing, Aimee. What we are saying is that he's changed." Aria's tone was low and soft. "We just want you to be prepared if he's not the way he was the last time you saw him."

"Maybe everything caught up with him once he got home." My voice was calmer as I offered a possible reason for the change in Carter's attitude.

Declan shifted. "You could be right," he agreed. "He didn't take the time to go through Lacey's things for quite a while and then he dropped everything when I was in the hospital." He paused and then looked at me. "Maybe I should go with you to see how he's doing."

"I don't think you should." I said the words much too quickly, catching him by surprise.

His eyes widened and his forehead wrinkled. "Why not?"

"Because, you know... If Carter wanted you there, he'd ask you."

Declan smiled suspiciously. "And when did you get to know my brother so well?"

Aria interrupted. "I think she's right. Imagine how you might act if something happened to me. It wouldn't be easy. We both know how brooding you can be when things aren't going your way."

Declan scoffed at her comment, and everyone became quiet as we pondered our own thoughts.

"I'll tell you what." I broke the silence. "Once I'm there, I'll make a point to check on him. If I notice anything's off, I'll call you."

Aria gave Declan an inquisitive look. He looked back at her as he brought his glass to his lips and drained the contents. He then turned his attention to me. "You call me if it seems like it's more than a case of the blues."

"I promise."

"Don't let your feelings cloud your judgment."

"I won't. Wait, what do you mean? My feelings? I don't have any feelings. He's my friend." A traitorous flow of blood flushed my cheeks, creeping down my neck to spread across the exposed skin above my shirt. Aria smiled.

Declan didn't share her tact. "Yeah, right." His tone was mocking. My body had betrayed me, making me vulnerable.

"You don't have to hide it from us." Aria gave me a knowing look.

If my blush warmed my face before, now it was on fire. I shrugged my shoulders. "I'm not hiding anything." Declan laughed out loud, the dark timbre piercing the quiet roll of the waves. As Aria shot him a look of warning, he masked his laughter with a feigned cough. I glared at him. "Shut up, Declan. If it makes you feel better, I don't think he notices me like that."

Aria ignored her husband laughing at my expense. She reached for my hand, giving it a comforting squeeze. "You two would be lucky to have each other."

I looked out over the ocean, my emotions wavering in concert with the sea. When I was little, I used to pick up every penny I saw on the ground, hoping that luck would follow the simple act. There were always kids moving in and out of the social services office. I kept my little bag of lucky pennies in my pocket in the hopes that the right family would keep me. The older I got, the less likely it became I would find a permanent home. One with a mom and dad that loved me. A place to spend the holidays. A place to feel safe. It never happened. Everything I'd attained was because of my own efforts, and I'd worked my ass off. I had no lofty ideas that fate would make a man fall in love with me. If love—real love—were to find me, I was sure I'd have to work for it, just like I'd worked for everything else in my life. Luck would have nothing to do with it.

Chapter 12

Aimee

The time spent on the ride to Deep Creek fed my curiosity. I decided to go to Carter's house as soon as I arrived. Stopping by unannounced might not be the brightest idea I'd ever had, but I wanted to see for myself what Aria and Declan were talking about. Unless Carter had turned into a total tool, I didn't think my opinion of him would change. The drive was a long one, and I hadn't eaten. I planned to use my hunger as a convenient excuse to ask him to lunch. Anticipating he would be happy to see an old friend, I intended to tell him over a meal that we were now neighbors and also to make myself available should he ever need anything. I even had a contingency plan if he proved to be resistant; I wasn't familiar with the area's best restaurants and I needed him to help me get the lay of the land. What man wouldn't help out a damsel in distress? It was perfect.

The roads began to look more familiar as I neared Carter's house, using my GPS to guide me. I'd only been there once, when his wife died. I had stayed a few days along with Declan and Aria to help him through those first tough hours. Even though he was grieving, something had drawn me to him. I felt guilty being attracted to a man who'd just lost his wife, but there was a loneliness in him I identified with. I dismissed my feelings once we had all gone back to our busy lives, but when Declan needed him, Carter had dropped everything and came to live at the beach. Over the next year, we'd gotten to know each other well. I liked him, but I wasn't sure if he could tell. Although I knew many men, I had little experience with relationships. My heart beat faster as I pulled into his driveway. I didn't see any other vehicles except his truck, so I was pretty sure I wouldn't be interrupting him. I stepped out of the car and groaned at the limb stiffness caused by being confined in the same position for several hours. As I closed the door, I sighed and relaxed into a long stretch. I nearly fell on my face in Carter's driveway when something bumped me from behind. I reached to grab ahold of the offender, and I was met with a handful of fur. *Cody!* I squatted down to greet the big girl. She nuzzled me in dog-like delight.

"Hi, sweet girl! I missed you!" I had never had the luxury of having a pet, my childhood had been too transient. None of my foster homes had pets either. I guess they had enough to keep track of with kids, much less adding animals to the mix. Cody responded to my sentiment by wagging her tail, causing her whole hind end to wiggle uncontrollably. "What are you doing out here all by yourself?" I looked around as I hugged the giant fur ball. "Where's Carter?" I looked around to see if maybe he was outside instead of in, but there was no trace of him. I stood. "Let's go find your dad." Cody followed close behind me as I made my way up the porch steps to the front door. I took a moment to remember the beauty surrounding me. The Maryland mountains enveloped me with contentment. I took a deep breath, inhaling the crisp, clean air and exhaling months-worth of stress. The difference between New York and Deep Creek was the definition of polar opposites. Both had their charm, but the calming environment I currently found myself in was more than welcome to someone whose schedule had been too full.

I straightened my posture, and with Cody girl beside me to provide courage, I lifted the door knocker. As I gave a few solid hits, my stomach began to do major flips and somersaults. *Maybe he isn't home. Maybe he's out fishing.* Seconds seemed like long minutes, and I was just about to turn back to my car when the door opened. All tight and firm, six-foot-four-inches of Carter Sinclair stood deliciously shirtless in the doorway. His jeans were slung low and half unzipped; I knew instantly that unannounced company was the last thing he'd expected. He leaned against the doorframe once he recognized me. His lips were sexy as sin, and his eyes pinned me in place. His mouth tightened into a thin line, while mine went dry. I dropped my gaze, an apology forming on my lips. Instead, I was rendered speechless as I got a healthy view of his tight abs and the deeply toned vee that dipped down into his pants and my imagination. Tingling started in several pleasant locations. *Damn!*

After a moment, I broke the awkward silence. "Hi."

His eyes scanned me slowly from my head to my feet. "Hi, yourself," he replied, his voice rough and sexy.

"Umm... I was in the neighborhood." My joke was an attempt to lighten the mood as I turned to look at my car. He continued to stare. "Cody showed up as your welcoming committee. She almost knocked me over when I got out of the car." Confirming she knew I was talking about her, Cody rubbed up against my side.

"Hmm." Carter pulled his hands over his face and then ran them through his mussed hair. "Yeah, that's Cody." His tone was edgy.

"Oh." His whole demeanor was unwelcoming, making me queasy.

"I didn't mean that the way it sounded." He rolled his shoulders, apologizing in a less harsh tone. "I wasn't expecting anybody."

"No, I should be the one to apologize. I should have called." I backed away from the door. "I can go…"

"No. Aimee. Wait… shit."

I took a step toward the stairs, tears of hurt and embarrassment pricking my eyes. His hand cupped my shoulder. "I'm sorry. I just woke up. I was passed out on the sofa when you knocked." He placed the bottom of his foot against the door and pushed it wide open. "Ignore my smart-ass attitude and c'mon in."

Although apprehension flooded me, I tentatively stepped through the door. The slight brush of my arm against Carter's chest sent shivers over my skin. My cheeks heated. I hoped I wasn't turning as pink as my nail polish. I walked into the living room and was surprised that it was immaculate. I don't know what I was expecting—maybe empty beer cans, pizza boxes, or leftover containers of Chinese food—but certainly not a scene from *Better Homes & Gardens*. Most of the talk I'd overheard from other models was them complaining about men being messy. I'd had nothing to contribute to their conversations since I'd never been in a relationship. Maybe the guys they knew were pigs, but not this one. His house was filled with furniture gleaming from polish and hardwood floors that glowed warmly in the sunlight. The only things out of place were a pillow and a blanket on the sofa.

"Your house is beautiful." Inhaling his scent, my misfiring brain cells attempted to pull common words from my frazzled mind.

A puzzled look filled his expression. "You've been here before. Nothing's changed."

"I guess I didn't notice. You know, given the circumstances." I sank into a leather chair across from the sofa. It was comfortable, and I was still stiff from the ride so I closed my eyes and rolled my neck from side to side.

"Comfy?"

"It's great. It was a long ride, but you know that." I nodded toward the sofa. "I could ask you the same thing."

His reply was sober. "I sleep out here most nights. I rarely make it to my bed."

I had no reply because I was afraid I might open an emotional wound. Carter took a few steps, heading to the kitchen. "You thirsty?" he called to me over his shoulder.

"I'll take a water if you have one." I leaned forward in the chair to better see him and then sat back rapidly when I saw him coming my way. He caught me watching him and one corner of his mouth hooked into a sly smile. So much for me trying to act nonchalant. He handed me one of the bottles, then took a seat on the sofa. *This was what I wanted, right? Carter and me, alone.* He put a foot up on the table, causing the undone top of his zipper to expand over his toned abs. Suddenly I was parched and speechless, so I unscrewed the cap and placed the bottle to my lips.

"You okay?" he asked.

I nodded and downed half the bottle. As Carter stared at me, his brows arched, forming rippled lines on his forehead. Why did it I feel like I was walking on eggshells?

"So, what brings you up here? Last time I talked to my brother, he said you were super modeling all over the world."

"I am—or rather, I was," I stuttered. "I'm taking some time off."

He leaned back on the sofa, stretching an arm across the back of it, which gave me a nice view of his tanned and muscular chest. As before, I began to feel warm all over. My heart was beating so hard I was surprised it wasn't audible. "And you decided to come up here?" he asked, surprised.

"Well, yes. I came up here for a vacation—but I have other reasons for being here."

His raised brows begged me to continue. "Where are you staying?"

"A house over on Clark Lohr Road," I explained. "I was on my way there when I stopped here." I anxiously sipped my water and changed the subject. The prospect of revealing that we were neighbors no longer held the same appeal as it did while I was driving. "But enough about me," I countered. "Tell me what's going on with you. Declan said you opened your own business." He sat up tall, put both feet on the floor and spread them. With his knees opened I saw a small, worn hole on the inside of his thigh at the seam. I stared at it. *What was it about this man that made even a rip in his pants leg so sexy?* I tore my eyes away before he caught me.

"Yeah, me and two of my friends. We have a security company."

"A security company?"

"It kinda came to mind when Lacey died, but then I went down to Ocean City for Declan and I put it on the back burner. We didn't really put the whole plan together until I came back home."

"So..." I teased flippantly. "How's the bodyguard business?"

Carter's lukewarm expression suddenly cooled. Too late, I realized it sounded as though I was mocking him, and I felt terrible. Not that he would know this about me, but I teased or giggled when I was really nervous. Being alone with him, dressed the way he was, was making me nervous. Correction. *He* was making me nervous.

"It's doing well, as a matter of fact, but it's a little more than being a bodyguard." His answer was clipped, indicating his irritation. "We've developed security plans. In case you aren't aware, you passed Thurmont on your way up here. Camp David is there. There are more bodyguards around than you realize." He emphasized the word *bodyguard* with a sarcastic tone.

I *had* offended him. "I wasn't making fun of you," I said apologetically.

He ignored the apology and glared at me, his voice growing increasingly loud and agitated. "It doesn't matter if you were or not. In today's world, you can't be too careful—or maybe you don't think about stuff like that."

"You're absolutely right. Everyone should take it seriously," I conceded. The last thing I wanted was Carter thinking I was belittling his business.

He picked at some unseen lint on his knee, not looking at me, and, thankfully, changed the subject. "What did you mean when you said that you had other reasons for being here?" He then gave me a look that unnerved me.

"Believe it or not, I bought the house where I'm staying. The one on Clark Lohr."

Carter's mouth dropped open and his eyes widened. "You're going to live up here?" Just as quickly as his surprise registered, he recovered and snapped his mouth closed with a firm jaw.

"I'm planning on it—at least when I'm not working."

"Why?" Carter's tone lowered to a near growl.

His reaction couldn't have stung more than if he'd slapped me. He certainly wasn't happy with my news. More like he was angry. Indignance stiffened my spine. "Why not?"

"Because you're alone. You don't have anybody up here!" He nearly shouted his disapproval.

"Apparently, I don't, and your comment sounds

kind of sexist!" I went on the defensive. "Do you interrogate all of your friends this way, or just me?"

Carter smirked with hostility. "I'm just saying, it's quite a big move for a pretty girl all by herself."

My blood began to boil. "For your information, I've been living on my own a long time. I don't need anybody. I'm just fine by myself." I stood, ready to walk away, but I faced him instead. "Just who the hell do you think you are, Carter? You have no say over what I do." I turned my back to him, grabbed my purse, and started toward the door.

He followed close behind and grabbed me, his fingers cuffing around the top of my arm. "Dammit, Aimee! You didn't think this through! I thought you were more responsible than this. What if you get sick? Or get hurt over there all by yourself? I'm not always going to be around. Do you even have a plan?"

I narrowed my eyes, looking from where his fingers held me captive up to his eyes. The intensity of my stare should have incinerated him into a pile of ash. I snapped my arm from his grasp. "Don't touch me." The words hissed through my clenched teeth. I flung open the door and ran down the steps.

Carter, still barefoot and shirtless, pursued me into the driveway. "Aimee!"

"What?" I snarled. I turned so suddenly that he backed up a step. My anger seemed to amuse him. He didn't even try to hide his smug look. I shook my head and got into my car as a comment escaped under my breath. "Bastard."

Carter laughed. "Don't go away mad, sweetheart. You haven't even told me where on Clark Lohr you're living. You know, so I can check up on you."

I gunned the engine. As I put the car into drive, he stood in front of it and crossed his arms over his chest. *So, he wants to play games, huh?* I put the car into reverse and looked over my shoulder. I nearly jumped when a loud *bang* came from the front of my car. The asshole had slammed his hands down on the hood. I rolled the window down. "What?"

"Where. Are. You. Staying?" He enunciated each word as if I hadn't heard his question. I'd heard him. I simply chose to ignore him.

A snarky idea popped into my head. He wanted to play games? I'd give him something. "In. A. Boat." I peeled wheels when I backed up and then threw the car into drive. As I sped off, I didn't even glance in the rearview mirror.

Chapter 13

Manuel

The plush hotel suite served well enough as a makeshift office and Manny was comfortable in the space. The only thing that wore on his patience was that the staff was slow. He chalked it up to the lackadaisical attitude that seemed prevalent in this country. There was no consistency in their schedule, which altered his. Even though it was early in the morning, he was already in an irritated mood.

Manny missed the comforts of home. There he had control. His staff in Colombia was efficient and had been trained to anticipate his every need. Traveling with a skeleton crew unnerved him. The kingpin of a drug cartel should be protected on all sides, but more men would only have brought unwanted attention. His thoughts were interrupted as a heavy knock sounded on the door. His assistant answered it and he relaxed into his chair when the visitor entered the room.

"It's about time you showed up."

"I was waiting until your entourage thinned out." Blade was Manny's number one enforcer, a tall man standing at well over six feet, with long, black hair that touched his shoulders. He was an imposing man, treacherous in skill and appearance. His arms were stony, showing bulging veins beneath the skin. His nickname came from the scar on his face, but it also signified the method by which he preferred to torture his victims. The look of fear he extracted from them fed the adrenaline that rushed through his veins. He and Manny were opposites. Manny thrived on power and prestige, while Blade focused on death. He walked over to the credenza and poured himself a cup of coffee. Relaxing into the chair across from Manny, he gave him his full attention. "I'm here now. What do you need me to do?"

"I have a few people I'd like you to take care of." Manny's tone was grave.

"Good. My fingers are twitchy." An evil grin crept onto Blade's face as the prospect of a fresh kill flooded him with craving.

Manny knew the look well. A baritone chuckle vibrated from his throat. "Patience, my friend. I want you to visit someone for me, but just as a warning."

Manny and Blade had been part of Carlos's enforcement crew. Manny had always used his fists, whereas Blade preferred the knife. There was a certain seductiveness of a honed piece of fine steel and Manny knew Blade enjoyed an unnatural love for it. He was an artist. Instead of boar's hair brushes, his creations were made with metal. He preferred skin to a canvas. Blood seemed to fascinate him. It was almost unnatural the way he could compel it to come to the surface of the skin with a razor thin cut. A victim's life essence created his masterpieces, while the playlists accompanying the deeds were made up of screams in place of musical notes. He rarely spoke when in the midst of a creative trance, a trait that unnerved his victims, but on those rare occasions when he did, his voice would cut glass with its brutal tone. To Blade, pleas for mercy were a potent aphrodisiac.

"As you know, Marianna has put herself in a precarious situation. She employed the services of an attorney who helped her build quite the real estate portfolio. I know Marianna. She does everything with an ulterior motive. What I don't understand is the fascination with the coastal housing market. She won't tell me why, and I suspect this man is hiding something for her. I intend to find out what."

A lascivious grin filled Blade's lips. "You want me to pay Marianna a visit?"

Manny gave Blade a glare that spoke death. "Marianna is mine to discipline. I want you to go see the *abogado*."

Blade shrugged his shoulders indifferently. "I'm

sure I could make Marianna talk. Then you'd have your answer straight from her."

The thought of Blade extracting information from Marianna sent a white-hot charge to Manny's brain. Along with the lightning bolt, his voice rolled like thunder. "I'll say this only once; touch her and you die."

Blade grinned and nodded his head. "Of course. Just trying to help." A pregnant silence filled the room and the tension slightly dissipated. Once he determined that it was safe to talk, Blade spoke. "So, what do you want me to do with the lawyer?"

"Encourage him to give full disclosure on his dealings with Marianna. I was polite when I gave him a chance to come clean. He might need a stronger touch. But I need him alive. We can't afford to compromise our efforts to have Marianna released into my care."

"Does the lawyer have a secretary?"

Manny sneered. "He does."

"At least I get to have some fun."

Manny shook his head slightly. "I don't care what you do, but keep it light, nothing permanent. As I said, we can't take any chances until Marianna is free."

Chapter 14

Manuel

As he and Marisol stared at each other, they began a competition of who would be the first to speak. Instead of how her thoughts normally ruled her tongue, he watched as his wife silently concentrated on how the cheap fabric of her uniform chafed her skin. After his last visit, she had seemed willing to play whatever game he wanted if it got her out of there. He knew she didn't delude herself into thinking that he wanted her free because he loved her. It couldn't be that simple. She had to know that, whatever his reason was, it had everything to do with him and little to do with her.

Manny's voice pierced the silence. "The attorneys think there is a good chance of getting you out of here." Marisol's cheeks flushed with color, but Manny put his hand up to halt any premature celebration. "Don't get excited, *mi amor*. You're not getting out tomorrow." As Marisol's smile melted into a frown, Manny chuckled at the abrupt mood change. "Ah! There's my beautiful wife!" he teased.

"Be quiet, Manny." She narrowed her eyes, giving him a sideways glance. "You aren't the one locked up. You dangle hopeful news in front of me like a carrot to a rabbit."

He reached for her hand, stroking the back of it in a comforting manner. "I could try to accelerate your release, mi amor. All you have to do is be honest with me."

Her eyes widened. "What haven't I been honest about? I've told you everything."

One eyebrow raised as he responded. "You shouldn't lie to me."

"How have I lied?" Marisol pulled her hand from his grasp and folded her arms across her chest. Indignance rolled off of her in waves as she braced for Manny's interrogation. They stared at each other for several strained minutes. She looked up at the ceiling, then slowly blinked as she gave her head a slight shake. "Fine. What do you want to know?"

Manny leaned in carefully, his warm breath bathing Marisol's cheek. "You can start by telling me why you were stockpiling real estate."

Marisol shrugged. "I wanted to expand my interests."

"Let me rephrase." Manny's tone dropped to grave depths. "I paid a visit to your attorney. Why were you stockpiling real estate?"

She cocked her head to one side. "Why do you find it so hard to believe I wanted to invest in property? Don't you think I'm smart enough to diversify?" They stared at each other, officially at a standstill. He wanted what she refused to give—information. Marisol was determined to find a way out of the corner in which she found herself and the best survival skill she had was manipulation. "Oh, Manny..." She threw her hands up in the air and squeezed a lone tear from her eye. "Do you have any idea what it's like for me? Women are jealous of me, men want to use me, and now, everyone thinks I'm a killer. You don't know how it feels. To have everything stripped away from you. To feel like you're an animal in a cage. To find yourself at the whims of your captors, no longer in control of your own fate."

"That's where you're wrong, Marianna. I know all too well. Because of your father."

Silence fell like the quiet aftermath of a bomb, until all that remained between them was the naked truth—that Carlos had treated him and Marianna like property. He had wielded his control over them until his death. They were slaves to his whims in equal measure, and both had suffered at his hands. "You have to tell me everything, Mari. There's no other option. Even with my influence, I can't order the justice system to release you. But, if you tell me the truth—all of it—I may be able to find a way to get you out. Now," he settled uncomfortably in the chair, "tell me about the real estate and your connection with the Sinclair family."

IT HAD TAKEN SOME TIME, but eventually Marisol was forthcoming. She disclosed everything. She even revealed the sordid details of her liaisons with other men. She used the excuse that her actions were necessary in order to achieve her goals.

Although Manny hated the thought of Marianna using her body to get what she wanted, he resigned himself to the fact that a man in her situation would have used whatever resources were available. She had done no less. He admired her ingenuity. But he vowed to kill the next man that touched her. "Now that I know your side of the story, let's discuss the hearsay. The information I have says the Sinclair brothers were out for revenge. That you were not only responsible for the death of Carter's wife, but also for the breakup of Declan and his wife, before they were married."

"That's not what happened." Marisol stiffened her posture as she defended herself. "I had a very, ah, close relationship with Declan. Aria interfered."

"Explain what you mean by *close.*" Manny's teeth ground together, his jaw so tight Marisol was afraid it might snap.

"Well, Manny, we're married, but we're not really married," she emphasized.

He nodded. "Go on. Tell me about the woman you attacked. Aria."

"It started in Hawaii." Marisol watched his eyes narrow. "If you want me to tell you the truth, then you have to be ready for it. I don't think for a minute that you haven't been with other women since I left Colombia, so stop acting like I cheated on you. Now, do you want the truth or not?" She paused as Manny took a breath and rolled his head from side to side to loosen his neck. Once she saw that his shoulders were slightly more relaxed, she continued. "I was in Hawaii to reconcile with Declan. What I didn't know was that Aria's friends had conspired to humiliate me. Unfortunately, they were successful." She turned her face away from him as she shrugged. "It doesn't matter anymore. They got what they wanted in the end."

"And what was that?" he asked.

Marisol looked him in the eye, her demeanor more serious than he could ever recall. "Think about the people involved. Aria's friend Aimee has stolen my career, and her friend Paige was able to expand her business because of me. Carter Sinclair needed someone to blame for his wife's death. I became a convenient scapegoat while he chased my sister to her grave."

"And the Vencedor Corporation?"

"The Vencedor Corporation was formed so I could

discreetly expand my interests and diversify my funds. That's the truth. I am a public figure who chose to conduct private business. If I had done it under my own name the press would have been all over it."

Manny took in everything, disseminating and dissecting the information. He had achieved his goal, listening intently as he weighed what was, and what was not, useful. When the end of visiting hours was announced, Marisol moved to stand. Manny stopped her, covering her hand with his. "Before you go, I need to know what was said to you when you were arrested. This is very important. Did you understand everything they said to you? Think carefully."

A thoughtful look crossed her face as she recalled the events of that night. "They acted like they had me. When they told me I was under arrest, I told them I didn't understand. In fact, I told them several times, but they paid no attention to me." She looked at Manny with genuine sadness. "I told you. Carter had it in for me."

As Manny watched Marisol disappear down the hallway, he was determined she would never wear that look again.

Chapter 15

Manuel

Manny made his way out of the facility and into the parking lot. Marisol's honesty had given him much to think about. *Damn her!* He felt an unfamiliar twist in his chest, something he hadn't experienced before. He reasoned that he must be getting soft and made a mental note to keep that feeling in check. The knowledge that she was confined, and he had no control over her fate made him feel a mixture of pity and anger. They had rekindled whatever relationship had been between them and the reminder of their legal binding gave Manny a sense of satisfaction. He'd been so focused on taking over the cartel he'd neglected Marianna. That would now change. She was the type of woman he needed on his arm, both for business and pleasure. Manny pulled out his cell phone and hit the speed dial number for his attorney.

"Manuel! What can I do for you?"

"I want you to pull the records from Marianna's arrest, Juan Carlos."

Manny's driver opened the car door. Without missing a beat, Manny slid into the back seat, the soft leather bowing beneath his weight. "I just had a conversation with her. If my speculation is correct, there may be a way to get her out of this."

Chapter 16

Carter

Three months later

"You're a prick!"

It had been awhile since I'd spoken with my brother. The conversation was not going in the direction I'd hoped. Declan was pissed off. He wasn't holding back on me. He and Aria hadn't spoken with Aimee until today and during their conversation, Aimee had divulged details of our previous encounter, and now I was on my brother's shit list. Truthfully, I was surprised she hadn't called them months ago.

"Why would you be so shitty to her? She's never done a thing to you!"

I kept quiet while he ranted, determined to let him blow off steam before I responded. Half listening, I stared down at the floor, specifically, at my bare feet on the floor. Every once in a while, I mentally checked back in to listen to what he was saying as he droned on.

"I thought you were her friend. Is that how you treat all your friends?"

It was a rhetorical question, but I fired back. "Yeah. You would know all about how to treat your friends, wouldn't you?" Sarcasm thickened my tone.

The phone went silent. Several seconds later, Declan spoke in an emotionless monotone. "That's a low blow... even for you."

I felt a flicker of remorse, but I also felt justified in my statement. Declan had been a self-centered asshole throughout his accident recovery. Everyone had fallen victim to his mood swings, me most of all. My pride wouldn't allow for an apology. "I call 'em as I see 'em, Dec."

More silence. I could hear Declan take a deep breath on the other end of the line. He was composed when he started speaking again. "Aimee's a friend of mine—and Aria's—and I thought she was a friend of yours, too. Seriously, what were you thinking? She said you acted like you were pissed off that she bought a house near you. That she should have gotten your permission. She also said that you acted like she needed to be taken care of. Which, my brother, insulted the hell out of her."

"I did not," I said in my defense, knowing full well I was lying.

"Look, Carter. You don't know Aimee like I do. She's pulled herself through some tough shit to get to where she is. She had it rough growing up, and she could have turned out a whole lot differently than the person she is. The business we're in causes some people to get caught up in their own egos. They get messed up in drugs or alcohol all the time, not to mention all the other shit that's offered to them, but she's squeaky clean."

"I might have mentioned that she should think about being up here alone. You know, I might not be around all the time—especially with the business."

"She wasn't looking for you to be her babysitter, dipshit. She's had a lot of responsibility thrown on her since Marisol was locked up. She's just looking for a nice quiet place where she can unwind. She likes the mountains and she loves the lake. Deep Creek was a no brainer for her."

I dragged my hand over my face. "I didn't mean to come off like that. I'll apologize if it'll make you happy."

"It would. Let me give you her number."

"I've got it in my phone, but I think I'll stop by in person. Apologize, check out her place, make sure it's safe." I grabbed a piece of paper. "What's her address?"

Chapter 17

Carter

I stared at the bizarre... house? Boat? I didn't know what the hell to call it and it had taken me forever to find. It was the craziest damn thing I'd ever seen. Her house was shaped like a boat on dry land. When Declan had given me Aimee's address, he purposely misled me by saying that she lived in a houseboat, but after the way I'd spoken to her, I couldn't blame him. I had to give him credit for being a smartass. He had me going around in circles trying to find her. I'd searched for days down at the water's edge, looking on the lake for a houseboat, not a boat-shaped house.

As I lifted my hand to knock on the door, I saw a knocker shaped like a life preserver. It had years of wear on it, but it fit the house. Kind of how I thought about Aimee. She was younger than Declan and me, but she fit with our crowd because she had an old soul. I lifted the iron and gave a few solid knocks. She had no idea I was coming. It would serve me right if she didn't bother to answer. I heard the floorboards creak on the other side of the door as Aimee approached. The footsteps stopped. I put my eye up to the peephole. "It's no use. I know you're in there."

I heard her curse under her breath as she twisted the locks. She opened the door slowly, pushing a few strands of hair back toward her ponytail as she came into view. She was a mess, but a beautiful one.

"What do you want?" Her tone dripped with sarcasm.

I leaned against the door frame, looked straight into her eyes, and gave her my best shit-eating grin. "I was in the neighborhood."

One corner of her mouth rose ever so slightly as I repeated, verbatim, the words she'd said to me when she showed up at my house. Aimee quickly recovered, dousing any amusement at the situation. She crossed her arms over her chest and stared at me for several long, uncomfortable moments.

"Let's get this out of the way. I know I was an ass. You know I was an ass. I'm sorry. End of story."

She continued staring, with her arms crossed.

"C'mon, Aim. Aren't you going to let me in? We are friends, after all."

She rolled her eyes at my plea. The smile she tried to deny forced a barely detectable curve on her lips.

"Friends, are we? You could have fooled me. Why should I let you in?"

I straightened, forcing her to look up at me. I placed two fingers under her chin and tipped it up further. "Because when you showed up at my place, I let you in. Tit for tat."

"Yeah, right!" She spat the words and then turned to walk away from me. The fact that she hadn't slammed the door in my face was more than enough invitation for me to follow her in. Once we were in the living room, she turned to me, her eyes narrowed. "Why are you really here, Carter? You made it clear I wasn't welcome in your territory—unless that's the way you treat all your friends."

I nodded. "It absolutely is." My matter-of-fact attitude prickled her.

"Damn you, Carter. You really pissed me off." I heard hurt in her confession.

"That's why I'm here. To do damage control." I followed her as she paced along the perimeter of the living room. It was apparent she was struggling with my apology. "Oh, for God's sake, how long are you going to chew on this, Aim?" She turned to me and I cocked a wicked grin and stretched out my arms. "You know, we could hug it out."

"Um... no. Thanks."

I walked toward her with outstretched arms.

"Stay away from me." She smiled as she walked backward in an attempt to widen the space between us. Seeing that she was smiling, I moved my legs forward in a Frankenstein-like walk. Her back hit the wall, and I pulled her in, earning a lighthearted giggle.

"Stop! I get it! You're sorry. Now get off me." She pushed me away and seated herself at the end of the couch. I sat in an adjacent chair.

"Seriously. Can we call a truce?" Aimee didn't seem to be the kind of person who held grudges. In the time I'd known her, I'd witnessed hurt cross her expression many times and saw her forgiveness issued in equal measure.

"You hurt my feelings, but it's okay."

Her admission tore at a tiny corner of my heart. I leaned back in the chair. "I didn't mean to. I can be an ass sometimes."

"It seems when things aren't going your way, you and your brother share the same trait."

She was referring to Declan's behavior after his accident. I remembered it all too well. "Yeah, we do."

Her shoulders relaxed. "You were a real grouch when I showed up at your house."

"What'd you expect? You woke me up from a nap!"

"Yeah, well, at least the dog was happy to see me. Where is Cody, by the way?"

"Home. If you want, I'll bring her next time. I didn't know if you'd want a dog in here."

A burst of laughter escaped her. She waved her arms around the room. "Seriously? Does this look like the Taj Mahal?" She gently shook her head in disbelief. "She's welcome whenever you want to bring her."

I felt myself smiling in return. "Before I let the time get away from me, let me cut to the chase. I came here to apologize and ask you to dinner." She cocked a suspicious brow, making me grin. "That is, if supermodels are allowed to eat."

"Oh, I eat," she laughed.

I laughed too. Not just a chuckle, but a belly laugh. It was unexpected and foreign. When was the last time I'd laughed like that? Aimee pulled the elastic band from her ponytail and pushed her long, blonde hair into a haphazard pile on top of her head. As she once again secured the strands, she pulled her legs up on the sofa and leaned her arm on the bolstered sidearm. She wore a tank top and faded jeans, and her bare feet sported polished toes. So fucking sexy. I jolted upright, the thought searing through my mind like a hot poker. Immediately I tried to push it away. No such luck.

"So." Her voice interrupted my thoughts. "How'd you find me?" A smirk crossed her lips. "Use your state police contacts?"

"Not so cloak and dagger, sweetheart. Declan gave me your address, although it took me a while to find you. I've gotta admit, the house is kind of cool."

"Thanks. I think so." An awkward silence fell for a few moments, then Aimee slid her legs from the sofa to the floor and stood. "Want some iced tea? I just made some."

"Sure."

As she busied herself in the kitchen, I looked around. Most of the other rooms could be seen from where I was standing. Aimee had quite an eclectic mix of furniture. Funny, I always figured her house would be filled with expensive things. I couldn't have been more wrong. Everything invited you to stay for a visit. It was homey. I turned when I heard the sound of ice clinking into a glass and a few seconds later I heard a loud click. I leaned further to see an old refrigerator in the kitchen. It was severely outdated, but it blended in with everything else.

While I waited for Aimee to join me, an unusual table caught my eye. I'd never seen anything quite like it before, and above it was an odd arrangement of crosses of every size. Some of them were painted or stained, while others were shiny or weathered metal. One in particular caught my eye. It was huge, made of copper covered in a green patina that most people would think of as a piece of trash. I was impressed at how Aimee had taken something most would discard and made it look so good. The table complemented the arrangement on the wall so well that the entire space looked like a work of art. The table was made of arched windows, probably from an old church. The paint was chipped, and the wood weathered. I'd never seen anything quite like it. As I studied the whole wall, Aimee came up beside me. I moved my head in the table's direction. "Did you make this?"

She smiled warmly as she ran her hand over the surface. Her fingers caressed the worn wood as they moved toward a blue Mason jar filled with wildflowers. "I did. It's one of my favorites." She tipped her chin up as a stray, blonde lock fell over her cheek. "Do you like it?"

I nodded.

"I found the arched church windows in an antique shop. They were in a dusty corner, begging to be brought home and shown a little love. I had to have them. They needed a new life."

"It's an interesting piece." By her expression, it was evident she appreciated my compliment.

"This is just an old piece of barn wood I found with a pile of stuff in the house. Once I sanded and oiled it, I knew it was perfect to top the windows. They belonged together." She looked at me with wistful eyes. "Not everyone appreciates how I married them."

The corners of my mouth lifted. "Everyone?" I teased.

"Well, honestly, no one has been here except delivery people and the mailman."

I pointed to the crosses. "Religious?"

"I'm not what you would call religious, but I have an intense faith." She walked back to the sofa and tucked her legs under her as she sat down. I followed and sat at the opposite end. She continued. "I don't really like religion. Too many rules and regulations."

"Really? You don't believe in any religion?"

"No. I don't believe in religion. I believe that there is a God and that everything is under His control."

"It's that simple for you, huh?"

She gave her shoulders a gentle shrug. "Religion isn't faith. I don't think God has a favorite religion, so neither do I."

Aimee's soft expression caused a strange and unexpected reaction. Although she looked into my eyes, I felt the tug in my chest. When I'd lived down at the beach, there were times when I thought of her as a brat, but it was evident I'd misjudged her. I ignored the sweat forming on my glass until I saw beads of water dripping. "Shit! I'm sorry, Aimee. This is dripping all over your couch."

She smiled. "This is exactly why I have a home and not a house." She reached to hand me a napkin. Her fingertips grazed my skin. At the moment of contact, our eyes met. The contact sparked, detonating something neither of us expected. We both pulled back at the same time.

I cleared my throat. "You remind me a little of my mom. I don't think we ever owned a set of anything, but somehow she pulled it all together." Aimee wore the same warm smile from a moment ago, and, again, I felt the same tug in my chest. I found it easier to talk than feel, so I steered the conversation to the rest of her house. "Did you make all of this stuff?"

"Most of it," she said proudly.

"I wouldn't have thought a prissy girl like you

would like messing around with this kind of thing. Sanding wood and all—"

"Then I guess you don't know me," she interrupted. "I like the idea of putting the unlikely together." She stood up and moved toward an old birdcage. "Just because something is discarded, doesn't mean it isn't useful, you know?" I looked at how she'd used the cage to house an array of plants. "Don't you ever ride by a junkyard and wonder about the people that used to drive the cars?"

"Can't say that I do."

"I do." She placed her hands on the cage, a tender expression softening her features. "When I see something old, I wonder about its former owner. Was it a gift? Probably. A woman owned it most likely. Maybe in the 1930s or 40s. And the bird? Was it a songbird? A parakeet? A canary? They were common back then. Usually a present for Easter or Mother's Day. I could go on, but you get the gist of what I'm saying. I let my mind wander."

Her imagination fascinated me and my stomach flipped as I watched her. Aimee looked at me like she could see through me and into my soul. Why had I never noticed her eyes? I'd been here with her for what? An hour? I couldn't have predicted how differently this visit would end from the way it started. I had intended to apologize, get my brother off my back, and be gone. Instead, I was enjoying getting to know Aimee in a different way than I had before. She wasn't as superficial as I'd initially thought, and I silently berated myself for being judgmental. I'd figured the modeling thing, especially with how popular she'd become lately, would have made her snobby or high-maintenance. Aimee wasn't that way at all. There was substance inside the beauty. "Your place is nice, Aim. Though I have to admit, the house itself is odd. All the different pieces you have here, I like them. Gives your place a down-to-earth feeling."

"I'm happy you like it. Most people take the word *home* for granted. I don't." She looked down into her lap and spoke quietly. "I never have."

I would have asked her to elaborate, but I was fixated on something else. A nervous habit, maybe? The more she talked about her house, the more she rubbed her palm up and down her thigh. She didn't even notice she was doing it, but I sensed that it was to self-soothe. I wanted to stop her. Make her feel better about whatever was bothering her. "Why are you nervous?" I couldn't help myself from asking.

Instantly she stopped the action. She pulled her knees up and placed her arms around them, gazing down toward her feet. "I'm not, really."

I moved closer to her and put my hand on her knee. "Aimee, look at me." My tone was gentle, as was my touch. "I'm glad I came over today—and I'm sorry for before. I'm not always the nicest person. Just ask my brother."

"Thank you for saying that." She peered at me

through thick, lush lashes. Her eyes glistened as a narrow ray of sun warmed her face. "I honestly thought you didn't like me."

The magnetic pull I'd previously felt gained strength with our close proximity. I looked from her eyes to her mouth—and found myself wanting to kiss her. The guilt that accompanied that thought pierced through any desire that had surfaced. I interrupted the quiet moment. "I think I should go." I removed my hand, hoping the severed connection would grant me a moment to regain rational thought. *Would it ever be right to feel again?*

"Oh, okay." I detected confusion in her words as she stood to walk me to the door. She tried to hide it, but there was a puzzled look in her eyes. "Just so you know, Carter, you're welcome anytime."

I didn't want to leave. Even though I thought I shouldn't, I wanted to see Aimee again. One foot was out the door as I turned toward her. "How about dinner? Let me make up for being a jackass."

"Another night, okay? Maybe Friday, if that works for you." Her voice was so soft that it could have carried on a butterfly wing. Her gaze went over my shoulder. "How did you get here? I don't see your truck."

"I walked." I took her hand and pulled her outside. Barefoot, she followed my lead to the back of the house. "See that slight clearing through the woods? If you go down that path, eventually you'll come to the back of my property."

"Wow! I didn't even notice it." She looked from the woods to me. "Is it far?"

I shrugged. "Nah. Just a good stretch of the legs."

Her hand was still in mine. It felt so small. Aimee said nothing, just looked around at the beauty surrounding us. She was more relaxed than I'd ever seen her, with a sweet expression that moved something inside of me. Something I thought had died along with Lacey. I didn't know what to call it, but I kind of liked it. I began to walk backward, letting go of her hand as I headed toward the woods.

"See you soon?" She held her hand up, waving softly.

I fought the urge to go back to her and enjoy more of our conversation. I wanted to learn more about her. I wanted to explore the woman behind my preconceived and wrong notions. I smiled and held up my hand to return the gesture, happy that her comment was an obvious invitation. "Probably sooner than you think."

Chapter 18

Carter

I continued to stare at the lackluster ceiling, although it provided no answers. A few days ago, I'd gone to see Aimee, and since then I'd spent every evening the same way. As if my fingers locked together beneath my head would somehow lift me to a higher consciousness, I stretched out on the sofa and quietly tried to sort out my thoughts. I had moved through a range of emotions, and each accompanied a question. The *how, why,* and *when* were the most troublesome. Lacey was gone, and I was left among the living and had to move forward. I thought that I had been doing just that when I threw myself into MarSin Falcon, but talking with Aimee that night had brought out more than just a desire to work. Aimee was like a breath of fresh air. As most men would, I found her beautiful, but after our conversation I realized she was so much more interesting. We'd never been alone, never had a one-on-one conversation until that night at her house. After seeing her, I'd gone home puzzled and full of questions, but mostly I examined my thoughts. I chastised myself for no longer thinking of her the same way my brother did, like a little sister. There was nothing sisterly about Aimee. The way my body had reacted to her dispelled that notion completely. It was the guilt that followed that was my enemy.

As I'd walked home through the woods that evening, all I could think about was when I'd see her again. The original plan had been to ask her to dinner that coming weekend. I felt quite good about it actually —until I arrived home. Once I walked through the door, it seemed that every corner held something that reminded me of Lacey. The feelings that hit were overwhelming. Misdirected shame at my betrayal of Lacey had washed over me, the thoughts corrosive as they took away any remnants of happiness I had gained just hours before. I didn't know how to handle it, so I didn't. Avoidance. It was the chicken-shit way out of dealing with my feelings. I was afraid to call Aimee, afraid of experiencing something that scared me. Who would have thought that being alone with a beautiful blonde with eyes the color of emeralds would scare the hell out of a man who carried a gun? I'd picked up the phone to call her—several times, in fact—but hung up before the call completed. It shouldn't have been a big deal. After all, it was only dinner. *Yeah, right!*

Once again, I turned my eyes up toward the ceiling. Cody lay beside me on the floor. She raised her head, looked me over, then laid it back down to rest on her front paws. I was familiar with the routine. It was her way of assuring herself I was okay and all was well. Ever since Lacey had died, Cody was rarely absent from my side. She was a good judge of character too. If your dog is good natured and doesn't like someone, I'd say that's a sign to keep your distance. But if that same dog shows an unusual amount of affection for someone, that's a sign too, and Cody loved Aimee. I turned over, my hip bone sinking into the space between two cushions. Thoughts of Aimee refused to leave my mind, no matter what I tried. I closed my eyes. It was time to man up. I'd had promised her dinner and I never break a promise. Thoughts of her lulled me to sleep.

MIDMORNING. I couldn't believe it. When I'd opened my eyes and looked at the clock, I was surprised I'd slept for so long. I'd been suffering from insomnia since Lacey's death, so a few solid hours of sleep made me feel better than I had in a long time. In truth, it had been the first time in over a year I'd slept a full night.

The first thing I did was make some coffee. I expected my business partners to come over within the hour. Marcus and Falcon would be arriving soon for a weekly strategy meeting, and I wasn't at all prepared. I'd intended to be up early, but I wasn't going to complain now about the extra sleep. My thoughts were interrupted by a loud knock. Cody began incessantly barking and she didn't stop until she saw Marc. He held pizzas in his hands, and suddenly my dog became his best friend.

"Hey, girl." Marcus placed the boxes on the table and bent down to give her some love. "You missed me, gorgeous girl—you know you did. I promise my pizza crust has your name on it."

With the reassurance she would share in his meal, Cody turned toward her bed. The quiet was short lived as her excitement was roused once again by Falcon's arrival. Once he, too, had spent a few minutes with her, my big furball climbed back onto her bed and closed her eyes. The three of us went into the office, and I positioned the computer screen so all of us could see.

"So, what's the latest?" Falcon wasted no time getting down to business. "From the stats you sent us, it looks like we have six more companies on board."

He was right. Business was good, and it was growing. The figures reflected it. Most of the firms that had entertained our proposals were now clients. Even though MarSin Falcon was a new security firm, our reputation for practical solutions was growing fast. We were anticipating triple the expansion than we'd predicted.

Each of us gave a recap of our respective meetings over the past week, and once we were satisfied with our goals for the next month, the conversation turned away from business and more to bullshit.

"If you guys are just going to sit here and jerk off, I think I hear that pizza calling my name." Marcus left the office while Falcon and I followed close behind him. He flipped the top open on both boxes. The cheese and pepperoni pizzas were probably cold by now, but no matter. We grabbed drinks from the kitchen and made ourselves at home in the living room. We were shooting the shit about sports and hunting when a knock on the door interrupted us. I shrugged, just as puzzled as they were. No one came to my house except for the two of them, and as Marc and Fal watched, I got up to answer the door. When I opened it, I was met with warm eyes and a bright smile.

"I hope you don't mind. I just stopped by to give you this. I won't keep you." Aimee held out a plastic container with a handle. "I was in a baking mood and I think I overdid it. I hope you like homemade pound cake. It's my grandmother's recipe."

Color flushed her cheeks as she looked past me and saw my buddies. "Sorry for the interruption, gentlemen," she called out.

Marcus recovered quickly and was instantly by my side. He took the cake out of my hands and nearly knocked me into the back of the door. "You didn't interrupt anything, sweetheart. Just a bunch of guys chewing the fat. Want some pizza?"

As I glared at him, Aimee looked at me. I could tell she was unsure of what to do. I stepped back in front of him. "Why don't you stay?" I asked, inviting her in.

"Only if you're sure there's enough."

As she stepped inside, Marcus grabbed a plate and loaded it with a slice from each box while Falcon stood. "You want a drink, sweetheart?"

"Sure." There was a hesitancy in her tone as she placed a napkin across her lap. Marc handed the plate to her, and she extended her hand. "I'm Aimee."

"Marc," he responded in introduction, as her delicate hand disappeared within his large one.

Falcon returned from the kitchen and handed her a glass of iced tea with one hand, extending the other out to her. "Falcon—Fal for short."

I gave them both a warning stare, silently cautioning them to be on their best behavior. Cody had already curled herself into a ball at Aimee's feet. The gesture wasn't lost on the men.

"It looks like Cody's found a new friend." Marc jerked his chin toward the dog.

"She doesn't do that for just anyone," Falcon chimed in.

Aimee smiled and took a bite of pizza. An awkward silence filled the room. After she swallowed, she looked at me. "I didn't hear from you, so I ventured out on my own and found some nice places to eat."

"I'm sorry, Aim," I fumbled. "I've been busy."

Both men shot me inquiring looks, which I ignored.

"Me, too," she answered. "I lose track of time. I'll start on something at nine in the morning, and the next thing I know, it's nine at night."

Marcus cocked an inquisitive brow, dismissing me. "So, how is it that you know Carter?"

"We've been friends for a few years now. We met through his brother. Declan and I work together."

"You look familiar." Marc narrowed one eye as if to see her better.

"I was around during the funeral. I helped out with the luncheon. I just moved up here." She took another bite and looked over at me, masking her eyes in shyness.

Falcon threw me a disapproving look. "*Hmm.* Funny. Carter didn't mention that we had a new neighbor."

I glared, willing him to knock it off. "Don't pay attention to them, Aim. They're like old women in a small town, getting all up in my business."

Aimee laughed, diffusing the tension that had thickened the air. "Honestly, guys. There's no story to tell." She looked around at the three of us. "When I was here before, I really liked Deep Creek, so I bought a little place I'm renovating. A houseboat of sorts."

"So... you live on the lake?" Marc's curiosity was piqued.

"Not really, no. It's hard to describe." Aimee's voice

suddenly seemed guarded, but she recovered well enough not to offend. "I'll tell you what; when I'm all finished, Carter can bring you guys over, okay?"

"Cool. I'd like to see your handiwork."

Falcon's comment sounded more suggestive than I was comfortable with. In fact, both guys were just shy of hitting on her.

"Be careful, Aimee." My words hung heavy with warning. "They might look like nice guys, but they're pigs."

Everyone, including Aimee, laughed off my warning. She bent to give Cody a remnant of her pizza, and while her attention was elsewhere, I glared steel daggers at my friends. Once she'd petted and kissed Cody, she stood and began to remove the dirty plates and empty bottles. I reached to take them from her hands. "I got it, Aim."

"Don't be silly." Her lips pursed as she shook her head. "It's just a few plates." She turned to Marc and Fal. "If you guys want dessert, I'll put on some coffee." She looked over at me. "If that's okay with you."

I nodded. Aimee carried everything to the kitchen. Once I heard water running, I rounded on my friends. "What the hell do you think you're doing?" My voice was low, the words seethed through my teeth. Marcus gave me a sinister grin. I wanted to punch him.

"We're not doing anything, buddy. Just being nice to your friend." Marc laughed.

"Yeah, the one you never told us about," Falcon chimed in.

Aimee returned, carrying a tray with the cake and four mugs of coffee. Both men dug in, the only sound in the room the clinking of metal forks against the glass dishes. Once they'd gobbled down everything on their plates, the conversation resumed.

"Beautiful and a good cook too? Where's Carter been hiding you?" Falcon teased.

She grinned. "Cook? Not so much, but I like to bake—and he hasn't been hiding me."

Marcus was staring at her, a puzzled look on his face. Aimee caught him and dabbed at the corners of her mouth. "What? Do I have something on my face?"

"Have we met before? You look really familiar."

"Yeah, you do," Falcon's brow furrowed as he searched for the recollection.

She blushed. "I don't think so. I hadn't been up here before now. Well, other than the funeral. It could have been from there."

"No, it was somewhere else. I didn't make it to the funeral because I was out of the country," Marc answered.

I sighed, more annoyed than anything else. "Didn't you hear her say she works with my brother? She's a model, idiot. She's in commercials and magazines."

"That's it!" Enthusiastically, Marcus slapped his knee.

"I remember now," Falcon added. "We were

watching the football game, and you were on TV in one of the commercials. Matter of fact, Marc said he thought you were very sexy. Shit! No wonder Carter's been hiding you."

"Gorgeous and makes a cake like this? Sweetie, you can come bake for me anytime." Marcus winked at her suggestively.

Aimee smiled a shy smile, nothing like the dazzling one in the media. "Thank you, but I have to be going. It was nice meeting you both."

I followed her when she stood and walked her to the door. Leaving Marc and Falcon in the living room gave us a semi-private moment.

"I didn't mean to barge in without calling. I could tell it got awkward in there."

I dismissed her fears with a wave of my hand. "It's not your fault. They're morons."

"Still..." There was that shy smile again. I felt that pull in my chest that was becoming more familiar whenever I was around her. She rose up on her toes and brushed her lips against my cheek. The connection sent a jolt flaring through my veins, igniting a feeling that had lain dormant for too long. I inhaled her scent as she pulled back. "I promise, I'll call next time."

Before I had time to think, she was going down the front steps. I watched as she got in the car and closed the door. Once she pulled out and into the driveway, I turned on my heel and stalked back into the house to address my friends. "What the hell was that?" I glared at them both. "Christ! I wouldn't be surprised if she never comes back."

"Just being friendly, brother." The corner of Marcus's mouth hooked with a ribbing sneer.

"Yeah? Well, back off, assholes; she's a sweet girl." It sounded like an order. Unfortunately, my tone only enticed them to throw out a few more comments.

Falcon narrowed his eyes, his grin sly. "Yeah, I'd say she's sweet!"

Heat flicked my anger; the burn singed my neck and ears as my blood pulsed a violent beat. "Knock it off. She's not some trashy piece of ass you picked up."

"Sure, sure." Falcon raised both hands to assure me the message was received, then both he and Marc roared with laughter. I ground my teeth, a snarl tickling my tongue against the back of my mouth. I was ready to burst into beast mode knowing what kind of thoughts they were having about Aimee. I didn't like it. Not one bit.

Chapter 19

Carter

I never thought I'd need to ask for advice about a woman, especially from my baby brother, but here I was, phone and pride in hand.

"Hello?"

"Hey, Dec. You got a minute?" A tentative feeling gnawed at my gut. It pained me to have to do this, after all, I was everyone else's go-to person. Now I felt backed into a corner.

"I've got a few minutes," he answered. "What's up?"

"It's about Aimee."

Declan paused. "What about Aimee? Tell me you weren't an asshole again."

"It would probably be easier for me if I had been," I said and laughed.

"Oh, Christ. That doesn't sound good." There was a wariness in his voice. "Just spit it out, Carter."

"I want to take her out." My stomach felt as if I had eaten bad oysters.

"Seriously? You want to take her out?" He paused. The silence increased my anxiety. "Why?"

"Oh, I don't know! Why do you think?" I laced my words with sarcasm. "She's beautiful, sweet, and talented. She's a good cook. Want me to go on?"

"She's not a good cook," he interjected.

"That's where you're wrong, brother." I shook my head in deference to his comment.

"Aimee brought a cake over here that Marc, Fal, and I demolished in one night."

"She's a good baker, not a good cook, but I get what you're saying." I could hear the underlying thread of humor in his words. I rolled my eyes toward the heavens. He was playing with me. "So, what's the problem?"

That was a loaded question. *What exactly was the problem? She's single. I'm... single.* "I feel a little guilty, okay?"

"What the hell for?" His tone was bold, almost arrogant, and put me on the defensive.

"Because I feel like I'm cheating on my wife!" I said the words more explosively than I intended, firing them at him in rapid succession. There was no sound on the phone other than my brother's breathing. "Tell me I'm wrong."

"You're wrong, Carter."

The words unlocked chains of apprehension from my chest. I breathed in an unhindered breath, suddenly aware of how tightly I'd been holding myself. Declan spoke slowly and calmly, the words a healing balm for the gaping wound that I'd made a habit of ripping the bandage off of.

"You're not cheating on Lacey. I know you loved her, but she's gone. She would want you to move on. You know that."

I sat down at the table, the phone pressed to my ear. I scrubbed my hand over my face. "I think I do, but it feels weird to have feelings for another woman."

"I can't give you the answer," Declan advised, "but I can remind you that Lacey loved life. She wouldn't want you to stop living because she's not here."

"I don't know." I sounded like an exasperated teenager.

"Look, I'm no expert, but I don't think the grief ever goes away. You just figure out how to live with it and go on in spite of it."

A WEEK HAD GONE by since my conversation with Declan, and now I found myself standing at Aimee's front door. I thought it would have been harder, pushing myself to go on a date, but I was pleasantly surprised to find I felt good about it. I was really looking forward to spending an evening with her. It had been a long time since I'd put any thought into seeing a woman. Relying on the traditional route, I'd put on a suit and brought flowers. Now here I was, knocking on her door. Before I had any time to think, she appeared.

"*Wow.*"

The word fell from my mouth, and I quickly clapped it shut so I wouldn't drool. Aimee's body-hugging, light-blue dress accentuated her curves in the best possible way. Her long blonde hair fell in soft curls around her face and down her back. The color of her eyes was warmer than I'd previously thought, the gold specks in them sparkling like diamonds. She was so gorgeous it knocked the wind out of me. I swallowed hard as she smiled.

"I hope that's a good *wow* and not a bad one."

"Not at all." I continued staring.

"So, that means it's either not a good one or not a bad one," she teased. I looked at her helplessly. I was already screwing this up, but she took pity on me. "I'm just playing with you." Her lighthearted laugh accompanied a peck on the cheek. "Are those for me?" she asked, pointing to the flowers.

I almost forgot I was holding them. "Yeah, they're for you." I gave the bouquet to her, and she inhaled deeply.

"Thank you," she said as she brought her lips to my cheek again. After she backed away, she reached her hand up and rubbed where her lips had been. "Lipstick," she explained. "Can't have you going out with a mark on your cheek." Aimee walked into the kitchen with the flowers. "I'll put these in water before we go," she called over her shoulder. "What time are the reservations?"

I unbuttoned my jacket and followed her to the doorway of the kitchen. I could watch her all day. Leaning against the jamb, I placed my hands in my pockets. "Seven thirty. It's only six fifteen now, we have some time until we need to leave."

Aimee turned toward me with the blooms now neatly tucked into a vase. Pausing at the doorway, she leaned into me. "I'm really looking forward to tonight." Her breath caressed my cheek. It tempted my starving libido with wicked thoughts. Her fragrance wafted up my nose and into my bloodstream, much like I'd heard cocaine hits the first time to create an addict. I could easily become addicted to Aimee. She was tempting enough to make a celibate man rock hard. As she pulled back, I focused on her rose-colored lips. Full and plump. Blood rushed through me at a fiery pace. I grew hard imagining how they would feel as she took me between them. She grabbed her coat. "I think I'll need this."

"You're probably right. It gets chilly up here at night." For an instant, I hated that damned coat and the idea it might rob me of a chance to touch her. I shook off the thought. "You ready to go?"

"Yes, sir."

She was quiet during the drive, relaxing into the seat and enjoying the music.

"I would never have pictured you as a guy who'd listen to Amos Lee."

I arched an eyebrow, looking over at her. "What? You think all mountain boys listen to country?"

She scrunched up her nose in a playful way. "Kind of. You fit the stereotype."

"Oh, yeah?" I laughed. "I guess I need a shotgun and a tin of chewing tobacco to complete the image."

"No, I like you like this. You just surprise me, that's all." She reached over to pat my hand. As her fingers lingered, the connection sizzled. It remained there until I pulled into a parking spot. Aimee turned, placing her hand on the door handle.

"Don't you dare." My voice held enough warning that her head snapped around and her brows furrowed. She gave me a puzzled look as I exited the car. When I came around to her side of the vehicle and opened the door, her expression softened. She offered her hand to my outstretched one.

"Thank you, kind sir." Slipping her petite hand through my arm, she gently gripped my bicep.

We didn't sever our connection until we were seated at our table. The waiter handed us both a menu and told us he'd give us a few minutes to peruse the wine list. I waited for him to walk away. "I think you might like the Tasting and Pairing Experience."

She peeked over the wine list and cocked her head. "Mr. Sinclair, you are just full of surprises."

I shrugged. "I've had it. It's a good choice."

She placed the menu and the wine list down on the table. "You know what? I think I'd like you to order for me this evening, that is, if you don't mind."

I grinned. "I don't mind. Are you adventurous with your food?"

"I guess you could say that," she laughed. "I have a healthy appetite, and there isn't much I don't like."

"I thought supermodels existed on crackers and water."

"Oh, yes," Aimee said, suddenly serious. "I'm very adventurous with my crackers. Sesame, rosemary, sea salt, and whole wheat—I've tried them all." She leaned in with a mischievous look in her eye. "You tell me if you see the food police, okay? I don't want to get in trouble for being a rebel and eating something that might satisfy me."

I chuckled. She was beautiful and funny. The waiter returned, and I ordered for us both. Aimee listened with interest as I spoke. Once he was gone, I relaxed. Being with Aimee was proving to be easier than I thought. "I have a question. Why'd you agree to go out with me tonight?"

"Well," she quirked her lips and raised her brows in a playful expression. "Why not?"

I liked this side of her. Aimee leaned in closer, as if she were going to share a secret. I did the same, noticing how the light played with the glints of gold in her eyes. "The truth is..." she confessed in a whisper, "I know you mountain men like a good meal. We girls on crackers and water can't pass up real food. We may be pretty, but we aren't stupid. We never pass up a juicy piece of meat and a hot guy."

Christ! She's killing me! I shifted in my seat. She'd just sucked me into a mindset that could make it hard to get through dinner. Aimee's smile was sweet, but her sultry tone and seductive expression were anything but. She pushed my buttons in a good way—making my body behave in a bad way. Parts of me had a mind of their own, and my pants grew tight in response to her. My urges had been long-starved, and her behavior was oil to my rusty parts. In that moment, I decided I was going to have fun tonight instead of psychoanalyzing everything. Self-examination be damned.

Aimee reached across the table and gingerly placed her hand atop mine. I was beginning to like the feel of her touch. I felt a satisfied grin creep onto my lips. "The truth is, Carter, we had a rocky start, and I know it hasn't been easy for you. I'd like to put all of that behind us. If you're comfortable doing that, I will be too." She hooked her fingers into the fleshy space between my thumb and index finger and settled them there. "Fresh start, okay? You promised me dinner. I promise you you won't regret it." She made circles on my skin with her thumb.

Does she know how damn sexy she is?

I let my guard down. Any reservations or preconceived notions disappeared. I lost myself in her. Aimee's voice was seductive, the liquid velvet tone coaxing me into a semi-hypnotic state. My police training usually dictated that I absorb the details of my surroundings, but all I could focus on was her—and my thoughts of sinking deeply into her. I lifted her hand to my lips and placed a kiss on her fingers. Her eyes locked with mine as the air between us surged and sparked. "I'm gonna hold you to that, doll."

Chapter 20

Carter

The drive back to Aimee's house was comfortable. Quiet, yet peaceful. I was so content I didn't want to risk saying something to dispel the atmosphere that had dominated our evening. I parked and went around to the other side of the car to assist her. She squeezed my proffered hand.

"Why don't you come in for a little while?"

I didn't want the evening to end, so I followed her inside. Aimee poured herself some wine and handed me a beer. She was more observant than I thought because I noticed it was a brand I favored. Removing my suit jacket, I sat down on the far end of the sofa while she slipped off her heels. She made herself comfortable at the other end, tucking her feet under her in a posture I had noticed several times. She tipped her wine glass in my direction. "To new relationships."

I moved closer and tapped my bottle to her glass. "New relationships," I repeated.

I loosened my tie and unbuttoned the top buttons of my shirt.

"Was it as bad as you thought it would be?"

"What do you mean?" I asked.

She gave her shoulders a gentle shrug. "I'm just guessing, but was this your first date after losing Lacey?"

We were on the same wavelength because I'd just been thinking about that. I rested my arm against the back of the sofa and took a swig of the beer. She watched me as she waited for an answer. "It wasn't, and it is. As a matter of fact, I really enjoyed tonight. With you."

"This is a really crazy question to ask you, but do you think that Lacey would approve?"

Although surprised at the question, I appreciated her candor. "Of you? I think she would have liked you. I just don't know how she would have felt about me dating. It's a strange position to be in, because I also know she wouldn't want me to be alone."

She reached for my hand. "I want you to feel good about spending time with me. I don't want you to do it if it feels wrong to you." She smiled sweetly. "I know this is kind of personal, but do you sometimes feel like you died when she did?"

"Yes. It's strange how you try to sort things out when your partner dies. Some of the things you used to do, you only did because of them. Those parts of me died, and others grew numb." I placed my hand on her leg. "Then there are other parts of me that are learning to live again."

"You know I speak my mind, Carter. I really enjoyed tonight, and I'd be lying if I said that I didn't find you attractive."

"It's mutual, sweetheart."

"Do you think that we can do this again? We can just figure it out as we go."

I loved her candor. Aimee was proving to be a woman I could get used to being with. "I think that's a good idea."

WE SPENT several hours laughing and talking cars, sports, and renovations. When it was time for me to leave, she slipped her hand around my waist as she walked me to the door, while my arm hung lazily around her shoulders. "What are you doing next weekend?" I turned her to face me and ran my fingers through the hair at the back of her head.

She shrugged. "I don't have any plans that I know of."

"How about we take a hike through the woods? I'll make a lunch. We can even bring Cody."

"I like that idea." A pleasant smile hooked the corners of her mouth.

I didn't think, I just surrendered to the moment. Leaning down, I pressed my mouth to hers. It was sweet and yielding, a ripe peach for the taking. I ran my tongue across her lips, applying just enough force to tease them apart. We lingered there for a few moments, which seemed like an eternity.

Chapter 21

Aimee

A few walks and hikes were accompanied by a few lunches and dinners, and then I was seeing Carter nearly every day. We balanced each other out; I appreciated his serious side, and he seemed to enjoy my more carefree nature.

I felt at home in Deep Creek. I loved the small town feel and had made friends in town. The old man at the hardware store, the florist, and the kids who work at the ice cream shop were all on a first name basis with me. For the first time, I could actually say I loved my life.

I extended my vacation so that I could continue renovations on the boathouse. My latest project was a cute little nook in a cozy corner of the kitchen. The view from the window looked out at the forest between my house and Carter's. I wasn't yet familiar with the trails through the woods, but I looked forward to walking the path between our houses.

I was in the midst of putting the final coat on the benches when Carter arrived. Neither of us stood on ceremony anymore. Instead, we had an "open door" policy. I knew it was him just from the sound of his footsteps on the hardwood. His boots made a *click-shuffle* sound as he walked. A different noise alerted me to something else. Cody. Initially Carter was hesitant to bring her, thinking her size would get in my way. He said he could just imagine her knocking over paint and rolling around on the floor to get it off. More likely she would have eaten a paint brush or a rag, but I promised I would keep an eye on her. Now if Carter didn't bring Cody with him when he came by, I sent him home to get her. It didn't take long for her to feel as comfortable at my house as she did at home.

"Hey, pretty girl." Cody nudged me, the force tumbling me onto my rear end. I took the break, stretching my legs out in front of me. She interpreted that as an invitation to lay across my thighs.

"There's a picture." Carter's rumbling laughter warmed my insides until they were toasty.

"Best lap dog ever," I answered as I looked at her. "Did you miss me?" Carter offered me a hand up, but Cody wasn't moving. I shrugged, and he shook his head at both of us.

"You spoil her." He tugged on her collar, and she responded to her master. Again, he reached to help me up. I rose, but my legs felt like they were asleep. I staggered and fell into Carter's chest. Instantly, he wrapped an arm around me and pulled me close. The opening of my paint-covered flannel shirt widened. Our eyes locked. "Hi." His voice wrapped around me like a seductive blanket.

"Hi, yourself." My breathy voice betrayed me as I stared at his lips. We'd done lots of kissing. A few times, the kissing had led to touching, and the touching had fed my lust. My tummy fluttered when I thought of where the touching would lead. Eventually.

He pulled back, leaving me breathless as he tipped up my chin and kissed me on the nose. "I brought coffee and donuts."

"You're going to get me in trouble! I'm never going to fit in the designers' clothes when I go back to New York."

He answered by pulling me closer. He placed both hands around my waist so his fingers touched. "I think you're perfect."

I slid my hands over and down the muscular ridges of his chest, appreciating every inch. My voice fell seductively low. "I guess I could always become a plus-size model."

His eyes smoldered as his voice coated my skin with smoky tones. "I like curves."

The heated moment was interrupted when Cody

wiggled between us. Reluctantly, we separated. Carter went to get the donuts he'd left in the other room. When he came back, I drew his attention to my project. "So, what do you think?" I nodded toward the breakfast nook.

"I like it." He took one bite of the donut, tearing it nearly in half. He followed with a huge gulp of coffee and then wiped his mouth with his shirt sleeve, making that simple act a study of raw sexuality. "What are you going to do with the old table?"

"Donate it. Someone will be able to use it."

He set his cup down. "I can take it to the thrift store for you. I'll load it up in the truck when I leave."

I loved his thoughtfulness. "Thank you. That will save me a trip."

He waved me off as if his gesture was insignificant and then held the box out to me. "I got you a Boston Cream."

My heart melted. Carter didn't realize how much the little things meant to me. Butterflies took flight in my stomach, causing my heart to open like an unfurled flower. "Did you know they're my favorite?"

"As a matter of fact, I do. You might not notice, but I pay attention." Pride accentuated his handsome face. "I know a lot about what you like."

His tone was suggestive. I returned his gaze. Two could play this game. I lifted the donut from the box. Keeping my eyes on Carter's face, I slowly tore it in two. I teased some cream out with a crooked finger and placed it in my mouth. I took my time, sucking the filling in as I slowly pulled the digit between my lips. I repeated the act a second time and was about to do it a third when he grabbed my wrist. He pulled my hand toward him and mimicked my actions. I couldn't breathe. Two definitely could play this game. He released my hand, and grabbed my hips, forcing me to straddle him. I sank my fingers into his hair as he looked up at me. "You're such a tease."

His lips scorched the base of my throat as he peppered kisses toward my breasts. My head fell back as he taunted my skin. His kisses were accompanied by his tongue, and the combination left tingles in the wake of their trail. My breath quickened and my head fell to the side. He continued the delicious assault down my exposed neck, kissing, licking, and gently scraping from the small hollow behind my ear to my collarbone. My whimpers urged him on. He tugged at my shirt, causing it to fall over my shoulder. As my excitement grew, so did his. I felt his hardness beneath my bottom. All that separated us was denim. The possibilities simultaneously thrilled and frightened me. I had spent most of my life warding off men, but this man... I trusted him. I wanted him.

He wove his fingers into my hair, pulling me so close that barely a breath had space between us. He returned his lips to mine, and his tongue incited a craving that escalated. There was a wanton little minx inside of me. Imprisoned for too long, she wanted to come out and play. His lips left mine again, but I wasn't ready to sever our connection. I took his bottom lip between my teeth and gently nibbled as I ran my tongue across the surface. He grew harder beneath me. He ran his hand down my side, and as it traveled over my ribcage, I trembled. "Carter..." My whispered plea barely escaped.

Both of his hands slid up my back beneath my shirt, and he unhooked my bra. His eager palms came around to my chest, and he pushed until my breasts were free. Cupping them, he kneaded the globes and teased the tips until they were painfully hard. I closed my eyes, savoring the feel of his touch. He dipped his head for a taste, doing amazing things with his lips and tongue. My head drifted back, and I fell headfirst into the pleasurable sensations. A soft cry escaped as his teeth grazed my most sensitive parts. In one quick movement, he lowered me to the floor, holding me down as he gripped both my wrists above my head with one hand. He imprisoned my hips between his knees as he straddled me. With insistent fingers, he unbuttoned my jeans and pulled the zipper down. My breath came in quick gasps as he dipped a finger inside my folds.

"Carter."

"*Shh*, baby. Don't think, just feel."

I obeyed. I wanted this. I lifted my hips when I felt him tug to remove my jeans. My mind was swimming in a sea of sensations, the current of desire washing away any conscious thought. Tiny waves of lust gained strength as the denim was pulled down my thighs, then a sound caught the attention of both of us. Carter froze and my eyes popped open.

"Anybody home?"

Chapter 22

Marisol

"Manny, stop. Please."

The news that Manny had just delivered to Marisol was almost too much to process. The opportunity it presented was overwhelming. As he explained the possible loophole that could secure her freedom, Marisol tried to focus on his words. Knowing Manny had information that could manipulate the judge into rendering a decision in her favor gave her comfort. Manny had connections, money, and power. The combination of the three could secure anything he wanted.

"The paperwork is being drafted as we speak, chica. I'm in the process of getting the video of your interrogation. After you told me about what happened when the authorities arrested you, I took that information to the abogado. He said that if you did not compre-hend your Miranda rights, then the legality of your arrest is in question. Do you understand what this means?"

Marisol nodded. "They handcuffed me and started telling me I had a right to many things, but I didn't understand. I told them that they were making a mistake. They ignored everything I said. I specifically remember them asking me if I knew what they were saying and I answered 'no.' I was yelling at them."

Manny laughed. "Of that, I have no doubt!"

Marisol bit her lip, uncertainty clouding her thoughts. "I don't think that they appreciated my behavior. I remember telling Carter Sinclair he sounded like he had a mouthful of *mierda*."

Again, Manny laughed. "Did he know what that meant?"

She shrugged.

"You, *mi tesoro*, are priceless." A grin stretched his face as he reached for her hand.

The tender gesture warmed Marisol and brought a smile to her face. It occurred to her she'd taken connec-tions with others for granted. Since she'd been confined, she rarely had the luxury of a kind touch. "I was ranting in English and Spanish. I doubt they knew what I was saying."

"Exactly! That's what the lawyers are looking for."

His erupted exclamation was a little louder than intended, causing Marisol to look around to see if he had drawn any attention. Once she placed a finger to her lips to shush him, she adopted a puzzled expression. "Can you explain to me how my misunderstanding could compromise the case?"

His face was smug. "It's very simple, chica; if what you've told me is supported by the video of your arrest, it could be your ticket to freedom."

"But the United States... the *policia*—"

He interrupted her. "Are corrupt? Yes. There is corruption everywhere, mi amor. I have discovered that one of the arresting officers has accumulated quite a gambling debt. American football. I have sent a message to him that all of his problems could disappear if he's willing to compromise his morals. I have no reason to believe that he won't. There are many immigrants in the US. It's a matter of whether or not the government is doing all it can to help them learn the laws of the land without exploiting the language barriers."

Marisol's shoulders relaxed. "Thank you."

Manny appreciated her gentle tone. It pleased him to know she would be in his debt if his plan came to pass. "Thank me when it's finished. Then we'll celebrate." He watched intently as her eyes misted.

"What is it, Marianna? Are you happy or troubled?"

"It's nothing."

A prick of rage caused Manny to narrow his eyes. "Then why the tears? I told you I would fix this."

Marisol collected herself and looked down at Manny's strong hand holding hers. "And I know that you can, but the truth is, some things have been taken from me that you can never replace. Some people who should pay restitution for what they've done to me never will. You talk about corruption. I will never see justice done to those who made it their mission to destroy me."

Manny's jaw grew tight. His eyes clouded with a determined stare. He knew the people of whom she spoke. He'd done his research and had made a mental list of names. He intended to exact revenge on those who had discredited Marianna. While he had to admit that her behavior was unacceptable, it in no way justified the treatment she'd received. He leaned in close to her. "Dismiss your concerns, *mi amor*. I have it under control."

Chapter 23

Aimee

Heavy droplets fell as I stood in the shower. I hoped the water carried enough weight to wash away the embarrassment that had covered me just hours before. I had so much to learn. I was still adjusting to small town life, so I hadn't anticipated that my friendly delivery man would come around to the back door when no one answered the front. Carter and I could have ignored him if not for the four-pane window. I hadn't thought to cover it with curtains, so we'd found ourselves putting on a show for the man when he looked inside to see if I was home.

I put my head under the forceful spray and let it wash away my self-conscious thoughts. Instead, I concentrated on the events that had occurred before

Carter and I were interrupted. I'd almost stopped him at the point when I felt like I was losing control. When his hand had slipped inside my pants, and his fingers went to a place that had never felt a touch other than my own, my thoughts were convoluted. I'd never realized how closely excitement and anxiety were related. To say I was overwhelmed wouldn't be an accurate description. But the feelings. They were just... just... *more.*

Carter's words had been a potent tranquilizer. They calmed and intoxicated my anxious inhibitions until my jumbled thoughts melted away in a haze of wanton desire. After we'd jumped to our feet and arranged our clothing, the unspoken messages we exchanged with our eyes had me believing this was the last time our passion would be unmet. I leaned my head against the shower wall as the water eased the tension in my shoulders. Although I waited for anxious thoughts to consume me, none came. *How would I feel after I engaged in the act?* It was more curiosity than fear that caused me to ask myself that question. I'd never considered this before Carter. I hadn't been the typical teenager. My only security was what I had conjured for myself. Everything in my young life had been dictated by a foster care system that was woefully inadequate, and once I started working, Bella Matrix was in charge of my comings and goings. Throughout my life, I had little say regarding where I lived, what I ate, and when and where I would travel. As a result, I still held a steel-tight rein on the only things over which I did have control. My heart. My soul. My body.

The thought of giving those things to Carter filled me with a fragile sense of security. I remembered the feeling of his kisses as bubbles skated over my skin. The memory of his lips occupying the same space filled me with longing. Would making love with him feel as good as I imagined? Would the heaviness that I'd carried since a child take flight under the tutelage of his expert touch? The truth was, when I was with him, everything felt lighter—better—than I could ever have dreamed. Concerns about yesterday and tomorrow faded away as I happily lived in the moment. Falling in love with him released my self-inflicted doubts until they floated away into confidence. I didn't delude myself into believing he felt the same, but the possibility that he could one day, made me want to explore what was next. *But what if I get hurt?* Damn the voice inside my head! No matter what happened, I knew one thing for sure: I would survive. I would push forward. I craved the sensation of someone devouring me because they need me more than anything else, filling me with such rock-hard desire that I'd detonate into shattered and beautiful pieces of gratification.

I thought of Carter as I stepped out of the shower. I wanted him more than I'd ever wanted anyone. With me, he was stern, but soft; determined, but flexible;

demanding, but permissive. He was an orchestra of contradictions but having him near was a sweet sound to my lovesick soul. I doubted he knew any better than I where our relationship was going, but I was willing to take a chance.

Chapter 24

Carter

Feet up on the desk with my ass in a comfortable chair: that was my definition of peaceful solitude. As I looked out of the window, I could see the wind picking up. It tossed wishes and pine needles until they formed little orbs. I could hear it whistling as it moved through the treetops. I needed a little seclusion to clear my head. I was on my third beer since coming home from Aimee's. I'd always been good at figuring things out. I was a patient man. I took my time. I watched. I learned. My mom had praised my self-control growing up. I liked learning how things worked. Car motors, clocks, lawn mowers—I could take things apart and put them back together. But that didn't apply to women.

Aimee and I had clicked. She meant more to me than I expected would happen. Things with her were so different than they'd been with Lacey. I'd always felt like I had to impress my wife in order to earn her love. Since meeting Aimee, I've realized it had all been in my head, because with her, everything came naturally. Our relationship wasn't something we could have predicted. The way I felt about her had grown organically. The more time I spent with her, the more time I wanted to spend with her. It was easy to be me. Even though I probably shouldn't have, I couldn't help but to compare her to Lacey. More precisely, I compared the difference in the two relationships.

I read a quote once that said, "The greatest challenge in life is discovering who you are. The second greatest is being happy with what you find." I hadn't known who I was when I was younger. I tried to be who I thought people wanted me to be. In contrast, with Aimee, what you saw was what you got. I didn't try to figure her out, because I didn't need to, and she didn't expect any more of me than who I was. I pondered the places we'd gone and the things we'd done. Every dinner, lunch, hike, walk—hell, all of it—I enjoyed more because I was with her. I've learned from her that appearances can be deceiving. In magazines, she looks emotionally detached, but she's actually nothing of the sort. She's thoughtful, kind, sexy—and a mystery.

I closed my eyes and laid my head on the back of the chair. I heard the squeak of the screen door opening. Who needed a doorbell when an old door and

Cody were more than enough? I didn't move; instead, I focused on the footsteps of our visitor as the hardwood floors magnified the sounds. Cody went to investigate, her paws making a soft clomping impression.

"Hi."

Aimee's tone was resigned and quiet as she stood above me. I opened my eyes to look at her. Her hair was still damp from a recent shower, the blonde a little darker from wetness as it hugged around her shoulders. With the light in the room, she looked like an angel but, damn that woman, she tempted me like the devil.

"Are you mad?" She walked around to the front of the desk and leaned her hip against it.

"At you? No. Although, I wanted to hurt the guy at the door." I patted my knee in silent invitation. As she approached, my eyes roamed from the V-neck of her sweater, all the way down her denim-clad legs. The material was so worn that the jeans hugged her like a second skin. Lifting one leg, she draped her knee over my thigh. She repeated the motion as she straddled me, resting her rear end on the top of my legs. With both hands she cupped my head, tilting my chin. When she rested her forehead against mine, her hair fell around us both. The warmth in her eyes pulled me in. Their gold flecks flickered as they adjusted to the setting sun's light. She pressed her lips to mine. I loved this part of our dance.

I threaded my fingers through her hair and intensi-fied the connection. Her body molded to mine, the mounds beneath her sweater now pressing against my chest. Her legs relaxed until the crotch of her jeans met the reaction in mine. I wanted to give her one last chance. "I wouldn't have stopped."

She searched my eyes, knowing I was referring to what had happened between us just a few hours before. "I wouldn't have wanted you to."

I lifted her up and stood from the chair. Hooking her legs around me, I carried her into the bedroom. My boot met the bottom of the door as I kicked it open. Our lips never parted as I laid her down on the bed. I tugged her sweater up over her chest, only releasing her mouth long enough to pull it over her head, and then slid the straps of her bra over her shoulders to the top of her arms. I kissed her hard. Her soft moans encouraged me. There was no one here to interrupt us, so there was no need to rush. I unhooked the back of the bra. Sliding it off of her arms completely I took a step back to allow it to fall to the floor. Cupping her breast, I kneaded the soft globe. I explored her leisurely, knowing that our shared cravings would be satisfied. Her heart beat a supersonic pace under my fingertips as I shocked the pebbled tip with my tongue. I grew painfully rigid as I absorbed the erotic sound of her whimpers. Passion coursed like lava through my veins, and, for the moment, my sole purpose was her pleasure. Nothing else mattered except getting her naked and studying every soft curve of her. I lifted her waist, pushing at her panties and jeans until they fell down her legs to her ankles. They joined her other garments in a pile on the floor. Aimee's naked body lay before me like a golden-haired pagan sacrifice waiting on my will. I relished the sight. She returned my gaze with eyes reflecting desire. I swallowed the lump in my throat. "You are so beautiful."

She smiled, and I went under, the depth of emotion in her eyes drowning me. I wanted to commit her image to memory by etching every mark and freckle on her body like the treasure map I found it to be.

I pulled off my tee shirt and got out of my jeans in record time. With one foot, I kicked them out of the way. They landed near the pile of Aimee's discarded clothes. I reached into the drawer of the bedside table. Fumbling through the contents, I felt the serrated edges of a condom package. I quickly ripped the foil and sheathed myself. I watched Aimee's expression change as her gaze traveled down my chest. Her eyes widened as I took my erection in hand and guided myself into her. My blood coursed hard and hot as my flesh pulsated against my fingers. Aimee tugged her bottom lip between her teeth, sinking them into the tender flesh.

Wrapping both hands around her waist, I pulled her to me so she had one leg on each side of my hips. I rocked against her heat. The beat of my blood intensi-fied as I pressed into her. I fought myself to keep from plunging in too fast and deep. The ache of denying myself was painful, but the feeling of being inside her was bliss. I swallowed. Until this moment I'd only imagined how good she'd feel, but nothing prepared me for the flood of satisfaction at possessing her.

Aimee responded by mirroring my motion. Her hips undulated as her breath quickened. I pushed in further. Inch by inch I forged our connection. With slow intent, I moved inside of her and felt tiny muscle spasms as she gripped me from within. Suddenly, I could go no further. As I pressed in slightly, Aimee's eyes went wide, and I discovered her secret. The resistance I felt at the point of our connection was unmistakable. Aimee was a virgin.

"Aimee..."

My voice was hesitant. I would have stopped, but she pulled me closer. Her legs locked around me, and my thoughts scrambled. How my beauty had reached this point in her life still a virgin was a mystery to me. Casual sex was rampant in the modeling world, according to my brother. A collection of questions danced a jig in my head, but I quickly dismissed them as a feeling of ownership raced a shiver down my spine. The knowledge that I was her first gave me more pleasure than it should have. It was a possessive feeling. I meant to be gentle with her, but Aimee dug her heels into my backside. The urge to conquer her was animalistic. It would only take one hard thrust to destroy the barrier.

I kissed her. Our tongues tangled, and our teeth

clacked as our motions intensified. Lust sank sharp claws into me and resurrected the primal need inside of me. Every muscle in my body stiffened as I plunged the full length of my stone-hard sex inside of her. I didn't stop until I was balls deep.

Aimee didn't utter a sound. Her back went rigid. Her legs quivered. The part of her I now owned tightened around me in a death grip. I deepened our kiss, keeping her mouth captive until I felt her body relax and adjust to my size. I had just shattered her insides, but as she eased into the pain, she wordlessly handed over her trust to me. Surrendering, she kissed me back and gently rocked herself into our connection. As her appetite increased, she turned wanton, sucking my lip and digging her nails into my shoulders. Pain had subsided as pleasure seeped in.

I pulled out slowly, dragging myself against her walls for our mutual enjoyment. I shuddered against electrified nerves as muscle memory ignited. Initially our motion was awkward, and then we found a rhythm all our own. Once we began to move in synchronicity, a dance of desire dictated our steps. Aimee's faint moans grew bolder and the sound wrapped around my head, tearing at my thoughts like barbed wire. Her sweet tones of lust fed my soul and pierced my heart. The sounds sank deep into me, fueling my yearning for her. Any debris of hurt I harbored due to the loss of my wife poured out of me as newfound hope took its place. I surrendered myself to the divine blonde beauty splayed on the bed before me and reminded myself I was alive.

Aimee's chest rose and fell as she chased her newfound sensations. I grew drunk on the residual effect. A primitive growl vibrated deep in my throat as I struggled to contain my release. Sweat dripped off my hair, trailing down my back. Aimee's expression reflected that she was lost in feeling. Her response caused my heart rate to ratchet up as I felt the initial assault of her orgasm. Sweet sounds of ecstasy escaped in Aimee's passion-filled cry. She shuddered against me, her back arching gracefully as gratification pulled an arrow of bliss and let it fly free. Aimee's eyes clenched tight. The arresting sight and sound ruined me. Any fragment of composure that remained was crushed. My vision splintered as I became victim to the magnitude of my own satisfaction. I exploded into her as my body came undone.

The two of us yielded completely to the sweet violence we'd created. Time stood still as we rode our waves of pleasure toward the heavens. We surrendered to the aftershocks and then slowly descended back to earth.

Chapter 25

Carter

Exhaustion claimed us, and we both drifted off to sleep. I don't know for how long but when I opened my eyes, Aimee's breathing was still deep. Inching away from her body, I backed out of bed, all the while being careful not to disturb her slumber. The evening had turned to night, and a chill was in the air. I seriously needed to use the bathroom and wanted to clean up before I got back into bed with her. As I walked away, I heard the soft sounds that she made in her sleep. They forced a smile onto my lips and filled something inside of me long empty. Stepping into the bathroom, I closed the door behind me.

Before dozing off with Aimee, I'd knotted the condom in my hand and dropped it on the floor. As I prepared to dispose of it, I saw that it had leaked. *Shit!* I poked it with my finger. The contents oozed from the broken tip. *Shit! Shit! Shit!*

My heart thumped as I paced with closed fists. *How the hell could I have let something like this happen? How long had it been inside the drawer of my bedside table?* As I searched through my memory, it occurred to me that the box had been there for about six months before Lacey died. We'd discussed children, and she wanted to get off of the pill. We thought it best to use condoms until we were sure that enough of the chemical was out of her system. *Christ!*

With my head buried in business, I hadn't given any thought to sex, and when Aimee came into my life I didn't think to refresh my supply of rubbers! *Hell! Who was I kidding?* This screw-up was on me. My fault. For someone so detail oriented, I really fucked this up. My heart leaped into my throat, squeezing with icy fingers. *How was I going to tell her?*

I leaned my hand against the wall as I relieved myself. No clarity came, only an onslaught of thoughts and accusations of what I'd done wrong. It was bad enough I'd screwed up, but I had also put someone at risk who meant a lot to me. It seemed all I brought to Aimee was bad news. First, I'd offended her, then I seduced her, and now, just when I wanted to explore a future with her, I had compromised her. *How could I be so fucking irresponsible?*

My jaw hurt as I ground my teeth together. Ceaseless accusations mixed with words I knew I should say. They taunted and tortured as I tried to play out my speech. *Would Aimee blow my head off with hateful words? Would she ever want to see me again? Would she think me so careless her opinion of me would change?*

I sat down on the closed lid and clutched my aching skull. My options were limited, and I hated it. Better to face the truth and just tell her outright the condom had broken. What a joke! It was such a fucking cliché even I would have laughed, and not with the joy-filled kind, rather with the nervous sound that happens when you get hit with the unexpected. I wasn't good at jokes. Hated them, in fact. Especially when they were at someone else's expense. I walked over to the sink and splashed cold water on my face. There was only one possibility that she would forgive this, and that was if she'd protected herself. She had to be on the pill. This was the age of the modern women. They didn't wait on anyone for anything. Hell, most of them didn't want to rely on men at all. Aimee had been taking care of herself for a long time. Surely, she was on the pill or some other kind of birth control. *Or was she?*

I winced. Not in my wildest imagination would I have thought I'd be bedding a virgin, yet it had happened. It was incredible that someone like Aimee, who was as gorgeous on the inside as she was on the outside, would rebuke every opportunity for sex that came her way, only to give her virginity away to some poor bastard in McHenry, Maryland.

I closed my eyes and saw her face. The peaceful expression I'd lingered on just moments ago. I wanted to go wake her. I wanted to hold her in my arms as I told her my mistake and listen as she told me I had nothing to worry about, that my agony over my error was just a waste of time. I looked at myself in the mirror and sucked in a few deep breaths. There was no way I was going to tell her tonight. I wouldn't blame her if she threw me away like a piece of garbage. If I never saw her again, at least I'd have the memory of tonight and the knowledge I hadn't become an emotional cripple because of what had happened to my wife. If tonight had been our first and last time, I wanted the memory because I'm a selfish bastard who believes that lightning might strike twice. I needed this. I wanted to hold her close while she slept and savor the softness of her skin, her scent, her smile, and every other nuance that made her unforgettable. I decided to rein in my tattered hopes and let her have a night of peaceful sleep and a morning filled with afterglow. And then, once I was satisfied I'd taken care of her physical needs, I would shatter her.

Chapter 26

Aimee

I opened my eyes and treated my limbs to a yummy stretch. Sadly, the space beside me was empty. My first thought was Carter had gone into his office to work, but then I heard faint sounds coming from the kitchen as the aroma of fresh coffee wafted through the house. I sat up in bed and hugged my knees to my chest. Already the day held promise. I smiled as I entered the bathroom. Fresh fluffy towels and a new toothbrush waited for me on the counter. I turned the lever all the way to hot in the shower and the room filled with steam. My toes curled of their own accord as I gingerly stepped onto the cold tile floor of the shower, but the hot water felt great against my skin. Sore muscles eased under the forceful spray as recollections of the previous evening bathed my mind.

Once I'd finished, I pulled my hair into a messy bun and gathered my clothes from the bedroom. Carter had placed them, neatly folded, on a chair by the window. As I stepped into them, I gazed out. It was such a gorgeous day. The sun filtered through the trees, creating random patterns on the ground. A gentle wind swayed evergreen boughs, while cardinals and blue jays hopped from branch to branch. Color was everywhere, and I could see the lake. At the end of the narrow pier was a wide deck. Two chairs were placed side by side in silent invitation to sit and enjoy the view. There was a peace inside of me that soaked into my bones, the residual contentment filling my marrow. My decision to make Deep Creek my home had been confirmed with each passing day. I couldn't remember ever being so happy.

I left the bedroom, following the tempting scents into the kitchen. As I entered, Cody bumped my leg. I reached down to pet her as Carter approached with a cup of coffee. He placed a chaste kiss on my lips as he handed me the mug.

"How'd you sleep?"

"Amazingly well." My lips met the brim, and I sipped the scalding brew. Carter went back to the stove.

"How do you want your eggs?"

"Scrambled, please." I leaned on the counter, holding the cup between both hands as I watched

Carter whisk the eggs in a bowl and pour them into a cast iron skillet.

"I didn't know you cooked."

He looked over his shoulder at me, a smile in his expression. "A man's gotta eat, beauty." My heartbeat fluttered inside my chest at the sound of his voice. "And since my brother already warned me about your cooking skills, mine are the safer bet."

"Seriously? You're going there?"

"You keep baking cakes, and I'll cook. Deal?"

How could I refuse, especially when his comment had implications for the future? Carter set a plate full of eggs, bacon, and toast in front of me. He pulled a fork from the drawer and flipped it in his hand so that he presented the handle to me. I accepted it, stabbed at the eggs, and took a bite. "*Mmm.*" I savored the deliciousness. "Where did you learn to cook like this?"

He shrugged. "My mother. She was an excellent cook."

"It's delicious." I looked up toward the heavens. "Thank you, Carter's mom."

A deep rumble of laughter rolled from his chest, and I relished the sound. We ate the remainder of the meal in silence. I dabbed at my mouth with a napkin and reached for his empty plate. He pulled it back and took mine as well. "I got it, Aim. Just sit. Enjoy your coffee."

I followed him, leaning against the sink as he cleaned the dishes. His sleeves were rolled up to the elbow, and soap bubbles clung to his forearms. "You spoil me, Carter."

"Spoil you? I would have thought this is your norm: people feeding you and getting your clothes together."

"Not hardly," I laughed. "I do for myself, but if you're counting meals, I either order room service or eat whatever they put out for the crew on the shoots. Believe me, it's usually nothing as delicious as your cooking."

He shook his head. "You're dispelling all the myths of the glamorous life I thought you and my brother led."

"It's not like that. We work just like everybody else. I'll admit, the travel is nice, but it can also be lonely." I turned and leaned my hip against the counter to see him better. "Thank you. For breakfast. For last night. All of it."

He rinsed the last dish and placed it in the drainer. Grabbing a towel, Carter wiped his hands dry and then tossed the cloth over his shoulder. I detected something was bothering him by the grave look that came over his face.

"About last night, Aim. We have to talk."

My breath hitched. I didn't move. Instead, I braced myself for the worst. Memories came flooding back, their images turning my blood to ice water. I already bore scars on my heart, and with each inflection of Carter's deep voice, I felt the damaged organ tear open and bleed out any hope that had earlier brightened my morning. Why should today be different than the many others when people I'd allowed myself to love lulled me into a false sense of security? I should have prepared myself. I knew better than to trust so easily. Hadn't I done that too many times in my youth? Hadn't I molded myself into what was expected of me to gain acceptance and love, only to have my efforts thrown in my face, my heart crushed under a flawed government system that dispensed and took away in game-like fashion? I should have known, should have remembered that once I gave the best I had, I would no longer be needed. Carter wasn't the first to utter a similar phrase to me. I'd heard it too many times, and nothing good had ever come from it.

Chapter 27

Aimee

A knot formed in my stomach. It rolled around brutally, convulsing my insides until I felt like I was going to be sick. Was this Carter's way of breaking the news to me that I'd just been a one-night stand?

He'd turned away from me as he rinsed the last dish and placed it on the drain board. I quietly watched as he dried his hands and waited for him to turn around and look me in the eye. We were separated by a few feet of space and a world uncertainty.

Once he had completed his task, he narrowed the distance between us with a few steps and tipped up my chin. Even in my distress, his fingers electrified my skin. My nerves were taut, stretched thin enough to snap under the slightest pressure. I studied his face, but learned very little, as Carter was an expert at masking his emotions. What I could detect was an apologetic expression, indicating to me that something terrible was about to happen. The bottom dropped out of my stomach, leaving a hollow feeling in its wake.

"Sweetheart, something happened—something that shouldn't have—and it's my fault." He took my hand in his and placed the other one on top. "First, I want to tell you I'm sorry. I take full responsibility."

Panic ripped like wildfire through every cell in my body. His words formed ghoulish fingers, tightening around my throat until I could barely breathe. I couldn't discern the hidden message behind his tone, and the explanation wasn't coming fast enough for me. I pulled my hand from his grasp. Instinctively my arms wrapped around my middle but they offered no comfort. I ran to the bathroom and slammed the door behind me. I had barely enough time to flip up the lid on the toilet seat when I violently wretched, emptying the contents of my stomach. My ribs ached. My head blazed hot. I laid it down and rested my cheek on my hand. *How stupid am I? All I'd been to him was a one-night stand! But what had I expected? I was probably one of many. Carter had needs. Of course, he'd been with other women. I was just the most recent. What the hell was I thinking?* A soft tapping interrupted my anxiety-filled thoughts.

"Aimee? Are you okay?"

Carter sounded full of concern, but was he? Maybe it was a well-honed act, and he was trying to smooth things over. That wasn't going to work with me. I was nobody's one-night piece of ass!

"I'm fine," I croaked. My throat hurt, and barbed wire scratched my voice as a result of throwing up. "I ate something that didn't agree with me."

"Can I get you anything?" His question traveled through the door.

"No." Nerves and agitation blended, making my tone more distressed than I cared to let on.

"Okay. Yell if you need me."

Resignation lay thick in his remark, making my thoughts spin out of control with insecurity and doubt. He had used the word mistake. *What was a mistake? Last night? Having sex? Letting something physical interfere with our friendship? Did we even have a remnant of that left? What now? Go back to being friends?* It had taken months to develop the relationship. We'd become such good friends. A flirty friendship, but precious to me, and now it was over. I had let it happen and I shouldn't have. Anger burned a corrosive trail from my belly to my brain. I was pissed off at Carter, but also with myself. I'd read more into our relationship than I should have.

Pulling myself up on shaky legs, I looked in the mirror. Tears had left a trail on my face from the strain of upchucking my food. I splashed some cold water on my cheeks in preparation for facing Carter. There was no way around it. I could only hope I'd maintain a shred of dignity and use it to leave gracefully. Although

I wanted to stay in the bathroom and hide away, the simple fact was I couldn't remain there all day. I checked myself in the mirror once more, attempting to shield my feelings with a composed veneer. The only makeup I'd put on my face before breakfast was a little mascara. Lucky for me that's all it was. I cleaned up the dark streaks under my eyes and rinsed my mouth. I quietly eased the door open and peeked out to see if Carter was nearby. Once satisfied he wasn't, I silently slipped out and went to the bedroom to check for any of my things I'd left there. The bed stared me in the face. It taunted me, mocking me with the jumbled sheets from a night of lovemaking. *Lovemaking? Who was I kidding?* Love had nothing to do with it. It was an act—sex, pure and simple—and now I was disposable. Just like I'd been my whole life. I slipped my feet into my boots, turned away from the hurtful reminder, and walked out of the room. I needed to get the hell out of his house and away from him. In my mind, I rehearsed what I would say if he intercepted me. I steeled my spine as I prepared to tell him he meant to me what I did to him—nothing. I locked my tear ducts down, imprisoning them to ensure I revealed no emotion when he said that what happened between us last night had no meaning. My chest rose and fell as I breathed in a fresh supply of determination, reminding myself my whole life had prepared me for moments like this. Neither the act of rejection nor Carter Sinclair would break me.

The house was quiet as I stepped toward the door. The scuffing sounds of my boots echoed in the room. Carter turned to look at me. A frown had formed tense lines in his face, revealing he took no pleasure in the task he was about to execute. He opened his mouth to speak to me, but something caught his attention. His gaze passed over my shoulder. I turned slightly to see what had momentarily monopolized his focus. On the corner of the table, in a simple wooden frame, was a picture of he and Lacey smiling contentedly in the middle of a snowy forest. Clarity trickled like ice water through my veins. It hardened quickly in my mind and solidified into a glacier of hurt. A piece of me cracked, the fissure breaking my suddenly chilled heart and setting the fragment free to travel, jagged and adrift in my bloodstream. *How could I have been so blind?* He was still in love with his dead wife.

Dejection shrouded me as tears burned my eyes. Sandpaper abraded my hopes with a harsh edge and left no remnant of affection. The raw surface was bare of even a speck of tender thoughts. I didn't trust myself to speak as I walked toward the door. Words would undoubtedly be weapons if I employed them right now. I had no desire to hurl any. If I did, I was confident they would draw blood with their razor's edge. As I took a step, I could feel Carter's presence behind me.

"Aimee, stop."

His voice pierced my composure, turning me into someone I didn't recognize. Someone feral. "Save it!"

Two words released my bloodlust. "I don't want to hear it. I should have realized you were playing me."

He took a step back, his expression one of shock. "What? Playing you? No. I was trying to say—"

"You know what?" I interrupted, anger blazing the words off of my tongue. "I don't need the pathetic excuse you're about to give me." A sob bubbled up in my throat, nearly strangling me. "You should get an award, you know it? You're a great actor. I almost believed you cared."

Carter's hand reached out, but I slapped it away as it inched toward me. "Get the hell away from me!"

A fire fueled my footsteps as I ran toward the back door. I flung it open with both hands. The force slammed the wood into the railing behind it as I stormed out into the chilly air.

Chapter 28

Carter

I watched as Aimee stormed across the yard, headed for the woods, Cody trailing closely behind her. The force with which she'd left made the screen door strain against the hinges. My footsteps carried me quickly, as I fully intended to chase after her. I was interrupted by the ringing of my cell phone.

"Not now!" The force in my words escaped through gritted teeth.

"Mr. Sinclair? It's Dr. Zais at Perkins hospital." The voice on the other end sounded shocked by my tone.

"I can't talk right now." I issued the response as I followed after Aimee. She was a few yards ahead of me and about to enter the wooded trail.

"Okay, Mr. Sinclair. I can call back. I just thought

you'd want to know there's a strong possibility that Ms. Franzi is going to be released."

My feet cemented in place. "What?"

"Yes. I've been told that proper procedure was not followed when she was taken into custody, and she may be leaving us soon. I thought you'd want to know."

I couldn't move. I couldn't breathe. Anger built in my stomach and blazed quickly. It was a sucker punch I didn't want to deal with now. I needed to go after Aimee, but I couldn't will myself to move due to the information I'd just received. As I watched her disappear into the trees, I saw Cody was still following her. My mind rested knowing she wasn't alone. I reasoned that I should let her go. She probably needed to get some air. We could straighten this out later. I pressed my ear to the phone, focused on learning details. "What's this? Marisol Franzi is getting out?"

Chapter 29

Aimee

W*ho the hell did he think he was?* It served Carter right, my walking out on him. As my angered footsteps pounded into the dirt, the exertion shortened my breath. I huffed as I made my way up the trail. Decomposing leaves and dead grass made a feeble attempt to cling to my boots. Tiny particles of dried mud and dust accompanied my pace, darkening the light tan color of my boots to a more brownish hue. Indignation pumped adrenaline through my system, and I angrily thrust away the branches in my path. In my wake, the tinier ones fell in a random pattern. I halted half a step as I heard leaves crunch behind me. Someone was following me. Thinking it was Carter, my hopeful heart beat a little faster, that is, until I felt a big bump hit against the lower part of my leg. I looked down and saw fur. It was Cody, not her master, on my trail.

"I love you, too, girl." Her tail affectionately wagged as I took hold of her collar. I bent down to bury my face in her fur. "Your master is a jackass, you know that?"

As I released the dog, I saw that, in my anger, I'd strayed from the trail and veered off into the woods. I had no idea where I was. *Damn it!* I hadn't paid attention to where I was going. The only consoling thought was I had Cody with me. I was sure she'd traveled these woods before and would get me either to my house or back to Carter's the moment she grew hungry. I ambled, tracing my footsteps backward, trying to decipher my location while looking for clues that would lead me to the original path.

I smiled at Cody's playful nature. As she walked alongside me, she'd abandon me momentarily to leap over rocks and tree stumps, or to attempt to snatch the full, bushy tail of a little squirrel. The burning anger that had accompanied my quick departure from Carter's slowly faded as the dog amused me. Her joy at the simplest things had a soothing effect. My breathing went from rapid and fuming to deep and even-keeled. Cody suddenly sprinted ahead of me, leading me to believe we were close to someone or something familiar. I hurried to catch up, still not out of the thick of the trees. I had only taken a few steps when a loud snapping sound came from behind me. I whipped around, sure that a tree limb was about to fall. Carter had warned me to pay attention to the sounds of the woods so I wouldn't be at the mercy of dead trees and broken branches, but as I scoped out my surroundings, I didn't see anything of the kind. My imagination toyed with my sensitized nerves, and I imagined what I would do if a bear suddenly appeared. The sky had grown overcast and the little sunlight that filtered through the clouds was barely bright enough to see through the trees. It had been risky for me to take the shortcut through the woods. I'd only walked the trails a few times, and it had always been in bright sunlight and with Carter. *Where did Cody go?*

I continued to walk, searching for anything that looked familiar. I then spun in a circle, navigating over a stump and the fallen tree in front of it. *Finally!* A speck of light drew my attention to the window where it shined. It was my house. Although it was still a bit of distance away, I had only to follow it, and, hopefully, in a few minutes, I'd arrive safely at my house. I took a deep breath, feeling much better than when I'd stormed out on Carter. Maybe in a few days, Carter and I would—

WHACK!

My vision disintegrated, exploding into a billion fragments of tin foil that floated before my eyes. They were all I could see or think of as what remained of my thoughts fled. I'd been hit, and the blow to the back of my head sent me reeling. Stumbling forward, I struggled to catch my breath and right my disoriented footsteps. Adrenaline spiked my fear. Electricity sizzled through my veins. My thoughts returned but became primal as a pounding fear thudded in my chest. Moments ago, I'd been dealing with affairs of the heart, and now I feared for my survival. I fell to my knees. As I struggled to pull myself up, a different kind of pain took hold of me as something lifted me by my hair. I screamed, the sound ripping from my throat as strands of hair and patches of skin tore away from my scalp. The pulling stopped as I was suddenly set upright. I clumsily tried to turn my body to see what had ahold of me. Before I could collect my thoughts something thick and heavy smashed into my face. The impact across my cheekbone and jaw completely collapsed my vision into minuscule slivers.

My attacker laughed, dispelling the thought that I was at the mercy of an animal. His strength was inhuman, but the sound of his voice left no doubt he was a man. He held me suspended above the ground, my toes barely touching the earth, like a marionette attached to strings. No matter how hard I tried to twist away, I still hung in space. He pulled me backward. My spine collided with something substantial. Every bump of every disk told me I was being held against the man's bare chest. Terror registered. Synapses in my brain detonated with horrific blasts. His physical violence joined forces with the fury of my fear, and a battle ensued. Survival instinct took over every part of my body. I trembled as my breath quickened into ragged gasps. I struggled as panic reared up my ribcage like a venomous snake about to strike. I reacted on the most basic human level, kicking wildly, my legs never stopping. They were savage in their quest and finally my foot connected with something. It had to be his knee because I fell as it collapsed and sent us both down. More machine than man, he immediately pushed himself to an upright position and staggered. His hold loosened on me, and I fell face first into the prickly arms of an evergreen tree. I ricocheted off the springy boughs and tripped over my own feet. I stopped when my face hit the ground.

I don't know why I didn't bolt at that moment, that split second when opportunity showed up as a getaway car and invited me to escape. Instead, I stole the chance to command my body into a position where I could look at my attacker. I wanted to sear every detail of his appearance to memory so that justice could sniff him out. I promised myself I would see him pay for hurting me—*if* I survived.

As my eyes trailed down his face, my breath strangled me. The air caught in my throat. The man looking back at me bore death in his eyes. I didn't recognize him, but his image would be burned forever in my memory. The first thing I noticed about him was the scar on his face. It slithered down from eye to jaw, pausing in white, knotted bumps along its trail. It hissed at the top of his cheek where it taunted me with its forked tongue ending in two lines. A quick glance down the rest of his body proved that he was scarred elsewhere. His skin was a map of tattoos, and his belt held several knives. He reeked of every sinister nightmare known to man.

"Who are you?" My voice was barely recognizable. Though I screamed the question, it came out weak and feeble and held a terror I'd never heard before.

He lunged at me, my momentary action of studying him providing him the second opportunity to assault me. Once again, he was fast, grabbing my hair before I could move away. He used it as a weapon against me, yanking and jerking me back and forth. My teeth rattled from the power, so much so I thought he was going to break my neck. He pulled me in his direction, while taking hold of my throat with his other hand. He squeezed it tight in a firm grip. His calloused fingers dug into my neck as he held me in a chokehold. I gagged, unable to breathe as he leaned into me. He pressed his nose to my face.

"Who am I?" The sneer revealed dingy teeth as evil dripped through his accent. Still rabid for details about him, I registered that the sound indicated Latin descent. "I'm the friend of your enemy," he spat.

My enemy? Who hates me?

He pulled me closer, and I felt his slimy lips

against my cheek. He licked my tears as he breathed in the scent of my terror. His breath was putrid. It charred my skin as his mouth grazed my ear. Bile rose in my throat in an acidic bubble as he whispered. "She doesn't like you, chica—but I do."

It was settled. I was going to die.

Chapter 30

Aimee

Fear like I'd never felt before whipped my thoughts. A vision of Carter appeared, and I started sobbing. He would find me dead.

My attacker smacked me again as he wrapped my hair around his forearm and enclosed my ponytail in his fist. He flung me like a pebble, and as if launched by a slingshot, I hit the trunk of a nearby tree. The impact was blinding as my skin shredded against the shards of wood. How I remained conscious, I didn't know. My body was stunned; my fingers fumbled against what was left of my cheek, the flesh burning as the touch blazed fire against the tattered mess that remained. Bloody specks stuck to my fingertips. My mouth was dry and filled with the metallic taste of blood.

I became a grotesque ragdoll as he continued his rampage. Keeping me off balance seemed to please him. Once he was done with bouncing me against the tree's surface, he plunged a weighty fist into my stomach. The hollow between my ribs collapsed, and the breath rushed out of me. The remnants of breakfast that I hadn't already thrown up while at Carter's house splattered on his arm. He backed away from the vomit and dropped me like a stone. I collapsed on the ground, panting as I struggled to breathe.

Carter. I invoked his name like a prayer. I hoped he was coming after me. I prayed he'd look for me once he realized I'd never arrived home. He was my only hope. If he wasn't looking for me, I was dead.

My legs vibrated in a staccato as my attacker dragged me away from the path and into a patchy thicket. I detected the scent of mountain laurel and pines. I whimpered as my hope of rescue waned. The light of home that had been my beacon disappeared from view. I'd been so close. The noises of the forest faded. In the silence, I realized that birds no longer sang and the wind wasn't even a whisper. It was eerily quiet. The only sounds I could hear were the pulse of blood in my ears and the rasping breath of my attacker. But then I heard something else.

Cody!

She snarled like a ferocious animal and threw her one-hundred-plus-pound body at the man. It unbalanced him. Curses flew, and he let me fall to the ground as he turned toward my furry savior. She leaped over me and took a protective posture. Her jaws snapped violently open and closed as she barked, her bared, white teeth ghastly as her upper lip rose in a rabid grimace.

I couldn't see what was happening because of the swelling of my eyelids. I struggled to open them, but only had slits for vision. Cody put up a good fight. She bit at the man's wrists and ankles as she dodged his fists. For several minutes it appeared she was winning, and then something transformed her from near victor to victim. Her yelp of pain stopped my breathing. In an instant, my attacker gained the upper hand. The toe of his boot sank into her fur as he mercilessly kicked the dog. Cody made pitiful noises as I lay helpless. I used what was left of my voice to scream as the man pulled a knife from his belt and prepared to plunge it into her.

With the last of my energy reserves, I managed to move my leg in front of his foot and cause him to stumble. Thankfully the point of his knife missed Cody's head, but it sank into her side instead. She made a noise that could best be described as a scream and was able to escape into the trees. He took a few steps after her but then turned back. He stalked over to me with rage-filled eyes. As he grabbed me, I scratched and tore at any flesh within my reach. He crashed his fist into my face.

After that, the world faded. I drifted in and out from behind a black curtain. I had no energy reserves left, as my body had become a lump of bruised and battered flesh and bone. My assailant made a sound of victory that roared above the trees, proving he was an animal. As he dragged me over a rough stump, I felt the crack of a rib, and I screamed. There was no one to hear me as despair covered me like a shroud. My attacker slapped my face to keep me from drifting into darkness.

"Ah, ah, ah, *puta*. No going to sleep yet."

He pulled the front of my blood-soaked sweater as he chastised me and rolled me onto my back. I lay help-less as he undid my jeans and yanked them down to my ankles. With precise measured cuts, he sliced off my sweater and bra and then cut the material clean through the crotch of my jeans. I couldn't go to my death without knowing the answer to my final ques-tion. "Why?"

His voice was thick as he answered with an evil laugh. It was the last thing I heard as I sank into obliv-ion. "Why not?"

Chapter 31

Carter

I punched Aimee's number over and over. I got nothing. Just voicemail. *She must really be pissed at me.*

After the initial shock of the phone call regarding Marisol had worn off, I cut my conversation with Dr. Zais short by taking his number and promising to call back. The possibility of Marisol's release was bullshit. I planned to investigate, but right now I wanted to talk to Aimee.

I wasn't sure what had pissed her off, but whatever it was, had been a misunderstanding. I wanted to tell her about the condom breaking and assure her I loved her in case anything came of it, but when I overheard her throwing up in the bathroom, I figured the news could wait. *What the hell went wrong?* I retraced the events that had transpired. I'd been on my way back to the kitchen after hearing her in the bathroom. She'd just come out, and I was about to look her in the eye and man up for being so complacent about updating my stash of birth control. I then glanced at the picture of Lacey and me. It was a good one. We'd been hiking, and one of her former students had snapped the shot. It was the first time I'd looked at it without feeling sad. That was because of Aimee. Then the shit hit the fan. *Fuck!*

She'd had stormed out before I had a chance to say anything. I should have followed her instead of answering my phone. *Dammit!* Marisol had screwed up enough of my life, and here she was getting in my way again, albeit indirectly. If I hadn't stopped for that call, I'd have caught up with Aimee. I'd have explained, and we could have moved on. *So, why isn't she answering her phone?*

Although I knew I was in love with Aimee, over the past few months, I'd discovered there were two sides to her. She was usually a complete sweetheart, but sometimes she had a nasty temper. *Damn! Voicemail again!* Aimee was ignoring me. At first, I thought that maybe she had left her phone behind. Now I wasn't so sure. I walked through the house as I dialed, trying to detect a ringing sound, but heard nothing. I tried once more. Again voicemail. *Damn her!*

Her behavior was childish, and Cody, the little traitor, had run out right behind her. She had to be with Aimee because I hadn't seen hide nor hair of her since Aimee left. *This is ridiculous.* My temper flared. Childish games weren't my thing, and this was pissing me off. It'd been a while since they'd both disappeared into the trees, and now the sun was beginning to set. I knew the mountains better than Aimee did. The temperature drop at night was substantial this time of year. Since Aimee didn't know the trails, I had a nagging concern she might still be out there. I hit redial on the phone and waited impatiently for some connection with her. It again went to voicemail. I paced as I debated whether to go after her or ignore her. It didn't take long for concern and curiosity to win, so I went back to my office to grab a jacket. I slipped my arms into the sleeves as I walked toward the back door. The zipper was pulled halfway up when I stopped. A chilling sound commanded my attention. Listening carefully, I zeroed in on its direction. *Fuck!*

I rushed outside to see Cody limping toward the house from the woods. She stumbled and uttered cries of pain as she approached. Blood trickled down her side, matting her fur with its wet trail. Black bears were prevalent in the area and raccoons could be vicious when cornered. I suspected one of them had gotten to her and I reached out a hand to grab her collar as I approached. She tucked her head and moved away from me. For each step I took forward, she took one back.

"C'mere, girl." I used a gentle tone as I tried to coax

her to come to me, but she refused. I halted my steps to set her fears to rest. I tried to lunge fast enough to get a grip on her, but she ran. I followed as she turned back into the woods with an awkward hobble. I slowed, afraid if she expended too much energy, the blood would flow more freely. Every time I got close to her, a burst of energy kept her a few paces ahead of me. Something was wrong. Instinct punched me in the gut with a fist full of fear. Cody would never run away from me. She was leading me somewhere. Trying to tell me something. I followed as she went deeper into the woods. The forest grew denser with each step I took. She'd veered off of the main path and into some brush. The evergreens here were older, taller, and broader. They blocked what was left of the sun as dusk quickly approached. The lack of warm rays made this part of the woods colder. I feared I might lose sight of Cody, so I pulled my phone out of my pocket, preparing to use the flashlight function.

Finally, her pace slowed. I reasoned it was either from exhaustion or pain. If she couldn't make it back to the house, I'd hoist her across my shoulders. There was no way I was going to leave her. She stopped, lying on her belly with her head on her outstretched paws. I paused as well, hoping that if I moved very slowly that she wouldn't try to run away again. It was quiet. If silence were a color, then it would have been black. With each step I took toward Cody, sound magnified. Cody's shallow and rapid breaths combined in a dance of desperation. I noticed that her breathing kept time with a faint, buzzing beat. I strained to hear it. The buzzing wasn't like bees, but a syncopated vibration. I activated the flashlight and shined the beam into the shadows surrounding us. Something blue, faded, and crumpled lying on the ground caught my eye. It looked like a pair of jeans. I kicked it with the toe of my boot. *Shit!* Aimee's phone fell free of the material and landed on the ground. It pulsated from missed calls. My missed calls. I looked at the fabric I'd kicked away and saw blood.

"Aimee!"

Chapter 32

Carter

I turned in every direction, frantically searching for more signs of her. Evidence of an assault was everywhere. I scanned the trees and found a piece of what looked like the sweater Aimee had been wearing. It was hooked on a branch and stained with blood. I looked below it to the ground and spotted her bra.

"Aimee!" I shouted her name again, my voice a mixture of rage and fear. I fought with trees as I flung aside branches. In desperation, I issued uppercuts and rib punches against limbs of bark and leaves. I looked for anything that would reveal another clue. *Jesus Christ, where is she?*

The lump in my throat choked me, throttling the muscles until I could barely issue a sound. I had to find her. I saw traces of blood on the trees and on the ground—so much blood. My senses were on high alert. Engaging every one of them, a pack of bloodhounds raced through my blood. I would find her, and I would kill whatever or whoever had hurt her. I would sniff him out, hunt him down, and maul the shit out of him as I made him pay retribution. There would be nowhere he could hide.

I then noticed an almost perfect, circular patch of dried blood. I raced to the spot and scanned the area, first left and then right. I saw her. My mind detonated. My brain became a brilliant explosion of horror and fear as the scene shattered my rational thought into a million crystals of glass. She was covered in blood, her lifeless body slumped over the remains of a tree. From that moment, everything became surreal. I felt as if time passed in slow motion. I couldn't get my legs to go fast enough to reach her. What was left of her clothing hung in tattered strips, and not much of it covered her pale skin. Her beautiful hair formed a curtain of blood as it hung matted and limp, covering her face. Her skin was tinged blue from the evening air.

She didn't move as I approached. I checked for breathing by placing my ear on her chest. Though the movement was barely there, at least it existed. I hesitated to lift her, but if I didn't, she would surely die. Tormented thoughts violated what sanity I had left. My mind muddled with possible scenarios. The damage to her body was extensive, yet the many wounds, and how they'd been inflicted, remained a mystery. I put my arm around her neck and gently lifted her head. Her face was covered with a sticky substance. It emitted the smell of sap mixed with blood, and, possibly, vomit. I'd thought, initially, some kind of animal had attacked her, but this bore no resemblance to what I knew of bear attacks. If she had encountered a bear, she'd have had maul marks on her skin or distinct claw marks. This was not the carnage left by the black bears common at Deep Creek. No, this was the work of something worse than an animal. A madman.

With a feathered touch, I moved the matted hair away from her face. The cuts were deep. The swelling gave her a bloated appearance. Bruises on her face and neck were forming in differing shades of blue. Just hours before, I'd been looking into her beautiful eyes as she lay beside me. The recent memory was so fresh it made me choke with emotion. As my gaze trailed down from her throat and to her chest, more cuts revealed themselves. There were scratches on her skin and thin lines of crimson that looked to have come from a knife. Her breasts were a mass of destruction. I couldn't tell where one wound began and the other ended. I had to get her home quickly. I pulled my phone from my pocket, but had no signal. I picked up Aimee's phone to try it, but the battery was dead. Nobody would hear me if I yelled, and leaving Aimee here while I ran to get help was not an option. Her best chance was for me to carry her to the house and then call 911. I just hoped we were closer to home than it seemed. The crescent moon was making an appearance, alerting me I had a very short window before total nightfall, and there was little light here as it was. I couldn't take the chance I'd soon be in the dark in unfamiliar surroundings. I had no idea how far from the trail we were, but I had to get her help soon. She couldn't handle much more exposure to the cold as her skin was showing early signs of hypothermia.

"Hang in there." My voice choked with emotion as I ripped my jacket off and draped it over her to ward off the chill. I lifted her arm and put it around my neck, and she whimpered. Burning tears stung my eyes. My insides twisted and made me feel like I was going to be sick. How anyone could hurt her this badly was beyond my comprehension, but years in law enforcement had taught me that men were the worst kind of animals. They took pleasure in destruction, while animals only attacked when threatened or too feed. There was nothing threatening about Aimee. She was beautiful and kind and all good things I didn't deserve. She had to survive this. She just had to.

"Sweetheart—Aimee," I whispered in her ear. "It's me, honey. I'm going to pick you up."

She responded with a guttural groan. The sound drove a knife through my heart.

The cop in me committed the scene to memory. There was evidence of struggle everywhere as shreds of clothing lay out of place amongst broken twigs and sinewy vines. In the dirt leading to a tree stump were drag marks, probably from Aimee's boots. Long clumps of blood-tinged, blonde hair were lying in haphazard places along my path. Bits of skin and scalp littered the ground. A tree to my right wore chunks of bloody bark. As I ran in the direction of my house, a sticky wetness rubbed against my arm. I was sure she had been raped. I was going to kill the bastard who did it—this slowly and painfully. And I would enjoy every minute of it. My temper raged and went wild with thoughts of the brutality she must have suffered at the hands of a monster; but for her sake, I had to stay focused. Vengeance could wait. "I'm going to get you home soon, baby," I said as she moaned again. A growl escaped me, and I realized I would turn into a more dangerous beast than Aimee's attacker could ever hope to be.

I tried to immobilize her as much as possible as I ran, praying I wouldn't cause her to puncture a lung. The tackiness on my arms rubbed against her raw wounds, abrading her skin even further. My muscles grew tight. I held her as rigidly as possible as I struggled to buffer her body with my own. Keeping my focus forward, I found the well-worn trail and concentrated on reaching my house. I didn't dare look down at her again for fear I'd lose it. The last time I'd looked at her, I was grateful she was unconscious. Refusing to give into my strained and burning biceps, I repeated a mantra in my head, reminding myself I was her only hope. The cadence of her breathing helped to carry me along. I tried to triple and quadruple my steps in time to the sound so I would move faster. My house was finally in sight, just about one hundred feet ahead.

Crossing the distance quickly, I nudged my foot against the door to open it and turned sideways to get Aimee through. I laid her down on the sofa and wasted no time ripping my cell out and dialing for help.

"911. What's your emergency?"

"This is Carter Sinclair. I have a female, mid-twenties, who was attacked in the woods. She's covered with lacerations and puncture marks. She may have internal bleeding. I need you to send an ambulance now!"

Once I relayed the location, my mind went numb. I wasn't sure what questions were asked or answered. The voice on the other end sounded like it was miles away. I focused on only one thought—keeping Aimee alive.

I knelt on the floor beside her as I waited to hear the sirens. That was when I remembered Cody. *Shit!* I ran my hands through my hair, trying to concentrate on what needed to be done. I had to get someone to go into the woods and get her. Someone who wouldn't scare her and who knew the terrain. I dialed Marc. He answered on the third ring.

"What do you want, Sinclair?"

"Aimee and Cody were attacked in the woods. I managed to get to the house with Aimee—EMTs are on the way—but I need someone to go get Cody."

"Shit," he answered.

"Can you get her?"

"Already on my way."

I dropped my phone on the floor beside my leg. I focused on Aimee, watching every breath she took. "Help's on the way, babe. Just hold on." I stumbled over my words, and my voice caught in my throat. "Please, Aim. I can't lose you. Not now." I gently pressed my forehead to hers and measured time in anxious thoughts. In the distance, I could hear the shrill wailing of a siren.

Chapter 33

Carter

Everything was moving in slow motion as I covered Aimee with a blanket from the back of the sofa. I felt so fucking inadequate. As I waited for help to arrive, a clock ticked in the background. I counted the shallow rise and fall of Aimee's chest as I sat on the floor with her hand in mine. A chill ran through my blood as I willed my body heat into hers. Though I wanted to touch her skin and gently rub it, I dared not, fearing I would cause her more pain. Comfort was all I could offer her now. The paramedics arrived just as Marcus did.

"Jesus, Carter." The expression on his face told that he was horrorstruck. Marc knelt down next to me as one of the EMTs took Aimee's vitals. As he turned toward me, he placed his hand on my shoulder. "Carter —what the hell?"

"I don't know." I lacked information, and what I had wasn't processing properly. Like a tower of blocks, I tried to construct a scene, but my emotions got in the way and sent them tumbling into a pile of rubble every time I heard Aimee moan in pain. I tried to explain, but the words wouldn't come out with any clarity. "Aimee, Cody, they were attacked. I don't know much." I looked up at him with pleading eyes. "Just help Cody. She's still out there."

"Got it." Marc didn't ask any more questions; he just took action. He headed toward the back of the house to retrace my steps. I didn't doubt he would find my dog and get help for her—if she wasn't dead by now. The thought paralyzed me. I loved that dog like she was my child. I couldn't imagine having anything happen to her. We'd been through too much together.

As I returned my attention to Aimee, the EMTs were trying to stabilize her on a back board. They moved slowly, taking necessary precautions as they slipped a collar around her neck and began flooding her dehydrated body with intravenous fluids.

"Do you have any idea what happened to her, Mr. Sinclair?"

The question sent me into a deeper introspection. Though I'd tried to piece together the attack scene and clues, I couldn't put compose a coherent thought as to why anyone would want to attack Aimee. She wasn't a threat to anyone. I had been asking myself since I happened upon the nightmarish scene if it was a random attack or a targeted one. I shook my head. "No. I don't have a clue." I struggled with the confession that, I, a former State Trooper and owner of a security company, couldn't imagine who would have done this. I felt as helpless as I did the day Lacey had died.

"You can ride with us if you like." The female paramedic had a note of compassion in her voice as she read the concern on my face.

Damn right I was going with them! There was no way I would leave Aimee alone. I nodded. I'd stay with her until she regained consciousness. I could get Marc or Falcon to bring me whatever I needed in the interim. I followed behind as the paramedics lifted the stretcher and made ready to slide it into the back of the ambulance. As they locked the frame into place, it jostled Aimee's broken body. A sob escaped, breaking my heart. "Take it easy with her!"

My demand went unanswered as they rolled the stretcher into the ambulance. I climbed inside and sat next to her. As the female paramedic watched over Aimee, I covered her bruised, bloody hand with mine. My mind raced. Questions without answers peppered my thoughts. *Has she lost too much blood? What bones are broken? Will they heal? Who the fuck did this to her?*

I covered my face with my hands as tears stung my eyes. Aimee was the brightest light to come into my life since Lacey, and I was terrified of losing her. The ambulance bumped down the mountain road. During the transport, guilt made an appearance and convicted me. All of this was my fault. I should have ignored the phone and gone after Aimee. If I'd followed her instead, maybe this would not have happened. I should have caught up with her and made her come back to the house. I should have explained. She wouldn't have gotten hurt if I'd only intercepted her. I tortured myself. Anguish whipped me and left a blood trail of guilt as each lash cut me deeply with questions. *Why did I let her go?*

It seemed like it took forever to reach the hospital. Upon arrival, the ambulance doors opened to complete chaos. Doctors and nurses appeared. The paramedics relayed information in a monotone fashion about Aimee's condition. I felt like I was in a dream. Everything was a blur. I followed the stretcher down the hall. A nurse stepped into my path and stopped me.

"Sir? I'm going to take you to a waiting room. Someone will come and get you as soon as they stabilize her."

"I'm going with her."

The nurse offered a sympathetic smile as I issued my decree. "I know you don't want to leave her, sir, but you have to let us do our job. It's the best chance she has."

The kindness in her voice made me nod helplessly.

I was numb. The nurse led me by the arm to a small room where a television played.

"Can I get you anything?" she asked.

I didn't know how to answer her question. The only thing I wanted was to know Aimee wasn't irreparably broken. Other than that, the whole world could go to hell.

Chapter 34

Carter

The urges inside of me were animalistic. I had no choice but to wait for information, but I wanted to hunt. I wanted to find the son of a bitch who'd attacked Aimee and left her to die in the woods. I paced. I sat. I peered down the hallway to see if anyone was looking for me. Finally, the same nurse that'd approached me when I'd arrived, walked toward me.

"Mr. Sinclair, they're still working on her. I've been checking for news, but all I know is that, at the moment, she's stable. I promise someone will continue to keep you apprised of her condition."

I numbly watched as she disappeared through a set of automatic doors. The whooshing sound reminded me of the wind as it blew through the tall trees on top of the mountain. The television on the wall showed a wrestling match. The sound was hard to hear and droned in a low tone. It comingled with the hospital speaker system. I tried to organize my thoughts, figure out who I needed to notify on Aimee's behalf. As far as I knew, she had no family. What I did know for sure was her relationship with Declan. I made a mental note to call him after I called the vet about Cody. Marcus had sent a text telling me he'd found her and taken her to Dr. Karls.

I punched the numbers into my cell phone. It was after hours at the clinic, but I knew that Lauri Karls would answer. She didn't work according to the numbers on a clock, but in devotion to her patients. I'd known Lauri a long time and had become friends with her over the years. I'd sometimes run across an injured animal or find a litter of puppies or kittens when I'd been a Trooper. Lauri always took them in and fixed them up. She would usually find good homes for the strays I rounded up. There was no one I trusted more with Cody than Dr. Karls. If anyone could make my giant fur ball well, she could. The phone rang several times before she answered.

"Hello?"

"Hey, Lauri. How's Cody?"

Lauri exhaled a sigh. "She's good. Better than she should be, but she's an amazing dog. I think Marc was worse off than Cody when he brought her in. He said you didn't know much about what happened to her. Luckily the puncture wound in her side didn't hit her organs. I stitched her up. My guess is that she was also kicked or hit. I'm giving her pain meds to keep her comfortable."

"Thank God." I took a deep breath. Some of my tension released as I let it out. "There was so much blood. I couldn't tell where it was coming from."

"Honestly, don't worry. Cody's had x-rays. Whatever it was beat her up pretty good, but there's no permanent damage."

I rested my forehead against my palm. The tension of the past few hours was inching a headache up my neck. Now that Cody was taken care of, I could fully concentrate on Aimee. "Thanks, Lauri."

"No problem. I'll keep her here for a couple of days. Marc told me about Aimee. You've got enough on your hands."

"I think Cody might have gone after the person who hurt Aimee."

"Cody will be fine with me. Take care of Aimee and keep me updated."

"I appreciate it. Thanks."

"And Carter? Aimee's in my prayers."

My throat constricted as I realized the long road ahead. Aimee could use all the prayers she could get.

SEVEN HOURS, thirty-seven minutes.

That was the amount of time I waited before Aimee's surgeon came out to inform me of her progress. I rose from my seat and stood on stiff legs as the doctor approached me.

"Mr. Sinclair." He extended his hand, and I did the same. "I'm Dr. Harris.

Please. Sit." He motioned to the chairs. "I understand you were the person who brought Ms. Vincent to the ER. Does she have any family here?" Dr. Harris looked over my shoulder to the left and to the right as he spoke.

"No. No one. Just me."

His expression grew serious as we locked eyes. "Ms. Vincent has multiple injuries. X-rays were done before taking her into surgery. The damage was varied and extensive: a broken jaw, nose, rib, and two others with cracks. Her left hand has a broken thumb and two broken fingers. She has a stab wound in her stomach, but it isn't deep. It's as if her attacker wanted her to bleed out slowly. We repaired that damage in surgery. The area around her spleen is bruised, and I suspect it will be extremely tender for a while. She also suffered other bruises and contusions. There were more knife wounds, but most were superficial. Only one, in front of her ear, was deep enough to require a few stitches. She's also missing a tooth and has a few tear wounds on her scalp where hair is missing. The pattern indicates that she was pulled in different directions. We put a soft collar on her as a preventive measure, so she doesn't strain her neck if she tries to move."

My mind was a minefield of detonated thoughts. I forced myself to focus. "But she'll recover?"

Dr. Harris took a deep breath. "We're hopeful. A lot will depend on her. Her injuries have been repaired, but she was in shock when she arrived. I think it will be some time before she fully recovers." He lowered his voice. "There's also no doubt she was sexually assaulted. Her examination revealed vaginal and anal tears consistent with rape. I had the nurses use a rape kit. It's the best chance of catching her attacker."

The doctor's lips tightened into a thin line, evidence that his thoughts and mine were the same. It took everything I had to keep myself together. A thirsty beast raged inside me that only justice could satisfy. I put him on lockdown while I finished the formalities befitting a civilized setting. He would get his. Death would be the easy way out for him, so I'd be the one to cuff him and throw him into a cell darker than the color of my bloodlust. But Aimee needed me now. She came first.

"When can I see her?"

"I'll have the nurse come get you. You can sit with Ms. Vincent in the PACU until we have a room ready for her. She'll be here for a while."

"How long?" I asked.

"I can't say, Mr. Sinclair. Again, most of it will depend on her—and what kind of help she has at home. She's going to need someone to take care of her."

"She's got someone. She's got me."

Chapter 35

Carter

I t wasn't long before a nurse came out to take me to Aimee's bedside. Nothing I'd been through on the police force prepared me for how I felt when I saw her. She was a shattered angel. Like pieces of a mosaic, Aimee was broken, yet beautiful. Bruises of various shades and hues provided the background for the thin dark lines defining the path of the knife. There were too many cuts to count on her arms and legs. I was sure there were also many more hidden beneath the blanket and hospital gown. Although the blood had been washed from her skin, the scrapes and brush burns that marred the surface left her with too much red for my comfort. It taunted the raging bull inside of me. There was only one thing—one thought—that kept the beast in control. She'd survived.

For hours, I had been sitting by Aimee's side, monitoring the gentle rise and fall of her chest. My inspection went back and forth between there and her swollen eyes. I held her limp hand in mine, running my thumb over the small joints and digits while being careful not to bump the broken ones. I lifted her hand and placed a gentle kiss on the back of it. Just as my lips touched her skin, her eyes opened ever so slightly. The swelling limited her vision, but I could see her looking at me through the slits. I sensed her confusion and wanted to let her know she was safe.

"Can you hear me, baby?" I whispered. I barely recognized my own voice as I spoke in a hushed tone. For hours, anger and concern had torn at my throat. The raspy sound betrayed any attempt of hiding my fears.

Aimee responded with a weak squeeze on my fingers.

"I'm here, baby. I'm not going anywhere. You just close your eyes and get some rest. I'll be here when you wake up."

As Aimee drifted back into unconsciousness, tears stung my eyes. I closed them to talk to a God I wasn't sure I still believed in. One who'd left the first woman I'd loved all by herself on a back road to die alone. One whose comfort I hadn't felt in years. One who I hoped would listen to a hypocrite like me.

I don't know if I even believe. I don't know if you'll take the time to listen to me. But Aimee believes, so I'm asking you to give me this one. Make her better. You screwed me over last time with Lacey, so give me Aimee and we'll call it even. Because I need her.

I laid my head down on her bed. The crisp sheets were cool beneath my cheek. My thoughts began to float as I lost the fight against exhaustion. As I listened to the monitors, their orchestration made a weird composition of notes. Together they made a symphony, the tempo peaceful and comforting, lulling me. The beeps and buzzes contented me with the affirmation that, despite the odds, Aimee was indeed alive.

Chapter 36

Manuel

Manny's eyes watched each measured step as a guard led Marianna to the visitor's area. She dragged her feet as she walked along the corridor, a clear indication her spirits were waning. Hopefully, the news he had to tell her would lighten her mood. She had so much to learn about self-control and appearances. Manny smiled at the thought of teaching her those lessons.

As she approached, he noticed her long black hair falling over her shoulders. There were only a few times he could recall seeing Marianna's face au naturel. Even without makeup, she was a beautiful woman. If the trappings of the fashion industry were taken away from his wife, she'd still outshine any in her gender. He was eager for the day when he would take her from here.

He assured himself the time would come soon. A smile crossed his lips as he painted a mental picture of how the press would react. The guard moved back against the wall as Marianna sat down.

"Hola, chica. ¿Como estas?" His tone was loving and elicited a weak smile from her.

"Bien, gracias, Manny."

His wife's manner was most ladylike, a stark contrast to her usual, entitled demeanor. Manny pushed away from the edge of the table to allow himself some space to stretch out and better observe her. He hated his visits to this place. Only for his wife and the plans he had with regard to her would he subject himself to such scrutiny and inconvenience. Marianna deserved personalized attention—his attention—but, right now, he was forced to let others provide it. He'd been working diligently to gain her release. He'd secured the best legal defense that money could buy, all in the hopes of laying the groundwork for his goddess to rise from the ashes like the phoenix she was. Marianna wouldn't like the obligations that would be attached to his help. Manny controlled her fate, and he needed her to believe he was her savior, that he was the only person able to meet her needs. He'd gone to great lengths to ensure her continued imprisonment until she understood what he'd require as payback. The details had proven to be a pain in the ass; no one else in the world warranted such favor from him. Although his possession of Marianna served as motivation, he had expectations of her. She'd either agree to his conditions, or he would leave her to rot in this godforsaken place. The distance between them was slight as the table wasn't very wide. It was already uncomfortably warm, and he could feel the heat from her breath as she exhaled. Everything about this building was antiquated. Even the air was dry and stale. He studied Marianna intently as she pushed an errant lock of hair away from her face. She then tugged at the neckline of her oversized shirt.

"You look uncomfortable." Manny brushed his foot against hers under the table.

She responded with a shrug and a weak smile. "I'm fine. What about you?"

Incarceration had tempered Marianna's fiery attitude. Before her arrest, she would never have concerned herself with anyone other than herself. It pleased him. Her spirit was slightly chipped, but he had plans to break it. With discipline and training, she would be a valuable asset to him. He could use her for his pleasure, and perhaps utilize her talents to broker some business deals. The thought of controlling Marianna caused a rush of blood to stiffen him. He would reduce her to a pile of rubble before he was through, and he'd take equal pleasure in rebuilding her to his specifications. Her return to power would rival that of Eva Peron.

"I'm fine, *chica. Gracias.*" His tone was tender. He brushed her hand with his fingertips.

"*¿Tienes noticias?*" Marianna was starving for any information that Manny could provide, gossip or any other communication that came from the outside. What she truly thirsted for was any news that would reveal efforts made for her release.

"I do have news." He leaned in and captured her hand with his own, giving it a comforting squeeze. "I have secured video of your arrest. It is camera footage from the police station, taken upon your arrival there."

"I don't see what good that will do. No one was listening to me. They ignored everything about me to serve their own purposes. What that video shows is the evidence of a fiasco."

A chuckle escaped him. "I assure you, there is much good that can come from the recording. I will also say, in this instance, I'm pleased that you have a stubborn nature."

Marianna's furrowed brow exposed her confusion, so Manny lowered his voice to explain. "Chica, in that fiasco of a video, you indicated over and over you required a Spanish-speaking interpreter. In fact, you also asked for a Spanish-speaking lawyer."

Puzzled, she cocked her head to one side. "That's true, but I didn't get one until the day after my arrest."

Manny's lips split into a wide grin. "Yes, my sweet. And that was where the police made their mistake. They ignored your request. Even after explicitly stating your need, they continued badgering you with their asinine questions." He leaned back again. "I've watched the video with our attorneys. The answers you provided were fragmented at best—and forced. When the police asked if you understood what they were saying to you, you raised your voice, called them names, and reiterated you didn't understand the charges. I lost count of how many times you declared your innocence. The video shows you made it clear to them you didn't want to talk without a lawyer and translator. When they read the charges to you and asked if you understood them, you spat at them, went on a tirade in Spanish, and asked them if they understood you! I have to tell you, Mari, I had a good laugh at that."

Marianna didn't share Manny's amusement. Instead, her hands were clasped tightly together, her knuckles so white, the skin was nearly transparent. "I'm glad you find this amusing."

"Marianna, my sweet, there's no need for you to worry." Manny placed one hand on both of hers. "The error was theirs. The police not only neglected to inform you of your rights, but they also attempted to coerce a false statement. They rushed through the process and didn't follow proper protocol. You were entitled to the aid of a translator, and they ignored that need. In other words, they fucked up."

As the truth began to sink in, the corners of Marianna's mouth lifted. A satisfied grin graced her lips. "So, they shouldn't have taken me into custody?" After a moment a thought occurred to her. "I could sue them for false arrest!" Her grin quickly morphed into a sneer.

"Slow down, chica. I didn't say that. They had the right to take you in for questioning as a person of interest. The mistake they made was in treating you as if you had waived your rights and confessed to the crime."

"I didn't confess to anything!"

Her raised voice earned her a stern look. "Marianna, get ahold of yourself. Now."

A paper-thin slice of submission compelled her to glance at the floor. "Fine."

Manny waited a moment to allow her time to regain her composure. Once he was satisfied misplaced enthusiasm had drained from her expression, he continued. "We are interested in the facts right now. Not your vengeance. They passed a form across the table to you. That form stated your rights. They were pressuring you to sign it, even though you told them you wanted an interpreter. You were never read your rights, nor did you sign them away. Our attorneys are arguing that anything you said—any statement that you made—was without a full understanding of the implication of your words. You were coerced. Those are the facts we've gathered from the video. With this information, your arrest could be negated."

Once again, the possibility of freedom saturated Marianna. She tried, but was unable, to curb her enthusiasm. "You did this! I'm getting out of here; I just know it."

"This is far from over." Manny's tone was thick with warning as he shook his head to dissuade any false hope. Although he was confident he would have Marianna freed, he didn't want her to be. If she didn't conduct herself appropriately, she could undermine the progress he'd made. "You must remain well-behaved. The best behavior you can muster. Any disruption could jeopardize our efforts."

"I will. I promise." In contrast to her usual, guarded veneer, it pleased Manny to see her enthusiasm. He only hoped it would continue to cultivate her indebtedness to him. She wrapped her arms around her middle and hugged herself. "I can't wait to get out of here! I miss taking a bath and having my hair done." She looked up at him through thick lashes. "I want my own clothes. I hate wearing these scratchy things. If you can make this happen, I promise I'll make it up to you."

The words were precisely what Manny hoped to hear. Marianna's appreciation would go far beyond a special dinner or any other token she'd deem sufficient. Retribution would be paid. If the plans worked the way he hoped, Marianna would owe her life to him. He made a mental note to secure a stipulation that remanded Marianna into his care once she was released.

"I only have one problem."

Her comment roused Manny from his thoughts. "And that is?"

"I don't know what I'll do when I get out of here. My reputation has been trashed by the press. Advertising agencies will shy away from me, not to mention I've been replaced. That little blonde bitch, Aimee, has stolen my identity. It's her face I see in the ads."

Manny stared silently. He tried to suppress any look that would give away the fact he had the matter well in hand.

"Don't act so concerned, Manny. It isn't as if you need to worry about your work or social life." The words dripped venomously from her lips.

"I'm not concerned at all, Marianna, because I have everything under control." His eyes narrowed. "Trust me."

Chapter 37

Marisol

If looks were daggers, Manny would have been dead from multiple stab wounds. Marisol stared at her husband's back as he exited the room. She had no choice. She had to play nice until he got her out of there, but his audacity made her blood simmer. How dare he walk away from her! Marisol was anxious to get out of the visitor's area. Anger fueled an underlying rage as she was escorted back to her room.

The calming quiet of her quarters was more conducive to strategizing. As soon as the lock clicked, indicating she'd have several uninterrupted hours, Marisol reclined on the bed and stared at the ceiling. Mental images emerged of exacting her revenge on the host of people who were responsible for putting her in this place. Satisfaction flooded her, flowing through her veins. The sedative effect nearly made her drunk with bloodlust. If she were to put any of these plans into action, she'd need to play Manny's game.

Perhaps he had a game of his own, an agenda that didn't fit hers. The thought deserved contemplation. If he didn't have a plan for her, then she would be disposable. That was how her father had thought, and he'd been Manny's mentor. There was also the possibility Manny wanted a woman who understood him, and who better than her? It made perfect sense. The egos of all men were fragile. If a woman could feed their pride while pretending to further their agendas, they could be useful. Although some men might deny it or not recognize it, Manny had an appetite for power, prestige, and respect.

Marisol contemplated how she and Manny could benefit each other as she mentally outlined a plan. Starting with his next visit, she would do her best to adopt a new attitude. She was a chameleon at heart, always appearing to give people what they expected from her. On the outside, she complemented the colors of her surroundings, while inside, her heart was the dark shade of narcissism. She would douse Manny with appreciative tones and affectionate lines, telling him how she couldn't survive this ordeal without him. She would paint herself as the epitome of helpless femininity. The scenario was distasteful, but she was confident it would work. It only required discipline. She had to keep her sights set on her goals.

Chapter 38

Carter

Declan's tone was barely above a whisper. He stood beside me, his eyes on Aimee. I'd been sitting in a chair at her bedside since they moved her to a private room.

"How is she?"

"Not as good as I'd like, but the doc says she's a strong woman. She'll recover." I stroked Aimee's cheek without looking up at my brother, then leaned over and pressed a gentle kiss to her head. She reeked of antiseptic, not the sweet scent I was used to inhaling. Standing, I placed a hand on his shoulder. "Let's talk out in the hall."

Declan nodded and followed behind me. "I gotta tell you. It was crazy at the hospital entrance. Once Aimee stepped into Marisol's shoes, her profile shot to the top. There are newspaper reporters and paparazzi everywhere. They're clamoring for information, but the guards seem to be keeping them at bay. My guess is that's your doing."

I nodded. "Whatever's necessary to assure her safety and privacy. I don't know how you do it. They're rabid for information."

"I know it's bad, but it could be worse."

"Worse?" I snapped. "Did you see her? She barely resembles herself!"

"I'm not talking about Aimee. I'm talking about the press. If this had happened in New York, this place would be crawling with them." His tone switched from slightly irritated to comforting. "Calm down, Carter. I'm here to help. I can handle the press."

"I don't want anyone getting pictures of her," I warned, my tone clipped with agitation.

Declan guided me to a more secluded spot in the hall. "You need to take it down a notch. Have you been home at all?"

I looked down at my disheveled clothes. Falcon had thrown a few things in a duffle bag for me and brought them to the hospital. I'd been living out of it for two days, but I couldn't care less about my appearance. "I'm not leaving her."

Declan heard the insistence in my tone. "I get that. I wouldn't want to leave Aria. All I'm saying is you can go home and grab a shower. Get something decent to eat. I'm here."

"Are you outta your fucking mind? I don't give a shit if you're here. I'm not leaving her."

"How long?" Declan's response to my outburst had me puzzled.

"What?"

"How long have you been in love with Aimee?"

As he clarified his question, I searched for an answer. *Do I even know?* I couldn't pinpoint a day, date, or time, but, somehow, Aimee had found a home inside my heart—at least what was left of it after Lacey died.

"A while," I answered, surprising myself.

Silence fell between us like a rising fog. Neither of us knew what to say. The unexpected revelation caught us both by surprise. As we stumbled through the awkward mist, Declan was the first to emerge. "Can I make a suggestion?"

I cocked an inquisitive brow.

"You stay with Aimee. I won't try to get you to leave but let me handle the press. I can spin it so it takes some attention away from her. That way you can go home if you want. There won't be a shitload of people hanging at the front entrance to pounce on you or Aimee. Will you let me do that?" "Please."

Everything about my body language projected tension and mistrust, but I heard Declan's calm plea.

I listened to his plan, and though I hated to admit it, it had merit. The press knew of Declan and Aimee's connection, but had no clue about me. They only thought of me as a police presence. Declan wanted to spin the story his way, and then leave the hospital with someone who looked like Aimee. If he led their attention away from the hospital and to her house, we could keep them away from mine. That way Aimee could recuperate in peace.

"Are you willing to stay here for a while to keep up the pretense? No one will believe that you'd drop her off and go. They'll dig for information if they suspect your concern is superficial."

"Aria is with me. Both of us are going to Aimee's house. We'll stay for a few weeks. It will simply look like we're helping out a friend. After some of the interest dies off, we'll revisit the issue, okay? Wait and see how Aimee's doing."

I weighed the proposition. It just might work. "Thank you." My voice was ragged. I was losing my battle with exhaustion.

"She doesn't have any family. Did she ever tell you that? I'm her emergency contact."

I nodded. "I just recently found out."

"Go grab a shower and some clean clothes," Declan suggested.

"I have to get Cody. She's been staying with the vet. I want to get her home. I'll have Marc and Falcon check on her while I'm here."

"I'll call you if she wakes up."

We walked to Aimee's room in silence, but before we reached her door, I turned to my brother. "I don't know when it happened. I just know I love her." I'd never been a man given to displays of emotion. Although I'd completely lost it when my wife died, my temperament had always been intense, yet calm. Not so since finding Aimee in the woods. That image would forever be burned into my memory. All I wanted was for her to recover so I could have her in my life. Loving her had hit me out of nowhere, but I refused to fight it. I'd do whatever was necessary to keep her. Although I'd vowed I'd never marry again, Aimee made me rethink everything. I wasn't looking for love, yet it found me. My brother knew me better than anyone, and I could tell by his expression the sincerity of my words had resonated with him.

"I'm glad you found her." Declan placed a hand on my shoulder. "In more ways than one."

Chapter 39

Aimee

It was comforting when I first opened my eyes and saw Carter at my bedside. This morning, the doctors had allowed me the freedom to use the bathroom, but only if someone accompanied me. Carter insisted on being that someone.

When my doctor told me I could have the intravenous medications and fluids removed, Carter had his friends bring fresh pajamas and underwear to the hospital. He knew that I'd would feel better if I could get out of the hospital gown. Marcus and Falcon raised no suspicions with the reporters in front of the hospital. No one had any idea of a possible connection between them and me.

At first, I thought that I'd be self-conscious when Carter helped me, but I didn't have the energy to object. He'd waited outside the bathroom door while I showered, and then helped me dry off. Carter was a realist and paid no attention to any attempt I made toward modesty. He anticipated my needs before I even thought of them and was always taking steps to protect my privacy. The intimate kindnesses Carter displayed touched my heart. If not for him, I'd have had to rely on hospital staff for the most minuscule tasks. No one had ever cared for me in the way he did. As a child, I was left to fend for myself by self-absorbed foster parents.

As I held onto Carter's shoulders for support, I realized the contrast between my past and present. It was comforting, yet foreign to me, to feel secure. Carter's steadfast demeanor never wavered. The air in the hospital room was so thick with his concern for me it was nearly palpable. I needed his assistance, as I was still unsteady on my feet, and even the smallest act had the largest impact on me. I placed first one leg and then the other into my pajamas. As Carter had predicted, once I was in my own clothes, I felt better. Although my lips were still tender and healing, I brushed them lightly against his hair with a gentle kiss.

"Thank you."

"No problem." He took my hand. "Let's get you back to bed."

I hadn't yet seen my face. If I looked anything like I felt, I was a disaster. For someone working in my industry, marred features were a death sentence. I leaned into Carter. "I want to see myself in the mirror."

His forehead tightened with a frown. "I don't think you should, not yet." Carter's posture stiffened as he tried to guide me back to bed.

My tone was as firm as my resolve. "I want to see."

Carter gave me a stern look. A silent battle of wills took place within those few moments. Finally, he gave a sigh of surrender. He held my hand as he helped me back toward the bathroom. Once I stood inside, he turned on the light so I could better see my reflection. The moment the room illuminated, I realized I should have listened to him; I should have trusted his judgment. But I thought I knew best. I was wrong.

I swallowed the lump that instantly formed in my throat. I didn't recognize the face looking back at me. My jaw was bruised. My lips were swollen and cracked. My eyes looked like they belonged to someone else, the blue color a stark contrast to red broken blood vessels in the white. My lips parted. The quick intake of oxygen felt cold on my tongue. Because of the injury to my cheekbone, it was distended and affected my facial symmetry. My nose was off-kilter, cantilevered to one side, while what remained was a patchwork of wounds and scrapes. I was used to the artistry of makeup accentuating my features. The different shades and hues of foundation and blush helped make me beautiful. As I looked at my naked skin, I realized I'd never seen so many colors of devastation. My face was a portrait of violence. My eyes burned as they flooded with bitter tears.

"Carter." I said his name so softly I barely heard my own voice. However quiet the sound carried, he heard my cry for help. My strength wavered, causing my knees to weaken. He caught me in his arms, turning me as I hid my face against his chest and bathed him with mournful tears.

THE NEXT DAY, I asked Carter to do something for me. He'd gone home the night before. I'd insisted he get a full night's sleep in his own bed. Unfortunately, I'd had lain awake, thinking, for most of the night. I recalled the difficult circumstances I'd faced all of my life. I needed the reminders. Those hard times had made me a survivor. Even though the situation was different, I was not. I still had the same inner strength and confidence. But even survivors have setbacks.

"Did you bring it?" Carter had barely breached the doorway when I asked the question.

"Yes." His tone reminded me of his disapproval. "I don't know why you want to do this to yourself. Can you just wait for a few days or even a few weeks?"

"I want to face this head-on. I know you don't understand, but if I look at them all—categorize them— then as my outside heals, maybe my inner strength will as well. Please don't give me a hard time about this. I need your help."

Carter nodded. Whether he understood or not, he supported me. As he sat beside me on the bed, we took inventory of my injuries together. The hand mirror was just the right size for investigating each point of damage individually while not tormenting me with the big picture. As each gash, bump, and stitch was catalogued, Carter reminded me of the doctor's comments.

Each day we repeated this task. Not much changed within a twenty-four-hour period, yet I was healing. I pivoted on an imaginary emotional scale—one day positive, one day negative—and after a few weeks had passed, I realized I would never be the beautiful girl I once was. I'd have scars, even if they were slight. Because my career required physical perfection, defeat washed over me in varying waves. Hope and despair rode side-by-side on the crest of possible outcomes. I could employ the best plastic surgeon, but if I couldn't see myself as beautiful, I would never be able to convince a critical public.

Depression blanketed me, and I curled into a ball beneath the covers of my bed. I pulled my knees to my chest and rocked back and forth to soothe myself while I cried. Losing track of time, I fell asleep. I woke to the chill of a cold washcloth against my face. My pillow was damp, and my eyelids were itchy and swollen. Although I knew the hand holding the cloth belonged to Carter, I didn't open my eyes.

"Please go home. I don't want you to look at me."

He was undaunted by my request and instead gathered me in his arms. "Are you finished?"

"I don't know. Maybe." I hiccupped. I felt the rumble in his chest as he chuckled. "What's so funny?" I tilted my face up and opened my eyes. His warm brown eyes met my blue ones.

"You are." He pulled me closer, and my legs dangled over his thigh. "I'm only laughing at your stuffy nose, nothing else."

"How can you stand looking at me?" Emotion mangled my words. "I can barely stand to look at myself."

"Well, that's a damn shame. I don't know what you see, but I see a brave and beautiful woman. One that is stronger and fiercer than I deserve. One that I love."

His admission left me speechless; my eyes widened in surprise, saying what I couldn't.

"I'll never forget how you looked when I found you, Aim. I was sure you were dead but prayed you weren't. The minute I saw you take a breath, nothing else mattered to me, and nothing else does now. I think you're beautiful. But, honestly? I don't give a shit what you look like. All I know is I have you. You're alive. You're mine. That's enough for me."

"It really doesn't bother you?" I asked in a quiet whisper.

He shook his head. "No, it doesn't. Time will heal your cuts and bruises, but I love the whole woman. Not just the looks. I'm sure that in time, you'll be the same as you were. Don't worry."

He thought he had me figured out, assuming I was only concerned about what I looked like. What he didn't know was those soulless eyes had begun to invade my dreams, turning them into nightmares and scaring me awake. Even though my skin was healing, my mind presented horrific images. Whenever I opened my eyes, I saw a woman who'd been transformed into a monster by the beast who'd attacked her. Despite my attempts toward bravery, those visions made me fearful of what was to come.

My shoulders slumped, and I rested my head on his chest. "That's where you're wrong. I'm not sure I'll ever be the same."

Chapter 40

Aimee

Twelve weeks.

Twelve. Whole. Weeks.

Four of those had been spent in the hospital. When I was released at last, Carter had insisted I recover at his house. At first, my moods were mercurial. I wavered between anger and numbness, but somehow Carter managed to pierce through the desolation of my thoughts. He followed my lead, bouncing between my mixed emotions as they shifted between dark and light. His constant presence offered the security I so desperately craved. As time passed, we both learned that even a fragile relationship could grow strong with one element.

Love.

One night, Carter came in to check on me. He

fluffed my pillows and sat beside me on the bed. He also made sure I'd taken my pain medicine on schedule. I found comfort lying in his arms. He made me feel so cared for, so loved. As I began to fall asleep, he climbed out of bed to sleep in the other room. He was afraid he would hurt me by moving around in the same bed.

"Don't go."

"I'll be right outside." His tone was calm and reassuring.

"Please? I feel better when you're here."

He relented, snuggling behind me. Our spooned position was like we were an old married couple. He kissed the top of my ear. "Tell me what's wrong. I'll stay, but you have to talk to me."

I shrugged. Opening up wasn't something I did easily. From the time I was a child, I'd learned if you divulged your secrets, people judged you. "I don't like the dark. I sleep with a nightlight at home."

Instead of making fun of me, he soothed me, stroking my arm from my shoulder down to my fingertips. "Why are you afraid?"

Again, I shrugged. "My mom and dad weren't the best people in the world. When I was young, my father left. I think I was five when I last saw my mother. After that, I went into foster care. Each house was different, each bedroom strange. I never stayed in one place long enough to get used to house noises." My memories were mixed. Vague and specific. I'd never spoken to anyone of my fears. Not to psychiatrists, counselors, or friends. Until Carter.

"Declan never said anything to me." He pulled me close.

"He doesn't know much," I confessed. "All he knows is I was a foster kid. I've never talked about my childhood to anyone. You're the first."

"You can tell me anything, Aim."

I couldn't see his eyes. Usually, I was good at gauging a person's intentions if I could look at their eyes, but Carter was different. I wanted to confess my secrets to this man. He made me feel safe enough to trust him. "My most vivid memories are of the first night in every one of those houses. Each one was different. Curtains, bedspreads—all of it. The one thing they all had in common was they were dark and scary."

"I'm sorry, baby." Compassion filled his words.

"You had your brother when you were growing up. Imagine if you had no one and the people you lived with knew nothing about you but your name—which they only learned a few hours before you arrived." I revisited mental images, and my breathing quickened. "They took a little girl, put her in a dark room, and expected her not to cry. If I did, I was reminded how lucky I was to have a roof over my head."

Carter squeezed my hand. "Aimee, if you want to leave a light on, then you leave the damn light on. Hell, you can leave every light in the house on if you want. This is your home as much as it is mine."

I huffed out a snort. "Right. You don't know what you're saying, Carter. I come with some baggage."

"So, we'll get rid of your old baggage and get some new. In case you haven't noticed, I'm not so perfect myself."

"Well, that's true," I laughed. "You take a little getting used to. You're so damn intense!"

"Well, shit," he drawled. "You didn't have to agree with me!"

As I drifted to sleep, Carter pressed a featherlight kiss on my neck and placed his lips to my ear. "I want you here with me, Aimee. Not just while you recover, but every day."

With each passing day, Carter confirmed to me, in little ways, his words were real, and I continued to grow stronger. For the first time, I was going to dress in real clothes. I'd spent weeks in either pajamas or sweats, and I smiled as I anticipated the reaction I'd would receive when he saw me. I fixed my hair and put on a little makeup. It was incredible how much better I felt with those little touches.

After I finished my tasks, I looked at the calendar. It was almost Christmas. Time had slipped away from me. I grabbed a blanket and curled up on the window seat. Carter had stoked and replenished a fire in the bedroom fireplace. As I looked out the window, I took in the scene that was like a picture from a *Currier & Ives* holiday card. Winter in the mountains was breathtakingly beautiful. Snow nestled on the boughs of the trees. The lake was frozen over in the shallow parts, leaving just enough water for the birds to skittle in for a drink or a bath. At the edge of the pier were two Adirondack chairs with a few inches of fresh, fluffy powder coating the arms and seats. Except for memories of the attack, I loved it here.

I don't know how long I sat there enjoying the scene, but my legs were beginning to cramp. Thankfully, the master suite was on the first floor, and I didn't have to tackle the stairs several times a day. I made my way to the living room and saw Carter also had a fire going in there. He was never far away from me, but recently had become more comfortable leaving me by myself so he could put in a few hours of work. I entered the kitchen and suddenly had a craving for hot chocolate. I hadn't cooked or baked anything in months. I found the ingredients I needed and got a pot going on the stove. Soon the house smelled heavenly, thick with the aroma of cocoa. I stirred the warming liquid while my thoughts drifted. Steam rose from the pot, and as I poured the drink into a cup, I compared the color to the rich brown of Carter's eyes. Looking into them had become a frequent pastime, and they bathed me with a secure feeling. A smile formed as I plopped a few marshmallows into the cup. The minute I placed it to my lips, Cody came up beside me and nudged my leg.

"You need to go out, girl?" I asked.

She answered by prancing around in a circle.

Grabbing a throw from the back of a kitchen chair, I followed Cody to the door. As I opened it, she flew down the steps and ran through the snow. It was so beautiful and so quiet, the cushioning silence you only experience when clouds and snow combine. I desperately desired to take in a few breaths of crisp air. I had been cooped up for so long. I opened the door, placed one foot on the top step, and held onto the railing. As I took another step down with the other foot, a strange feeling came over me. I gripped the wood beneath my hands. Snow melted upon impact with my body heat and sent a cold puddle between my fingers. A strange, gradual tightening weaved its way around my ribs. The iron-like weight made me double over at the waist. I struggled helplessly against its force. It squeezed my lungs, making oxygen a precious commodity. Invisible talons formed in my throat and clawed at lost air. Vertigo disoriented me. I froze in place, knowing that if I didn't turn around and go back inside I'd fall victim to a new assailant—fear.

Chapter 41

M *anuel*

MANNY WAS AN INTIMIDATING figure on his own, but today he had a companion. Mr. Dietz was sweating, his eyes jumping between Manny and the brooding man who leaned against the wall behind him. The stranger twirled a long-bladed, shiny knife between his fingers, anticipation gleaming in his eyes. The lawyer's fear didn't escape Manny's notice. He was confident his desire would be met by Mr. Dietz before he left his office today.

"Mr. Dietz."

"Mr. Vallega." Although the smaller man attempted composure, his voice wavered. The cracking inflection gave away his nervousness. "May I ask the name of your friend?" Mr. Dietz tipped his chin in the direction of the scarred man.

Manny glanced over his shoulder at Blade. "Who, him?"

Blade's mouth twisted. With a smirk, he pointed the tip of his knife toward Mr. Dietz.

"I apologize, Mr. Dietz. My friend tends to fidget. Situations like this make him uneasy."

"And why would your friend be uneasy?" Mr. Dietz watched as Blade sheathed his knife and folded his arms across his chest.

"Well, his level of unease will be decided by your response to my request, Mr. Dietz. Let's talk business, shall we?" Manny's tone was condescending. Today wasn't the first instance he'd had Blade become familiar with the attorney, but Mr. Dietz didn't know that. Unbeknownst to the lawyer, Blade was the man who'd attacked him about two months back. He was hooded at the time. As the poor older man had lain breathless against the hood of his car, Blade had disappeared down the dark street. Manny enjoyed Mr. Dietz's discomfort as he tried not to stare at Blade.

Feeling confident the lawyer was suitably intimidated, Manny proceeded to get to the point of this meeting—Marianna's real estate holdings. For the next fifteen minutes, he directed what he wanted to be done with the properties. "Do we understand each other, Mr. Dietz? I want all of the properties held by The

Vencedor Corporation liquidated, and the monies deposited into the account I've provided."

"I understand, Mr. Vallega, but..." He took in a long breath and then let it out. "Ms. Franzi is my client. I have to run this by her."

A violent red color crept up Manny's neck, stopping just above the collar of his shirt. He was disappointed in the attorney. It seemed more convincing was necessary.

Manny stood and placed both hands on the front of Mr. Dietz's desk. His height was imposing as he towered over the seated man. He glared, and his eyes narrowed into slits. "Are you suggesting your opinion better serves my wife than mine? If so, Mr. Dietz, you imply that I'm incompetent." Manny looked up at the ceiling and took a deep breath. After a moment of pause, he brought his hands up and slammed them on the desk. "My wife's business is my business, Mr. Dietz!"

The assault on his desk and the tone of Manny's voice caused Mr. Dietz to tremble. Rendered speechless, the man could only nod.

Manny straightened his posture and adjusted his tie. He took a moment to regain his composure. "I find it frustrating I'm constantly clarifying myself to you." He crossed powerful arms across his chest. "As of this moment, your interest in my wife's well-being is over. I decide what actions will, or will not, be taken for her benefit." He reached into the breast pocket of his jacket, pulled out an envelope, and threw it on the desk. "Here's a power of attorney. Don't question me again." He nodded toward Blade. "If you feel tempted to question my judgment, you can speak with my associate."

Chapter 42

Aimee

Breathe.

Just breathe.

I couldn't figure out what was wrong with me. I needed to take a deep breath. I desperately needed oxygen, but my body wouldn't obey. Invisible chains wrapped tightly around my chest. I was being attacked a second time, but this monster came from within. The entity torturing me had no physical form. It alternated its attack by numbing some sensations and exacerbating others. A cocktail of fear and incapacitation began to slowly snake its way through my body. Vertigo slapped me viciously, and I grabbed onto the railing to keep from falling. I lost my grip on the blanket around my shoulders. It fluttered to the ground in slow motion. I froze in place as another crisp dose of fear invaded me, twisting my insides with an icy knife. It was a sucker punch, unannounced and unwelcome. Seconds dragged like hours as I fought against the panic. Terror blistered my reality, igniting every nerve until they blazed.

I wasn't sure what to do. My mind told me to run, but there was no escape. The invading fear made the progress of my recovery seem insignificant and worthless. All at once I felt helpless and hopeless. The two formed a deadly poison which infected me. I'd worked so hard to rebuild my sense of security, but it was new and fragile and couldn't withstand the message that played in a loop over and over in my head: *I am going to die.*

I struggled with the magnitude of the moment. My mind writhed in agony while I rode the wave of fear. I held onto the railing until I was finally able to take a deep breath. The cold air burned my lungs, but I welcomed the fire. Placing one hand over the other, I pulled myself up the steps. My only goal was to reach the door. If I could just accomplish that one task, safety would be waiting for me on the other side.

I reached for the knob, and just as I did I felt Cody's head nudging me the rest of the way. I looped my fingers through her collar. The ice balls in her fur made my hand tingle with the cold. My feet felt so heavy the dragging sensation gave me a new understanding of the word exhaustion. A few more labored steps and I was finally inside.

Slanting my shoulder against the door, I pushed it closed behind me and went to lean against the counter. I couldn't stand up straight. Bent over, I gripped the edge with both hands while I caught my breath. On shaky legs, I inhaled oxygen in deep, cleansing breaths. Confusion clouded me. I didn't understand. This had never happened before, and I wasn't sure what *this* was. A side effect of the medication? An aftershock of the attack? Something like post-traumatic stress?

Minutes ticked away, and my thoughts began to normalize as the racing of my brain slowed down. Cody was sitting beside me on the floor. "I am beginning to think you're my guardian angel," I whispered. She responded to my voice by wiggling her hind end. I wanted to lie down. I was exhausted. My arms and legs felt like limp noodles. But relief evaded me because as I started to walk into the next room, pain tore through my core with a blistering intensity. I doubled over just as Carter approached me.

"What's wrong?" The moment his eyes met mine he rushed toward me and hooked his arm around my waist.

I looked up. "I don't know!" Terror filled me as my stomach cramped relentlessly.

"You need to sit down," he ordered. He walked me to a chair and helped me take a seat. I looked at him and watched as worry filled his expression. Lines tensed his forehead and jaw as his eyes narrowed. I tried to follow his gaze, but as he knelt down, my view was obstructed. Another wave of pain had me holding onto his shoulder. I closed my eyes. *Was this a continuation of what happened to me outside?* Carter reached for his cell. "Babe, I need to get you to the hospital."

"What's wrong with me?" I heard the fearful desperation in my voice. Something had him alarmed, but he didn't know about the spell I'd had when I was outside. I didn't know what was causing the ripping sensation in my stomach. I was even more frightened than I'd been out in the cold. I lifted my head and looked into Carter's eyes, the color now darkened by concern.

"You're bleeding."

I looked over his shoulder and saw that I had left behind a trail of blood from the few steps I'd taken. The tide of fear that had been rising inside of me crested at the crimson sight. All at once the room began to spin. My scalp prickled while goosebumps raised on my skin. I was hot. I was cold. My body temperature fluctuated erratically as I once again struggled to breathe. I noticed for the first time a warm rush of blood from between my legs. Sparkles appeared before my eyes. Like golden punctuation marks, the commas danced in my vision while everything else in the background faded to black.

Chapter 43

Carter

When had I begun to love Aimee so much?

I didn't know the answer because I'd spent so much time trying to deny it. Until the day that she was assaulted, I reasoned with myself I didn't have time for a relationship. *The moment I found her in the woods.* That was it. That was when everything changed. Now she was in jeopardy again. It was painfully clear to me that I couldn't bear to lose her. I was too familiar with loss; I knew the cavernous feeling all too well.

Shifting uncomfortably in the waiting room for what felt like the hundredth time, I prayed for some distraction from my dark thoughts. I remembered how it felt when I lost my mother and then my wife. I didn't want to sink into that soulless, black pit again. I barely made it out of there with my sanity intact the last time. I dropped my head in my hands. Maybe God would pardon all the bad shit I'd done in my life and not let me lose another woman I loved.

I heard footsteps on the tile floor as the doctor walked toward me. "How is she?" I stood up to meet him. A lump formed in my throat and choked me, making my voice sound serrated and broken.

"Aimee is fine." He motioned for me to sit back down, and he sat across from me. "The bad news is that she miscarried. I'm sorry."

The shocking news stunned me into silence. The doctor instantly interpreted my confused look.

"You didn't know she was pregnant?"

I shook my head, mute.

"She was about ten weeks along. We performed a D&C, and, other than the blood loss, I don't expect any problems with her recovery. We're watching her to determine if she'll need a transfusion, especially in her weakened state.

I nodded. Miscarried? A baby?

The words were bittersweet as timelines and circumstances lined themselves up in my head. Babies are supposed to bring happiness. There was no way to tell who the father was. Selfish bastard that I am, I wasn't sorry to hear she'd miscarried. The doctor said she was about ten weeks. It had been about that long since we'd made love—and since her attacker raped her. I never got the chance to tell her that morning about the break in the condom. *Who the hell are you kidding? You didn't want to tell her!* She should know, and I should tell her, but I was conflicted. What purpose would it serve?

"Does she know?" I asked.

"No, not yet," the doctor answered. "She's in recovery but not fully coherent. It's possible she may not have been aware she was pregnant. Most women figure it out by the eight-week mark, but Aimee has been focused on recovering from her injuries. I looked at her chart. We did a rape kit on her when she was here before, but it would have been too early to determine a pregnancy."

I ran my hands over my face and through my hair as I exhaled a frustrated sigh. "Can I see her?"

"I'll have someone come out to take you back."

Suddenly at a loss for words, I could only nod. Anything I said would be littered with emotion.

"Carter, this might not be a bad thing. At least she won't have to make the decision to abort. Are you going to be with her as she continues recovery?"

"Yeah. She's coming home with me."

"Good. In the short time I've gotten to know her, I can see Aimee is a very determined woman. I don't want her to push herself too hard." He stood, extending his hand. "Give them a few minutes," he said as he smiled. "I'll have the nurse bring you back to the PACU. In light of what she's been through, I'd like to keep her a night or two for observation." He paused, taking note of my expression. "Carter, she's a fighter."

I nodded. *Aimee is a fighter.* I'd noticed it way back when I was living at the beach. It was around the same time I'd decided she was a pain in the ass. Although most of her act was smoke and mirrors, I was glad she had a double dose of determination to go along with it. This news might set her back a bit, but she would bring herself out of it kicking and screaming once she had some time to digest it.

"Hey, Doc?" I called to him as he walked down the hall. "Thanks. For everything."

The doctor tipped his chin, nodded, and smiled.

———————

IT WASN'T long after that I went into the PACU as they moved Aimee. She'd slipped in and out of consciousness as they'd wheeled her down the hall, but now that she was in her room, she was sleeping peacefully. I leaned forward. As I stroked her hair, a soft curl fell over her cheek. Brushing it away from her face, I touched my lips to her forehead. As I pulled back, I saw the flutter of her thick lashes.

"Hey, babe." As I softly spoke the words, the corners of her mouth barely curled into a weak smile. *She's so strong.* As I stared at Aimee in the hospital bed, I realized how much her appearance had changed.

She hadn't been able to tolerate much food until just recently. I'd always thought she was a little too thin to begin with, but I understood keeping her weight down was part of the job. Now she was so tiny she seemed frail. Dark circles under her eyes had begun to transform her pale skin, making it appear almost ghostly white. *Strong, but still fragile.*

Her lips were moving, but I couldn't make out the words.

"What is it, baby?" I whispered as I stroked her face.

"It hurts." She tried to lick her lips but winced as her tongue caught the skin because both were painfully dry.

"Be right back." I went to the sink and wet a washcloth that I took from a pile of clean linens placed in the bathroom for her. When I held it to her lips she raised her hand to it, eagerly pressing the damp fibers to her mouth. "Easy, baby." I took her hand in mine to control the pressure. Once she was satisfied, she pushed my hand and the cloth away. "Better?" I asked. She nodded so slightly she barely moved. I lightly placed my hand on top of hers, caressing the back of it with the pad of my thumb. Her eyes opened more fully, and she turned her head to look at me.

"Please don't leave me." Her tone was hushed.

I gave her hand a gentle squeeze. "I'm not going anywhere. I promise. I won't leave you alone."

Aimee took hold of the rail on the other side of the

bed and pulled herself over so she could lie on her side. The desire to hold her took over my common sense, and I quietly slipped onto the bed, behind her. The mattress dipped beneath my weight. I was terrified I'd hurt her, but I had to be as close as possible. Aimee calmed my fears as she pressed back against me. Instinctively, my arm closed around her waist. Exhaustion set in, and my eyelids grew heavy as I tucked her head beneath my chin. All I cared about was that I was with her, and she was safe. I closed my eyes as I pulled her tighter.

"Go to sleep, baby. I got you."

Chapter 44

Aimee

I cy twitches in my legs woke me as they scratched and clawed at me from the inside. They alternated with a strange, stinging soreness. I shivered beneath the covers. Although details were still jockeying for their proper position as I became more awake, I knew Carter had been here with me. I remembered that much.

Earlier, I'd woken, startled, then realized he was holding me, so I drifted back to sleep.

Now he was gone, and I hated the absence of his body against mine. I was cold, and I looked around for him. Just as I pulled the blanket around my shoulders, Carter walked out of the bathroom. When he realized I was awake, he pulled a chair up to the side of the bed. His fingertips caressed my cheek, and he tucked my sleep mussed hair behind my ear.

"How do you feel?"

"Like I got beat up," I croaked. "My back hurts."

Without missing a beat, and with a firm touch, he rubbed my lower back, massaging with long, careful strokes. I moaned in response, and he chuckled at the sound.

"Good?"

"*Mm-hmm*. Real good." He continued his ministrations, and I was content to stay on my side for as long as he wanted. As I became more fully awake, my curiosity piqued. "Tell me what happened."

"You were bleeding. I brought you to the Emergency Room." His tone was flat.

"Is that why I passed out?"

"Yeah." Again, his tone was void of inflection.

"There's something you're not telling me."

He didn't respond. I hadn't planned to tell him how panicky and terrified I'd felt when I let Cody out, but I didn't want to keep it from him either. I carefully repositioned myself on the bed, my motions tentative as I turned to face him. "Something did happen to me, though..."

His brows raised as I could see that he warred with himself. The expression on his face revealed he wanted and didn't want to know. Lines furrowed his forehead. It looked like he was bracing himself for my explanation.

"I wish I could tell you exactly what happened, but I don't really know what it was. I don't know what I would call it. All I know is that I was letting Cody out. I put a blanket around my shoulders so I could step outside and get some air—"

He interrupted me. "You didn't have to do that. I could have let Cody out."

"I know, but I was starting to feel better," I sighed out the statement. "I didn't think opening the kitchen door was a big deal."

"So, what happened? Did you fall down?"

"No. Nothing like that. It was my whole body. It was all so weird. Like I didn't have control anymore." I paused. How could I put into words what I didn't understand myself? I had to try. "I was afraid, Carter. It was a fear that came out of nowhere. I became afraid as soon as I stepped outside. No, *afraid* doesn't do it justice. I was terrified." Telling him brought back the memory of the all-encompassing fear, and with it came some of the feelings. My hand started to shake in his. "I was more afraid than I've ever been in my life. I was scared when that man attacked me, but I was busy trying to fight him off. This was different." My eyes misted, blurring my vision. "I couldn't breathe. I felt like something invisible was strangling me. I had goosebumps all over, but I was hot, too. My arms and legs wouldn't work. My body wouldn't pay attention to what my brain told it to do. I wanted to go back up the steps, but my feet felt like they were in cement. My hair felt like it was standing up on end." No longer able to control my tears, they spilled over the rims of my lower lids and burned a salty trail down my cheeks.

"Did you hear or see anything that would have scared you?" He was in cop mode. As he asked his questions, he sounded concerned but not alarmed. I knew he was trying to help me to remember the details.

"No one. At least, I didn't see anyone." My face scrunched up with worry, and I looked at him with pleading eyes. "I didn't hear anything either. What if it happens again?"

The lines around his eyes softened. He took my hand in one of his and stroked my face with the other. "It probably won't. Maybe the temperature shocked your body going from the house out into the cold. It was only about ten degrees outside."

Carter's words permeated my rationale and had just begun to reassure me when there was a knock on the door. The doctor poked his head in, interrupting our conversation. "How are you feeling today, Aimee?"

I shrugged and wiped the residual tears from my conversation with Carter away from my face with the sleeve of the hospital gown. "I'm not sure. My lower back is sore."

The doctor glanced at Carter, who tightened his grip on my hand as I waited for information.

"I can explain that." The doctor looked from Carter to me, and I saw Carter shake his head.

Puzzled at the exchange, I gave them both a look that demanded answers. "What's going on?"

"Aimee..." The doctor pulled over a chair and sat by Carter and me. "Did you know you were pregnant?"

The world fell like lead. *Pregnant?* I didn't need an explanation. My rapid speculation of when and how was more than I could bear. The room disappeared around me, and I felt like I was free falling. I was desperately grateful to be holding onto Carter's hand. He anchored me—tethered me—as a dizzy spell spun my world out of control. I shook my head, the action giving my answer.

"You miscarried. You're fine, but you lost a lot of blood. We gave you a transfusion after we performed a D&C. The procedure is most likely the cause of your backache. I can order something for the pain."

I choked on a sob as the pieces fell into place. I remembered Carter had used a condom when we'd made love. There was only one explanation. The rape. I'd gotten pregnant from the rape. "Oh, my God." The words barely registered sound, for no notes would grace them. Tears blinded me. I looked at the doctor. "I didn't know," I said in a whisper.

"The good news is the procedure went well." Dr. Williams smiled at us both. "Aimee, there's no reason to believe that you can't have children in the future." His tone was assuring. "Since Carter said you're going to continue recovery at his house, I'm discharging you today. I'm sure you'll be much more comfortable there than in the hospital. I'll send the nurse in with discharge instructions." He stood.

"Thanks, Doc." Carter gave him an appreciative glance while still holding my hand.

"You're welcome," the doctor answered. "I'll see you in a couple of weeks, Aimee. Until then, rest." He paused. "And if you want to talk to someone, I'd be happy to recommend a colleague. You've been through a lot. It might help."

Once the doctor left, I closed my eyes. Too many things clouded my mind and I let the tears flow freely. Carter caught the drops as he swiped them away from my cheeks with his finger. Something soft cradled the tip of my nose.

"Blow," he said.

Absentmindedly, I complied. I let my thoughts run away with me, and they sprinted through every emotion. *Seventy days.* For seventy-days my body had housed a piece of my rapist. I felt like I wanted to vomit. *How am I supposed to feel? Horrified? Relieved? Sad? Numb.*

Carter held my hands. "It's gonna be okay, baby." He drew me close, consoling me.

Would this nightmare ever end? I couldn't look anywhere but down. I avoided Carter's face. I couldn't bear it. My immediate view was his jean-clad knees, and, for once, I was glad that our eyes didn't meet. The position mirrored precisely how I felt. Disconnected.

Chapter 45

It was a quiet ride back to the lake house. I drove with one hand on the wheel and held Aimee's hand in the other as she stared blankly out the window. She seemed to have traveled somewhere else in her mind. I didn't try to make small talk. Sometimes conversation was overrated, and solitude could be a best friend. For so long after Lacey had died I tried to be the talkative person most people wanted and expected. When I'd finally realized my preference was to be left alone with my thoughts, I found some peace. Aimee deserved the same courtesy. I had no intention of imposing on her what had been imposed on me. Once she had some time and space to digest and process all that had happened, she would talk. Until then I was content to hold her hand and give her a quiet ride home away from the hospital and the memories it held.

As I pulled into the driveway, Cody ran to Aimee's door. Her fur-covered rear end bobbled with happiness. I looked over at Aimee, her lips now curved with a smile. She reached for Cody as I opened the car door.

"Hi, baby girl. Did you miss me?"

Aimee's voice was too weak for my liking. I reached in and helped her out of the car. As we walked into the house, her steps were slow. Her grip on my hand was tight. "Let's get you comfortable." I placed my arm around her waist for support. She stopped midstride and leaned her head back against my chest. Instinctively, I closed my arms around her. The gesture provided as much comfort to Aimee as it did me. "You okay, baby?"

She nodded, holding the posture for a moment. She then moved forward with cautious steps. I took her hand in mine to support her and to keep a skin-to-skin connection. I wanted to make all of this go away, to have Aimee bright and sunny and smart-mouthed again, but all I could do now was try and help her heal.

As I led her to our room, exhaustion etched lines on her face. I eased her into a sitting position on the bed, and her shoulders slumped. I knelt down and slipped her shoes off. Pausing, I massaged each foot and helped her into sweats and a T-shirt. She was as limp as a well-worn ragdoll as I lifted her arms and legs. When I tucked her in, the enormity of the bed and plush linens enveloped her, And she nearly disappeared. As she moved around to get comfortable, I started a fire to ward off the chill that had settled in the room during our absence. When I returned to check on her, she was asleep. Her golden hair had lost a little of its shine, but still fanned out beautifully behind her. She had the silhouette of a battered angel. As I took in her appearance, the magnitude of the events that caused such devastation to her hit me with full force. Exhaustion claimed me as a second victim. I gave into it and climbed into bed behind her. As I cradled Aimee in my arms, I succumbed to the rest my body so desperately needed.

I OPENED my eyes several hours later and saw that Aimee was still asleep in my arms. My mind wandered to thoughts of the past and future. The moment I'd admitted to myself that I loved her, I wanted to be her everything. As a former investigator, that also meant trying to figure out what made her tick. Although I was initially resistant to being in any relationship, I was happy to be a part of Aimee's life now. Somehow between the time she showed up at my door and the night I'd made love to her, I'd stopped being an idiot. Aimee and I were like mismatched bookends from one of the old antique stores she liked to frequent—opposite, but similar. Without realizing it, I'd changed, and I liked who I was when I was with her. I also liked that she wasn't the diva she appeared to be as a model and that she could let her guard down with me. Aimee saw through me and all of my macho bullshit because she was well aware she had her own smokescreen. She saw my rough edges, and still loved me. Aimee seemed to be a tough cookie, but some of it was an act. I later realized she was one of the most interesting and loving people I'd ever met. Now that I knew her better, I understood why Declan was so protective of her. *Shit! Declan!*

I hadn't called my brother to let him know of this latest development, and I didn't know if I should without talking to Aimee first. Declan would be pissed if I didn't make him aware of what was going on, but what the hell could I say? "Aimee was in the hospital again—and, oh, by the way, she had a miscarriage." *Hell no*. That was Aimee's decision, and I'd abide by whatever she wanted to do.

Since Aimee was still asleep, and the house was calm, I got out of bed and quietly busied myself with chores, like putting the dishes in the dishwasher and taking out the trash. Every time I completed a task I checked on her. I'd just taken off my coat from going outside to get firewood and when I tiptoed into the bedroom, Aimee was awake. She was sitting up in bed, silently staring out the window at the falling snow. I added wood and stoked the fire then sat down next to her. I eased my arm around her waist, and she snuggled into me. She said nothing, and I respected that. I knew she'd talk when she was ready. Eventually, she wouldn't be able to continue internalizing her thoughts. The crackle of the fire filled the silence as we leaned against the headboard and watched any green that remained in the landscape turn to white.

"Do you think God hates me?"

I was taken aback. Although the question was huge, Aimee's voice was so small I barely heard it. She'd asked it in the tiniest whisper, but the weight it carried crushed my heart. I measured my answer, careful not to add to her pain. "I'm not sure there is a God, but if there is, I don't see how He could." I kissed the back of her head and inhaled the fragrance of her hair as I spoke. "One of the things I love most about you, Aim, is your kind heart. So, if you believe what you tell me about God only looking at the motive of a person, then I don't think it's possible for Him to hate you." I paused, looking down at her. "Why do you ask? Do you think God hates you?"

She shrugged. "I don't know. I hope not, but I can't be sure."

I wasn't following her reasoning. "Why not?"

"Because I'm a cold-hearted bitch."

"Aim," I protested, my words coming out in an amused huff. "You're anything but a—"

"I *am* a cold-hearted bitch. At least I admit to it." She tipped her chin up to look at me. Her eyes were brimming with unshed tears. "How else can you explain that I have absolutely no feeling for a little baby who never had a chance? No pity?" A sudden chill made her shudder, and a few fat tears fell down her cheeks as she closed her eyes. The lump that had taken residence in my throat since that night at the hospital expanded until I nearly choked on it. Aimee was the victim, yet here she was confessing as if she were the one who'd committed a crime.

My heart crumbled. I couldn't fix this for her, and I felt helpless. "You can't beat yourself up about this, baby." I pulled her in tighter. "You didn't want this to happen—any of it."

"I don't know what to think anymore, Carter. I've always believed that life should be valued. If that's true, shouldn't every life be precious, and every death be mourned?"

I had no answers for her, so I held her as she cried. Her cries became sobs I hoped would wash her conscience clean. Although Aimee had said she had no feeling about the miscarriage, there was no doubt she was in mourning. *Cold-hearted bitch? Never.* I knew I should man-up and tell her about the broken condom, but what good would that do now? The tortured look in her eyes when she asked the question would always haunt me. Whether it was about the violence that had been inflicted on her or the loss of a life that had never drawn oxygen, I couldn't be sure. What I did know was she was far from heartless. A tender heart fosters tears, hate abandons them.

Chapter 46

Carter

Days passed uneventfully as they stretched into weeks and I was cautiously optimistic that Aimee was healing both physically and emotionally. Gone was the old Aimee: the boisterous, meddling, pain in the ass girl I had first met in Ocean City. In her place was a more serious woman. She was slowly rediscovering joy, and it was in the everyday things. Aimee had made enough money to live on for a lifetime. She was comfortable financially and didn't have to go back to work if she didn't want to. I offered her security in any way she would accept and asked nothing of her. If she graced me with a smile, I was a wealthy man.

I felt like I'd hit the lottery when merely sitting with her to watch the birds. As they took food from the feeders she'd sip coffee or hot chocolate at the window seat recanting what species had decided to be our neighbors for the day. I worked from home. MarSin Falcon had become so successful, that, with our carefully selected staff, it practically ran itself. Cody was content to have both of us nearby. As she lay in front of the fire she kept an eye on Aimee. She'd become quite protective of her and was always nearby.

Although I knew on an intellectual level Aimee was recovering, her episodes of melancholy ate at me. She and her doctors said that she was getting better, but I could tell something was lacking. She was down, and I felt helpless. Little did I know that something routine and utterly innocuous would finally perk her up.

We'd just eaten breakfast and were sitting at the dining room table, lingering over coffee. The front door burst open, and in walked Marc and Falcon with a Christmas tree. Every year, the three of us would go out into the woods and try to outdo each other with the most spectacular Douglas Firs we could fit in our houses. I had opted out this year to stay with Aimee, so the guys told me they'd bring one to us. I hadn't given it much thought until I saw Aimee's expression.

"Wow!" Her eyes widened, surprise washing over her and filling her cheeks with a pink glow. "That's the biggest Christmas tree I've ever seen!"

"Yep. You won't get one of these in the city, that's

for sure." Marcus's words were full of pride. I swear, his chest swelled.

"Where did you buy a tree so big?"

The excitement in Aimee's voice amused my friends. They shot each other cocky looks. "City girl!" Marcus teased. "You don't buy a tree like this. Real men cut down their trees." Falcon shared this opinion as evidenced by his playful smirk.

"Yeah, yeah, yeah," I said as I came up behind Aimee. She wasn't looking at them, instead inspecting the tree. "You guys are real macho men." I closed my arms around her waist. I felt her body shake with laughter. "You like it?" Her head bobbed up and down like a child's toy, and my heart swelled. It was the first time in a long time I'd seen her this happy. "I didn't know Christmas would excite you so much. Some people can't stand all the commercialism that goes along with it."

"I haven't had many Christmas trees. It all depended on who I was living with at the time."

Her comment was a slap in the face to every Christmas I'd taken for granted. Our mom had always made the holidays fun. It didn't matter what kind of budget we were on. Our Christmases had always been memorable. Suddenly, I had an idea. "Aim, why don't we have a Christmas party?"

"What?" She turned toward me, excitement toying with her question. "A party? Who would we invite?"

Falcon cleared his throat while Marc hitched an eyebrow. "Excuse me, ma'am. What are we? Chopped liver?"

"I'm sorry." Delight sparkled in her eyes, and playfulness colored her tone. "I didn't mean to offend you guys."

"Yeah, well whether you like it or not, sweetheart, you're stuck with us." Marcus winked. Aimee smiled in response, and turned toward me, thirsty for details.

My fingertips trailed down her cheek to skim the line of her jaw. "We can do this. We can invite Declan and Aria—all of our friends from the beach. There's more than enough room for everybody. We'll ask them to come up for the weekend."

Aimee hesitated, chewing on her bottom lip. "I don't know if I can." Lines furrowed her brow. "I know I'm getting better every day, but what if I have a panic attack? I don't know..." Her voice trailed off as she looked down at the floor.

"I don't expect you to do everything by yourself." I lifted her chin and looked into her eyes. "I'm going to help." I willed reassurance into her with the delivery of my words. Slowly her desire outweighed her fear, and her eyes held some of the sparkle I'd seen just moments ago. I smiled and gave her a mocking glance. "I might even let you cook." She smacked me on the arm. "Ow!" I rubbed the spot. "There's no need to get violent, woman!" I teased.

"Asshole!" Her accusation was accompanied by a smile and an overexaggerated eye roll.

"If you keep calling me that, I might have to do something about it."

She narrowed her eyes at me as I joked, then placed her hands on her hips. "What about decorations?"

"We'll get new ones. Yours and mine. This is *our* party, Aim, our first Christmas together." I looked tenderly into her eyes and rested my forehead on hers. "The first of many." I touched my finger to her bottom lip, which had a slight quiver. "We need to start making new memories, baby. Good ones. What better time of year than Christmas?"

Her eyes turned misty as she nodded. "You're right. It's time to move forward." She went up on tiptoe and kissed my cheek. "Thank you." The words were low enough no one heard them but me. I kissed her forehead just before she spun around. There was a newfound spark in her demeanor. She pointed at both Marcus and Falcon. "Well, what are you waiting for? Let's get this bad boy up!"

"Damn, woman! I thought you were sweet and quiet. You got awfully damn bossy all of a sudden!" Falcon crossed his arms over his chest, his legs shoulder-width apart and anchored to the floor.

Undeterred by his manly show of intimidation, Aimee walked over to him and kissed his cheek. "You get to work, and I'll get the beers. Deal?"

I watched as Falcon rubbed the spot where her lips had touched his face. A goofy grin appeared as Aimee went to the kitchen. It only took a moment for him to notice the amused looks on both mine and Marcus's face. His expression quickly morphed into a sneer. "You heard the lady. Let's get to work!"

Chapter 47

Aimee

My mood brightened in anticipation of the Christmas get together. I'd managed to get everything in the house decorated the way I wanted over about a two-week span of time. Carter was discovering precisely how much of a perfectionist I could be. We'd even gone shopping for decorations and ate lunch out; the anxiety that had previously plagued me faded away like snow beneath the sun.

Tolerant as always, Carter exercised patience as I dictated instructions on where, how high, and how carefully to place our holiday décor. He confessed to me he thought the holidays had become too commercial. But after a while, he also admitted to a newfound enjoyment, one that came from seeing my happiness.

How could he not? The house never looked more beautiful.

Once the decorations were all in place, I began to bake for the party. Cooking was not my forte, but give me flour, sugar, and eggs, and I could bake like a fiend. I baked for days. Carter would interrupt me under the guise of wanting to sample everything that came out of the oven, although I knew his true intent was to make sure I took frequent breaks. And it only made me love him more.

Finally, the Friday before Christmas arrived and our guests began to show up. Declan and Aria were the first, and I was pleasantly surprised to see Aria's mother, Jeannie, accompanying them. She wrapped me in her arms, and I melted. My friends might underestimate the power of a hug, but I knew all too well what the lack of them felt like. The familiar void of a mother's love was replaced by the warmth of Jeannie's affection. That small token of tenderness from her had more value to me than a gift under the Christmas tree.

Shortly after their arrival, Paige, Blake, and Katherine arrived. Marcus and Falcon followed behind them. The handsome men that I had begun to think of as brothers did not escape the notice of Katherine and Paige. As I watched the group dynamic change with the addition of Carter's sexy friends, I detected a difference in Blake's demeanor. Normally friendly, he seemed guarded. I shrugged it off, thinking that I might be hypersensitive. I was hopeful for a good weekend and reading too much into Blake's body language would only defeat that mindset.

Carter and I led our guests into the dining room. It had been a long ride from the beach and for convenience we'd set a buffet table filled with various holiday favorites prepared by a local caterer. This allowed everyone to serve themselves, and Carter and I to enjoy their company. We prepared the same layout for the bar, and it quickly became a favorite area. Voices grew more relaxed and animated as everyone made themselves at home. After their appetites were satisfied, we seemed to split into two separate groups. The guys focused on football, while the girls doted on me.

"Your tree is one of the most beautiful I've ever seen." Aria stood beside it, her eyes traveling its length. "You did a great job decorating it, Aim."

I smiled at the compliment. Jeannie joined us and took a seat beside me on the sofa. A feeling of bliss washed over me. In spite of the violence I'd suffered, joy now filled the holes in my soul. This was the type of Christmas I'd always dreamed of as a child. The happiness of having friends who felt more like family together in a place that was feeling more like home to me every day was a feeling that inflated my spirit until it floated. Carter didn't know I'd spent the last four Christmases alone. Eating takeout and watching holiday movies on television was how I'd passed the time, all the while living vicariously through the characters on the screen. Some foster homes were more accommodating than others during the holidays, but there had been no consistency. No security of having a home base to return to for the holidays. Today I realized how lonely I'd been for what all of my friends took for granted.

The night before everyone arrived, Carter and I had sat in front of the fireplace. All of our preparations were complete. As the flames dwindled to glowing embers, I felt contentment like I'd never known. Holiday carols softly played in the background as we sipped hot chocolate. As he'd promised me this would be the first of many holidays we'd spend together, tears stung my eyes. His words melted away the guard I'd put in place over my emotions. The memory of Carter standing on the ladder to string the tree in lights would be forever tattooed on my heart. Once more I was consumed with hope for the future.

"It seems you have a reason to smile," Jeannie said to me as I looked at Carter.

"I do. He's been wonderful." My confession was momentarily overshadowed by a familiar pang of doubt. "I'm afraid the dark clouds might come back, though."

Jeannie took my hand. "Now you listen to me," she commanded in a motherly tone. "Choose your happiness. You can't change what happened yesterday, and you can't predict what will come tomorrow. All any of us have is today. Find your bliss in the little things, sweet girl. Soon, they'll outnumber the stars."

Jeannie was right. All I had to do was look forward to the future and keep reminding myself of my blessings. I'd experienced enough pain for two lifetimes, and Carter and I were finding our own way through past hurts. I loved what we were becoming together. While the others chatted, I thought about how far we'd already come. First friends, now a couple. When we had met at the beach, I thought he was handsome, but arrogant; he thought I was a pain in the ass. As we'd lain in each other's arms one recent night, he confessed that, although he'd loved Lacey, I was the first person he had ever felt *real* with. I sensed how difficult it was for him to admit that to me. It didn't negate the love he'd felt for his wife, but merely indicated he'd done some thinking about the man he was now. I'd followed up with a confession of my own and admitted that, although Declan was as close as a brother, the love I felt for Carter was the first honest to God sense of family I'd ever known. Somehow his love for me had gotten through to my inner layer—the layer I hadn't known existed. Our mutual revelations surprised us both. It was our story. A new beginning.

Just as I pulled my thoughts from past to present, I caught Carter looking at me. He smiled and moved away from the men. He took a seat between Jeannie and me. Lifting my hand, he pressed a kiss to the back of it. The touch of his lips against my skin sent tingles throughout my body.

"You doing okay, babe?" He searched my face for signs of fatigue. "Are you getting tired?"

I shook my head, reassuring him. "No. I'm fine. I'm just happy. I'm glad I'm here."

He sensed my meaning. I wasn't just happy to be at this party, I was happy to be alive. He leaned down and placed a gentle kiss on my lips. "Me, too."

The beat of my heart quickened. I wasn't the only one who'd been changed by what had happened to me. Carter's previously guarded and standoffish exterior was gone. I wasn't sure who knew what about us, but these open displays of affection made a huge statement. I hadn't detailed our relationship to anyone, but it was now clear we were in one. Marc and Falcon obviously knew, but I'd only spoken about Carter in general terms to Declan and Aria. But this... these simple gestures in front of everyone made a huge statement. With a kiss and a comment, Carter had silently declared me as his. To me, that was everything. I grinned up into his handsome face.

"What?" he asked, smiling back at me.

"Nothing. Just a thought."

"I'm a master at interrogation," he teased. "You might as well give it up."

I felt myself blush. "It's silly, really. I just thought of how many ladies are going to be unhappy you're off the market."

"Sweetheart, there isn't a female alive that could rival you. It takes a strong woman to love a flawed man

—and you're the strongest woman I know." He kissed me again. "Those ladies will have to find their own crusty, old mother fucker. You're stuck with me."

A burst of laughter escaped me in response to his words. Jeannie cleared her throat. "Should I leave?" she joked.

"Sorry." We both replied in unison. We also shared a sheepish expression, but only I was blushing.

"No need for apologies." She kissed us both on our cheeks as she rose from the sofa and took Carter's arm. "C'mon." She nodded toward the table of food. "Let's get her something to put some meat back on her bones."

Chapter 48

Aimee

Waking to a house full of loved ones was a great feeling. All the more this morning because I had Carter beside me. As I lay in his arms, I felt happier than I had in months. *Remember back when everything you did irritated him?* I smiled at the recollection. That was then, and this was now. Back then, I'd felt hesitant and unsure, now I felt wonderful and scared and exciting and comforting and—I could go on and on.

Carter had been helping me deal with what had happened to me when I ventured outside with Cody. Both of us were learning about something we previously knew nothing about. Panic attacks. According to the doctor, it was perfectly normal to have some residual anxiety because of what I'd gone through. So far, I hadn't had any more monumental episodes, but I lived in constant fear of another one coming. There were times I became overwhelmed with flash panics. The doctor explained that the two went hand-in-hand because I was suffering from a form of post-traumatic stress disorder. Each person's trigger was as individual as a fingerprint. In my case, knowledge was power. Knowing there was a physiological reason for what was happening was reassuring. Because of this, everything seemed to be slowly returning to normal. The doctor had prescribed anti-anxiety medication and suggested a counselor, but I felt my personal life with Carter contributed the most to my inner peace.

In the quiet of the morning, the peaceful sound of Carter's breathing soothed me. The security I felt when I was with him was better than any therapy. In his unconscious state, his arm snaked around my waist and interrupted my thoughts. I enjoyed the diversion and snuggled closer for a few moments before slipping out of bed.

As I tiptoed to the bathroom, I peeked over my shoulder to take another look at him. His love and this calm life anchored me. I hadn't known those things were missing, but now that I'd sampled it, life without him in our beautiful mountains was unimaginable. The uneasiness I'd lived with all of my life was fading. Loving Carter gave me a reason to embrace the future. As I reached for my toothbrush, I turned to look out the large window over the claw-foot tub. Crisp color was everywhere. Evergreen branches bowed, weighed down with snow. They nearly kissed the ground and provided a gathering place for some little birds, while the slightly higher branches dripped icicles that glistened like pieces of crystal in the morning sun. I couldn't imagine ever going back to my old life. Although I might return to work on a part-time basis in the future, I preferred to push the world outside of Deep Creek Lake far from my mind.

I dressed quietly so I could go downstairs and start the coffee. Although everyone retired late last night, they'd soon be awake and hungry. I placed a pound cake and pastries on a baking sheet and put them into the oven on low so they would be warm for our guests. I made myself a cup of coffee and sat down at the dining room table and was sitting there when Katherine walked in with a cup of her own.

"My God, it smells good in here." She closed her eyes and lifted her nose in the air. "What is it?"

"Cinnamon rolls, pound cake, and cranberry bread." I pulled out the chair next to me and patted the seat. "Here, Kat. Sit." I watched her for a few moments. Katherine stirred her coffee a little longer than was necessary. She seemed preoccupied. Finally, she stopped and looked at me.

"How are you feeling—and before you answer, don't tell me what you think I want to hear."

I smiled wryly. "Feeling a little bossy?" I teased. "I'm fine." I gave her an assuring smile. "But it's early yet." My attempt at making the mood lighter had failed, apparently, as Katherine still seemed to be struggling.

"I want to tell you something—but it's hard." I patiently waited as she gathered her thoughts and courage. Then she looked up at me. "Did you know I was mugged?"

"No, I didn't." Surprise arched my brows.

"It was before I moved to the beach. I lived in Baltimore. I loved everything about it. My job. Where I lived. Anyway, every day, when I got home from work, I went walking. I just laced up my shoes and got out in the fresh air for an hour or two." She sucked in a breath, her gaze drifting off in the distance. "One day a man came up behind me and put a gun in my back. He wanted my money. I told him I didn't have any. It pissed him off." Her voice trailed away as remembered, pain etched her face with fine lines. She sipped her coffee and took another deep breath. Holding the cup with both hands, she stared down at it. "He beat me up. Punched me, kicked me, and knocked me out."

I placed a consoling hand on her arm, and she gave me a weak smile. "The first thing I remembered when I woke up was pain. The sound of the siren made my head shatter. Everything hurt—everything. There wasn't an inch of me that didn't scream in agony. I didn't know for sure until I got to the hospital that I'd been raped. I must have been unconscious at that point. They told me that someone was walking by and saw him zipping his pants. When they yelled at him he ran away. The guy that found me called 9-1-1."

"I'm so sorry, Kat," I whispered.

"Yeah. Me too." She laughed. "I could have died. I walked away with some broken teeth, lots of bruises, and a big dose of fear—but I survived."

"How are you now?" The word *fear* had raised a red flag, piquing my curiosity.

Katherine shrugged indifferently. "I'm fine, most of the time. It took a while for me to get things under control, but I manage." She paused, still hesitant. "I have a confession. Declan told me about your panic attacks because I'd told him about mine. I'm not trying to get into your business, I promise. I just want you to know that I'm here for you if you need me."

I sat quietly, processing everything I'd just heard. Katherine had just bared her soul, and I couldn't think of anything appropriate to say. Before I could respond, the timer on the oven chimed. I was grateful for the interruption. I left her alone with her thoughts, giving me a quiet moment to gather mine. I took the sweets from the oven, arranged them on a platter, and placed them on the table. Katherine watched me, gauging my reaction to all she'd told me.

"Aimee, please don't be mad at Carter." A look of concern colored Katherine's expression. "I don't know if he knows Declan told me about what was happening to you. I only said something to you in case I could help." She gave me a tender smile. "Ever since it happened to me, I keep a very small circle of friends. You're one of them."

"I'm not mad at anyone, Kat," I assured her, "but I'm not sure that now—today—is the time I want to talk about it. It's too new. I never know what little thing will trigger it, and I want to enjoy this weekend."

"Then don't talk about you. Let me tell you about me. Maybe something that I say will help if you have another attack." Katherine relaxed back into her chair. I looked around the room, glancing toward the stairs to assure myself we were still alone. When I saw that we were, I nodded for her to continue. "I was like you, Aim. I didn't want to talk about it to anyone. What I didn't realize was that by trying to ignore it I'd let it become a monster. The more I tried to avoid it, the more my fear fed it. I hid it from everyone, even my parents. My first panic attack happened as I was going to work. I had to walk past the place where I was attacked to catch the bus. Fear hit me in the face, and I ran home and hid. At first, that was the only place I avoided—that one spot. I was afraid that if I went near there again, I'd have another panic attack. Then one happened in my house as I was going out the door, so I didn't leave the house that day. A pattern formed. I would have an attack and then I avoided that particular place or circumstance. Unfortunately, one time became another, one day became two, and two became thirty. I lost my job because I became consumed with terrifying thoughts. I didn't go out with friends. I couldn't predict when an attack would come, and nothing made them go away, so I surrendered. My world got smaller as my fear grew. It was so bad that, if I was watching a television show when I had one, I didn't watch that show anymore. If I was cooking and had one, I wouldn't cook the same food again. I could go on and on, but you get the idea."

I nodded. Katherine was right. I understood all too well. I wasn't as bad as she described. What remained to be seen was if the two of us would share the same painful path.

Chapter 49

Aimee

As I took in elements of Katherine's story, my heart grew heavy. I identified with much of what she'd said. Suddenly, determination flooded me. I would get better, no matter what I had to do. Knowing I wasn't alone gave me back a little piece of my power.

"Kat, some of the same things have happened to me, but I haven't had another attack that was as bad as the first one. I will admit I won't allow myself to be alone. I always have someone with me—or I have the dog. I'm sure you know Cody probably saved me from dying in the woods. She's been my lifesaver, in more ways than one."

Katherine nodded. "I'll bet. She's a sweet dog."

I looked at her. "So, I'm not crazy?" I asked.

"No. Not at all," she assured me. "You seem to be

doing a lot better than I was. When I went through therapy I learned most people experience the same thing when they've gone through what we have. It's apparently very common after having any trauma."

"Yeah. My doctor said the same thing," I confessed.

"I didn't know you had a counselor. Declan didn't mention it. I wouldn't have brought it up if I'd known you had one."

"No counselor. I'm sticking with my doctor for now." I paused. "I'm glad you told me about your experience. I'll be the first to admit I don't understand all of it. The medicine that I'm taking helps me. I don't like to take it, though. I saw too many people on drugs when I was growing up. But I've been told its normal to fear becoming dependent on it."

"Take the medicine. You won't get hooked. Your doctor is monitoring you. They know what to look for, like if the dosage is too low or if it seems you're taking too much. Trust him. He'll help you."

I gave Katherine's hand a gentle squeeze. Our conversation ended as we heard the sound of voices. Declan, Aria, and Jeannie appeared. "Good morning." I greeted them with a smile as if the weighty conversation we'd just finished had never taken place.

"Everything smelled so good down here we couldn't stay in bed." Aria took a piece of pound cake from the platter and placed it in her mouth. "Declan told me you couldn't cook! What was he thinking?"

"I never said that she couldn't bake," Declan interjected.

Jeannie placed a kiss on my head. "How are you today, sweetie? It was a lovely party last night. You must be tired."

"I feel good today," I answered, convincing her all was well. "Everyone cleaned up after themselves. I only baked for the party. Carter took care of the rest."

"What are you saying about me?" As Carter entered the room, he walked over and gave me a kiss. His lips were warm against mine. When it ended, he headed straight for the coffee.

"It's about time you got your lazy ass out of bed," Declan joked.

"Shut up." The banter between the brothers was playful. He ignored further insults from Declan and turned his attention to me. "How are you this morning, babe?"

"I'm good."

He nuzzled my neck, speaking into my ear so only I could hear. "Need anything?" His coarse scruff abraded the delicate curve of my neck and shoulder.

"Oh, for God's sake, get a room," Declan teased. "Just because you two finally let us in on your big secret doesn't mean you can make out with her while we're all sitting at the table."

Carter gave him a hard look. "I thought I told you to shut up." He grinned as he issued his warning. "Why are you still talking?"

Everyone laughed at their playful antics. The connection between the two of them was something we all missed when Carter moved back to the mountains from the beach. I quickly scanned the table to see if I needed to refill coffee or sweets and saw Aria leaning over Katherine's lap to help herself to another piece of pound cake.

"Girl, you're going to get fat." Blake's comment entered the room before he did, causing Aria's expression to sour. She immediately pulled her hand back and stared down into her plate.

"What the hell is wrong with you?" Declan gave Blake a dirty look.

Blake looked at her face and attempted damage control. "Aria, I'm only playing," he apologized. "You always eat like a bird."

Declan gave Blake a threatening glare and then looked over at his wife. "Eat it, baby. Don't pay any attention to him." Aria looked up from her plate and gave her husband a weak smile. "See what you've done, Matthews? You made her self-conscious."

"Sweetie, I didn't mean to hurt your feelings," Blake explained. "I was only kidding."

Declan's attention was on his wife. He lifted her hand to his lips. As he kissed her fingertips, his brow arched. An unspoken question passed between them. Aria tipped her head to answer him. Declan turned to the group. "We were planning to exchange gifts after breakfast, but now seems as good a time as any." Both he and Aria were now looking at each other, their faces beaming. "We're going to have a baby."

Stunned silence lasted but a moment, and then chaos erupted as everyone expressed congratulations. Chatter filled the room. I sat quietly for a moment, my emotions mixed. Carter noticed and reached for my hand. I looked at him and saw understanding reflected in his eyes. The knowledge that I wasn't alone in my thoughts comforted me, but I couldn't help but wonder if the hurt inside would ever go away.

Chapter 50

Aimee

Time passed quickly as everyone opened their gifts. Then after some more coffee and conversation they went off on their own until dinner. Now that we were aware of Aria's pregnancy, we noticed how tired she looked. She and Declan retired to their room for an afternoon nap, their exit inviting some playful teasing from the group. Jeannie asked Blake to drive her into town so she could do some shopping. Since my assault, I was much more aware of people's moods. Blake seemed on edge to me, but I couldn't pinpoint the cause. I shook off the uneasy feeling once he and Jeannie left. Paige and Katherine lingered, talking to me as I wrapped leftovers from the table. When Falcon and Marc offered to take them for a hike in the snow, they wasted no time getting ready for an outing with the two men. I smiled, entertaining some matchmaking possibilities.

After I put away the remnants of food, Carter came up behind me and wrapped his arms around my waist. "You look tired, baby. Why don't you go lie down? I'll finish up here."

I would have argued with him, but he was right. I was tired. This weekend was the most activity I'd involved myself in for quite some time. Instead of dismissing his suggestion, I welcomed the help. "Thank you. I'm going to take a hot shower first. Wake me when everyone gets back, okay?"

He nodded and took a container from my hand. "Got it."

I kissed him and headed to the bedroom. As I undressed, I thought about Aria, Paige, and Katherine. They'd dressed festively, but comfortably, and all three looked beautiful. I stood before the mirror. The reflection staring back at me was no longer that of a top fashion model. I was a mess. Semi-healed scars covered my body. Instead of reminding myself I'd survived when I should have died, all I could do was question how Carter could stand to look at me.

I felt defeated. It was degrading to see myself this way. The cuts and bruises were slowly fading, but I was impatient for the healing to be complete. I'd been thin before, but now I was too skinny, even for my own liking. Six weeks on a liquid diet will do that to a person. I turned around to inspect my back. As I looked over my shoulder, I hated what I saw there as well. Twisted patterns from the knife my attacker had used were slowly transforming, again too slowly for my liking. Where they had once been an angry crimson, they were now beginning to turn into thin, red lines. The connections made some bizarre sort of tribal symbol. I resented them. They were constant reminders of all that had been taken from me. I mapped the mending wounds one by one, cringing as memories of my attacker resurfaced. It hadn't been long enough for the recollections to fade completely. Goosebumps raised on my flesh as the pleasure in my attacker's eyes became crystal clear in my mind. As I sucked in a breath, I remembered his foul odor. The flashback of the tar and nicotine stains on his teeth stoked my fears as it painted the inside of my mind with a dark and ominous brush. I felt the air slowly squeezing from my lungs. I could almost feel the frigid steel of the blade as it pierced my skin and I felt my sense of safety sinking beneath the panic. I fought to remind myself that my thoughts weren't real, but I was losing the battle.

Unwanted images flooded my mind, and the familiar anxiety began to overtake me. Prickly shivers raised the fine hairs on my body as fear began to rise within me. I grabbed my robe off the hook on the back of the door, threw it on quickly, and got under the covers, skipping the shower I'd promised myself. I pulled the sheet up to my neck and curled into a ball. Using the relaxation techniques I'd been taught, I made a vain attempt to quiet my mind, slow down my breathing, and ride out the attack until it was over.

Chapter 51

Carter

Once I'd finished cleaning up, I went to the bedroom to check on Aimee. Her eyes were closed, but I could tell she wasn't sleeping. I got into bed behind her, spooning her as I wrapped my arm around her. It was the first quiet moment we'd shared since before everyone arrived.

"Have I ever told you how beautiful you are?" I buried my nose in her hair.

She answered me with a tremble in her voice. "You always do. I just wish I believed it."

I detected how troubled she felt by her tone. "Tell me what you're thinking, Aim. Let me help."

Her breathing was shallow and quick. She buried her face in the pillow. "Will I ever be the same again?

Will things ever go back to the way they used to be? I feel so helpless when these attacks creep up, and I hate the way I look. The scars make me look like a monster."

I pulled the sash open on her robe and slipped my hand inside. Her skin was warm, despite the threatening anxiety. I ran a trail with my hand all the way from her breasts to her hip. She trembled beneath my touch. "I think you're beautiful. You're perfect just as you are."

She kept her eyes closed. A tear fell and landed on the back of my hand as it returned to cup her breast. "I don't understand you. How can you say that? These marks—they're ugly. Who knows if they'll ever go away? I'll never be able to work again. It's all about appearance in my business."

I moved my fingers over the scars. I stroked each spot on her shoulder, back, and hips where she'd been hurt. "Do you know what I see when I look at these?" I lingered on the path left by the knife. "I see how strong you are—what a fighter you are."

Tears now flowed freely. The pools in her eyes sparkled as she turned to face me. I gazed at her face, seeing plainly the beauty she refused to see. I planted tender kisses on her jaw, cheeks, and above her eyes.

"You might not know this, Aimee, but you are the most incredible woman I've ever met." I pressed my lips to her head and spoke the truth she needed to hear. "These lines—these scars—they tell the story. It's a story of bravery and resilience. A story of how hard you fought to come back from near death—back to me." The truth overwhelmed me. I choked on my confession. "If I'd just talked to you that morning. Just said what needed to be said and not bullshitted around, this would never have happened. It's my fault. I'm the reason you went into the woods." Raw pain and emotion wrapped like barbed wire around my vocal chords and ripped them to shreds.

Aimee responded by placing her fingers on my lips. "Stop. It's not true. I behaved like a child and stomped off to have a tantrum. There was no way either of us could have known what was going to happen that day. We were both stubborn. It's nobody's fault."

Her expression was full of compassion, and I fell helplessly into the love in her eyes. Even if I could have stopped myself from confessing the guilt I claimed, I wouldn't have. Aimee wasn't the one at fault. I'd acted like an ass that day, but I was determined to spend the rest of my life being the man she needed.

I pulled her to me, cupping her head with my hand, pressing my lips to hers. I was desperate to drive away the fear and let her feel my love. The kiss left her gasping for breath. In her eyes, I saw evidence of a fire beginning to spark and I wanted to stoke it. Hopefully, it would turn into a blaze and burn away any feelings that tortured her.

I was desperate for the touch of her. The skin-on-skin contact I'd tasted the night before her assault fed my lusty appetite. I cupped her breasts and teased her nipples with my thumbs. They pebbled from the connection. Her body arched into mine, and a sudden blood rush hardened me. Desire pulsated in my dick, and I craved plunging myself deeply into her core to drive away any doubt she had regarding my love for her. *But I have to think of Aimee.*

She pushed her body against mine. It took everything I had to pull myself away from her as her expression morphed from desire to confusion.

"Why are you—?" As doubt and insecurity cast a shadow over her, she looked away from me.

I had to break her destructive thoughts. I fisted my hand in her hair. "Because I don't want to hurt you. Because you've been through so much." I looked into her eyes, forcing her to connect with me. "Because I'm in love with you."

Her eyes widened in surprise. "Then I don't understand—"

"I want you more than I've ever wanted anything—but I don't want to hurt you." Her gaze softened. "When you've healed completely I want to love you, take my time loving you, without worrying if anyone will hear or interrupt us. I meant what I said, Aimee. You are the strongest woman I know, and you came back to me."

"And Lacey didn't," she whispered.

I felt myself scowl at her. "I didn't say that."

"But it's what you meant, isn't it?"

"I don't need you putting words in my mouth, but suppose it is true? Suppose in the back of my mind it's a subconscious thought? I can't forget her. I'll always love her. But the love I feel for you is not the same I had for Lacey. You aren't a substitute for her. You're a different woman, and she isn't here. I'll always be thankful for the time I had with her, but I'm trying to tell you I don't just love you—I'm *in* love with you."

I leaned back, exasperation forcing me to wipe my hand over my face. I wasn't a shrink. I had no idea if I resented Lacey for dying or not, but it didn't matter. She was my past. After losing her, and nearly losing Aimee, I wanted to live for now.

Aimee reached out her hand to touch my cheek, and I pulled back. "Please. Don't do that, Carter." Hurt was evident in her tone. "Isn't that how we got into trouble in the first place? By not communicating?"

Her words were a slap in the face because I knew she was right.

"It doesn't matter to me, Carter, if you still love Lacey. It isn't what you think, so hear me out. I've had a lot of time to think this through. I can't love a man who's in love with another woman. Especially one who's a ghost."

"Aimee." I wanted her to stop, to reconsider.

"Let me finish. Please." She paused, then looked into my eyes with tenderness. "When I was in the hospital, I knew I was in love with you, but I wasn't strong enough emotionally to fight the love you had for Lacey. I remember how you reacted when she died. I knew you'd always love her—that the two of you were a package deal. I had to reconcile myself to the facts. I know what I'm getting myself into."

I feared what she would say next as she placed her palm against my cheek. I turned my face into her hand, and an errant tear escaped.

"I realized I couldn't love you if I had to compete with Lacey, so I decided I would love you both."

I took in a shocked breath, my surprised look meeting her sweet one.

"I know you'll always love her, and that's okay. I would never expect you to separate that part of your life. It's what's made you who you are. It's also part of what I love about you. You've said you always tried to live up to what she wanted you to be. I admire you for being a man who'd sacrifice his own wants for the woman he loves. I'll always be grateful to Lacey for being a stepping stone for the man I'm in love with now.

Aimee's introspection left me speechless. I pulled her close to me. "I don't know what to say."

"You don't have to say anything. The man I love is a different man than the one Lacey married. Her version of Carter died when she did. The man you are today is mine—all mine."

I stretched out and pulled Aimee against me. She laid her head on my chest. As I wrapped my arms around her, she placed her leg over mine. Silently, we stayed intermingled, both of us reflecting on what had gone before and what lay ahead of us. Contentment filled me, and I held her close to my heart. I remembered to do something my mother always told Declan and me she did every night. I counted my blessings.

Chapter 52

What is it about good friends and good times that make your problems feel like they've disappeared?

All of us talking and laughing over food was making me feel more like my old self. But would my new normal always include the threat of panic attacks? I couldn't answer that question, but I felt stronger and lighter in the knowledge of Carter's love. I watched as Falcon flirted with Paige, much to Blake's dismay. Katherine and Marc were hitting it off, and ever observant these days, I watched as they stole a few minutes away from the crowd. After the conversation we'd had, I'd never again look at Katherine as a carefree girl, but as a woman who'd battled a demon and emerged a warrior. I also realized there was something to the saying "misery loves company," because knowing I wasn't the only one of my friends who struggled with something I couldn't control, I now felt like a pressure cooker after it released its steam. With Kat's assurance I wasn't going crazy, I began to feel safe again. The insecure hell of being betrayed by your own body and mind was probably the worst part of the panic attacks. Like most people, I had learned to rely on solving my own problems. There was no right answer as to what to do or not do when plagued by something you couldn't see. The responses were as individual as snowflakes.

As Carter and I enjoyed the company of our guests over the final meal of the weekend, I was filled with melancholy. I wanted everyone to leave so we could have time alone, but at the same time, I didn't want anyone to go. This was the best Christmas holiday I'd ever had. My first sense of family. The time was soon approaching to say goodbye, and I had bittersweet emotions.

"Why don't you come to the beach for New Year's?" Declan asked. "You two can stay with us."

Carter sat next to me, his hand resting on my thigh. He looked to me for an answer. As much as I wanted to go to the beach, I also had to follow my doctor's advice and rest. Carter read my expression and could feel my inner conflict.

"Thanks." He patted my leg. "I think we're just gonna spend a quiet New Year's Eve alone. Maybe another time."

Jeannie noticed my expression and changed the subject. "Let's clean up." She initiated the chore by taking everyone's empty plates to the kitchen, while Aria began wrapping and storing the leftovers. Not long after, everyone was packed and ready to go. One by one, they descended the stairs and rolled their luggage to the door.

Declan, Aria, and Jeannie were the first to leave. Declan wrapped Carter in a bear hug, slapping him on the back. I embraced Aria. "I'm so happy for you." I rested my hand on Aria's belly.

She looked down and smiled tenderly. "Thank you. I have no idea what we're in for. The doctor has listed me as a high-risk pregnancy, but if I've learned anything, it's to believe in miracles. This baby was conceived in the midst of a storm. It was while we were at your house, playing possum for the paparazzi. I was told by the doctors I'd most likely never conceive." She gave my hand a gentle squeeze. "Everything is going to be fine with this baby, and with you. I can feel it."

Her sweet thoughts caused a lump to form in my throat. I swallowed hard. "Thanks for that mental picture. That's just what I need to see in my head when I go back to my place."

"Oh, I don't think you'll be going home, Aimee. All I have to do is look at Carter's face to know that this is your home now. You might go there to visit, but not to stay."

My shoulders bunched up. "We'll see."

Aria smiled as Declan moved their luggage out the door. "Don't overthink it. Who knows? We might be sisters-in-law one day."

She and Jeannie gave final hugs, and Declan, playing the gentleman, opened the car door and closed it behind them both. Before Declan got in the driver's side, he turned to embrace Carter and me one last time.

"Take care of yourself, Aim—and him." He tilted his head toward Carter then looked into my eyes. "I love you, kid. I know it was a rocky start, but I think this is the best thing that could have happened to you both." He emphasized his statement by moving his finger in a circular motion between us.

"I know." I gave him a peck on the cheek. "Me, too."

Carter held my hand as we watched them pull away from the house and onto the main road. Then we headed back inside. I shivered as Carter took my coat and hung it on the hook. "It was a great weekend, Aimee. I think this was the best Christmas I've ever had." Carter's words were full of praise.

"I agree, but it isn't Christmas yet. I think it was good we planned the party for the weekend before."

"Yes, and tomorrow you and I are taking a little road trip to pick up your present."

I gave him an apprehensive look, indicating my trepidation over leaving the house.

"Calm down. It's just a day trip," he consoled.

"We'll leave in the morning and be back home by tomorrow night."

"What about Cody?" The dog puttered in to sit by my side when she heard her name.

"She can come, too." Carter kissed the frown lines that creased my forehead. "Just trust me, okay?"

Reluctantly, I nodded.

He led me to the sofa. I turned to position myself near him. Each night we talked about the day, and as had become my habit, I tucked my toes under his leg to keep them warm. Carter rested at the end and stretched out his legs. "Was all of this too much?" Now that the weekend was over, he exhaled a sigh of relief. He rubbed my knee and then gave it a gentle pat.

"No. I'm good. It was fun." I answered, then paused and changed the subject. "Did you know Katherine has an anxiety disorder?"

He nodded, then closed his eyes and rested his head against the back of the sofa. "Yeah, Declan told me. He asked if I minded him telling Katherine about you so she could share her experiences with you."

"She was mugged. She said her panic attacks started after that. She also told me to call her if I need to talk."

His eyes remained closed. For a minute I thought he'd dozed off. "You awake?" I nudged him with my foot.

"Damn, woman!" Carter's eyes snapped open and he gave me an ornery look. The next thing I knew, he grabbed me by the ankle and began tickling the bottom of my foot.

"Stop!" I squealed.

"No! You won't give a man any peace. I've been talking my ass off all weekend. I need a rest." He stopped tickling me when I jerked my foot away from him, and we both laughed.

"Go to sleep! I'll just sit here and amuse myself."

He patted my knee once again, and I repositioned, resting my head in his lap. We grew more relaxed as Carter again reclined his head, and I made myself comfortable. Within moments, Carter's breathing indicated he was asleep. I watched the yellow and orange flames as they danced and flickered in the fire. The shadows they cast formed patterns on the rug just beyond the logs. The house was refreshingly still after all the weekend's activity. Cody came to join us from wherever she'd been in the house, content to lay at Carter's feet. I reached down to pet her, and she stretched out on the floor beneath me. No anxious thoughts or panic attacks plagued me, and for that I was grateful. My mind and body were full of peace and restfulness. My final fleeting thought as I fell asleep was that happiness is truly the most abundant of gifts.

Chapter 53

Aimee

The next morning Carter rousted me from our warm bed at six a. m. He hurried me through breakfast and getting dressed and then ushered me into the car. After being been on the road for a few hours, and the further away from the house we got, my anxiousness continued to spike.

"Are we almost there?" I was jittery with a combination of nerves and anticipation.

A grin crept onto Carter's lips, but he kept his eyes on the road. "You're worse than a little kid, you know it?" His playful intolerance was evidenced by the shaking of his head.

I ignored him and probed anyway. "Are we minutes away or hours away?"

"We're in to Pennsylvania." He gave me a quick glance. "Happy?"

"Thanks for the clue, Sherlock. I kind of figured that out for myself when we passed the sign that said *Welcome to Pennsylvania.*" Sarcasm dripped from my words.

His laugh rumbled low in his chest. "Just sit back and enjoy the ride, will you?"

I let out a *humph* and turned away from him to look out the window. I continued doing so until we pulled into a driveway. The house was surrounded by trees and had a long porch across the front of it. As we stepped out of the car, I noticed a white sign. The word Amore was written in black calligraphy. "Amore? You brought me to a place called love?"

He didn't have time to answer before a woman appeared at the door. She stepped out onto the porch as she zipped her coat.

"Hey, Carter! How are you?"

"Hi, Lisa," he replied. "This is Aimee."

The woman extended her hand. "It's nice to meet you. I've heard a lot about you. All good, I promise."

I gave Carter a look. I was still confused but I followed as Lisa led us inside. Once there, my heart jumped for joy and my eyes widened. Fifteen Bernese Mountain Dog puppies yipped playfully. They ran toward us, tripping over their paws and wiggling their butts. One followed the other as they chased each other's tails. I couldn't decide which to focus my attention on until one little furball came up to me and planted its fluffy rear end on the top of my foot. I bent down and picked it up. As I snuggled it against me, I was rewarded with the smell of fresh puppy breath and kisses.

Carter extended his hand to pet the puppy in my arms. "Amore is the name of the kennel."

As he spoke, the pup in my arms stuck its nose beneath my hair and nuzzled my neck. "I'd say the name is appropriate. This one is very affectionate!" I giggled as it sniffed me with a cold nose and left a damp trail in its wake.

"Do you like it?" Carter asked.

"Who wouldn't love a puppy?" I pursed my lips and rolled my eyes.

"That's good because one of them is your Christmas present."

He smiled as shock registered in my expression. "Oh my gosh! Seriously?"

He nodded.

"Really?" I had to ask twice to be certain that he wasn't teasing me. I felt lucky to share Cody, but I'd never had a dog of my own.

Again, Carter nodded.

I turned my attention to Lisa. "The one in my arms; has anyone claimed it?"

"Not yet, because Carter asked me for the pick of the litter. If you want him, he's yours."

"A little boy." My tone was wistful as I moved the

puppy into a cradling position in my arms. "How would you like to come home with us, little guy?" He responded by throwing his chin over my arm. He gave a little sigh, yawned, and closed his eyes. I was in love.

"I guess you've met his approval," Lisa laughed.

As Carter gathered the care package that Lisa sent along with each of her pups, I held our newest addition to the family in my arms. With each moment that ticked by, he claimed a piece of my heart. I floated in a dreamlike state, tuning out Lisa and Carter's conversation as I watched my puppy sleep. It wasn't long before Carter had everything loaded in the car. I placed the puppy in the crate on the back seat. Carter had positioned it behind the driver's side so I could watch it during the drive. Cody was behind me. Carter had clipped her harness to the seat belt, and she was lying down, her nose a few inches from the crate. Like a new mother, she observed our little boy as he slept. Lisa had given Cody a blanket which she had rubbed all over the puppy's fur. She said that it would help Cody adjust to the new family member.

The ride home seemed to go faster than the ride to Lisa's house. Once there, Carter took care of setting everything up. The puppy, now wide awake, shadowed Cody's every move. We fed them in separate parts of the kitchen. Once they'd eaten, we brought them into the living room where Carter loaded wood into the fireplace and started a fire. Cody tolerated the puppy as he jumped all around her. I was hopeful the two would soon acclimate to each other when I saw him cuddle up with Cody and fall asleep. Happiness washed over me and I turned my attention to Carter.

"I heard you say at Lisa's that Cody was going to need company. What did you mean by that?"

"She *is* going to need company. You're going to be busy with me." He wrapped his arm around my waist and pulled me closer to him.

I gave him a puzzled look. "The last I checked, being with you wasn't a full-time job."

"It will be if all goes well," he responded.

"Why are you talking in riddles? Just tell me what you mean already."

He stood, pulling me up into a standing position as his hand encircled my wrist.

"What are you doing?"

He answered my question with a kiss. His lips pressed firmly to mine while his tongue sought entrance. I willingly complied. His actions filled me with a craving for more. He held me tightly with strong arms, chest to chest. When he released me, I felt the void, but the intensity in his gaze magnetized us.

"I want you to promise me that you'll remember everything about today, especially when you feel over-whelmed or afraid." The timbre of his voice was low and passionate.

Puzzled, I stared at him—until he lowered himself on one knee. Then my heart quickened to a banging drumbeat. He looked up at me as he held my hand.

"I know you're used to a high-speed world back in New York, so I decided I wanted to do this the old-fashioned way." He reached into his pocket and pulled something out of it with a closed hand. My mouth suddenly went dry, but my eyes did just the opposite. I looked down at him through a tear-filled mist.

"Aimee, you weren't my first love, but you'll be my last. We've been through more shit together than most couples go through in a lifetime. You are everything I never knew I wanted or needed in a woman. We can do this however you want—fast or slow—but no matter the pace, I want you with me forever. We know we're good together, and when I look at my future, you're all I see. You make me want to be a better man. When you're ready, I want to make this legal."

Tears trailed down my face and onto our joined hands. I searched his eyes and saw no hesitancy in his gaze. Emotion choked me, making it hard to speak. "Carter, I know you love me, but I'm more screwed up than you deserve."

"I don't know about that. You keep me sane; you ground me. I won't push a time limit on you. Promise. I just know that I'm shit without you." He stood, taking me into his arms. "This much I can promise you—I'll spend my life protecting you and trying to make you happy. It might not fix everything, but it's a good start."

I wanted to say yes, but something hindered me. "What if I never get better? What if I'm the person who's hurting me? Don't you deserve more?"

"I deserve to go through the rest of this life with the woman I love. If you never get better, then I'll hold you and help you when you're afraid. We'll get through it, Aimee. Say yes. We can do this. We can get through anything that comes our way as long as we're together."

I hesitated, and Carter began to pull away from me. "You don't have to answer now. If you need more—"

"Yes." My answer was quiet. Serious. Filled with honesty.

He searched my face. looking for any indication of wavering. "Really?"

I nodded my head and laughed. "Yes! I mean it."

Before I knew what was happening, he wrapped his arms around me and kissed me so hard I squealed. Startled, he pulled back. Relief softened his features as I dissolved into a pool of giggles. His smile was the reward for my laughter.

"I love you," he said. "More than you know."

"I can't promise you that I'll be great every day because I can't predict the future. These attacks—"

He cut me off. "It's okay, baby. We're going to be fine." He kissed my damp cheeks. The dogs heard the excitement in our voices. Cody pranced around the two of us in a never-ending circle, while the puppy hopped against my leg on his back paws. I looked down at him. Never in my childhood dreams would I have imagined my own dog or a man who wanted me just for myself.

"Justice."

Carter looked from the puppy to me. "What?"

I'd thought about it all day, and in one instant it came to me. I was never more confident in my life than I was at this moment. It was karma. She was giving me a portion of what I was due. Pieces of my life that were previously scattered finally came together to form a beautiful picture. I smiled at Carter while the puppy continued his quest for my attention.

"Justice. That's his name."

Chapter 54

Aimee

Outside, snowflakes skittered through the frosty air like fragments of tattered lace. Inside, the fire kept us toasty warm, a direct contradiction to the cold outdoors. Carter and I were alone, blissfully segregated from the rest of the world. As we traded in the old year for the new, we celebrated with a quiet evening and a candlelit dinner. Both of the dogs slept quietly in front of the fireplace while we watched the festivities in Times Square on television.

Days had passed into weeks, and weeks had turned into months. Carter and I no longer thought about our separate lives, but of our life together. Carter busied himself with his work, while I continued to heal and grow stronger. I didn't have to worry about money.

Modeling had given me a healthy bank account and afforded me the luxury to indulge myself in hobbies.

One day, Carter suggested I think about redecorating the house since I'd nixed his idea of us starting over in a new place. Although my body was healing at a healthy pace, my mind was another matter. I found that keeping myself busy helped. I wasn't one to sit long on an idea, so I started browsing catalogs and surfing the internet for renovation ideas. My spirits were elevated as I redecorated room-by-room, and when I finished the project, it was no longer his home, but ours.

The relationship Carter and I cultivated grew stronger every day. The security of his love healed me. Whenever anxiety or panic rose within me, he gently guided me back to sanity with a soothing voice and strong arms. As he guided my thoughts back to rational thinking, he never complained, only reassured. Most of my episodes were mild and easy to contain, but a particularly bad one was about to strike unannounced and unwelcome.

A cold wind had blown a fresh snowfall into drifts all around the house as spring buds struggled to emerge from the ground and on the tree branches. Neither Carter, Marcus, nor Falcon were there; they'd gone to visit potential clients. I was browsing seed catalogs with the hope of planning an herb garden, while Cody and Justice were sleeping. I was tapping a pencil against the page detailing the different varieties of mint and peering out the window. As I prepared to return my attention to the task at hand, my gaze was snagged by the back door. I'd not used it to enter or leave the house since my assault. Memories began to trickle over me, one-by-one. Before I knew it, I was drowning in adrenaline. An invisible hand wrapped around my throat with icy fingers. I struggled for air. As my lungs constricted, fear pulled me into darkness. I braced myself for the coming onslaught. The ruthless predator had no form; invisibility was its ally. The panic came quickly, slicing through my peace of mind. The control that I'd worked so hard to cultivate sank into an abyss of insecurity. My inner strength was still thin from months of suffering following my brutal assault. Memories of the past and their related fears flashed as they joined forces with this new bedfellow, holding my contentment hostage until sanity hung by a thread.

"This will pass. This will pass." I repeated the mantra over and over again, hoping that by saying the words aloud I'd give them more power. Unfortunately, panic seemed to be winning. I clung to the cold granite countertop, my fingertips turning white from the force of my grip. Wave after wave of sensory bombardment reached into the depths of my mind and body. I regressed into a jumble of nerves. Slick with sweat, I sank to the floor. "Do whatever you want to me, you son of a bitch!" I screamed the words, daring my hidden enemy to do its worst. "Do it! I've lived through you before, and I'll do it again. Just do it!"

Cody and Justice found me by the sound of my voice. My desperate tone unsettled them, and they rallied around me, ready to attack on my behalf if needed. I forced my arms and legs to go limp. My head slumped down onto my chest as I relinquished myself to the fear. The cognitive part of me knew I wouldn't die from a panic attack, and I relied on that knowledge to force myself to relax. I surrendered, and an astonishing thing happened. The anxiety vanished. Simply vanished. My energy was diminished, and I tried to figure out what had just happened. *Was it really that simple? Surrendering could set me free?* Understanding pierced my thoughts. That small fragment of power over my psyche was a soothing balm to my wounded mind.

I heard Carter's boots scrape the floor as he came in through the front door. The last twenty minutes had depleted my energy, and I struggled to get up off the floor. Carter hurried toward me and dropped to his knees. "I'm so sorry, baby. I'm so sorry." He pulled me into the comfort of his arms and repeated himself as he held me tightly.

"It's okay." My voice was shaky.

"No, it isn't. I shouldn't have left you alone."

I relished in his strength for a few moments before I scooted off his lap and sat beside him. I took his hand and gently squeezed. "As much as I know you'd like to, you can't protect me from this."

"I should have been here." His tone was riddled with guilt.

"And what would you have done?" I argued. "Carter, you can't chase the boogeyman away if he lives inside me." I laid a gentle hand upon his cheek. "I never feel as safe as I do when I'm with you," I soothed. "And this time, I learned something about myself. You know Newton's law? For every action, there is an equal and opposite reaction? Well, it works." I told him about how I'd just surrendered to the panic out of desperation. "I think I may have stumbled on a solution, or at least the start of one. I'll talk to my doctor about it, but in the meantime, I'm going to practice relaxing into the attacks."

"I'd prefer you don't have another one."

"Me too."

"You know, you don't have to be alone. I could—"

I cut Carter off midsentence. "No. You are not going to have your buddies keeping an eye on me when you aren't here."

He eyed me suspiciously as he made peace with my decision. "You have to promise to keep your phone on in case you need me."

"I will. I promise."

Chapter 55

Carter

The day was dreary and cold. It was a reflection of the way I felt inside. Lacey's death had colored the canvas of my existence in hues of black and grey. It wasn't until Aimee peeled away the darkness that I saw the more colorful tones. If I likened my world to the colors in a Crayola box, Lacey could be compared to the pastel shades, while everything about Marisol was represented by dark colors. When Aimee had burst into my world, she'd added streaks of joy to everyday things. Our life together had become a watercolor painting. However, today wasn't one that could be depicted as a piece of art. Today was black. Today was Marisol.

As I drove toward my destination, the quiet hum of

the road provided some solace. It was the perfect back-drop to take me on a mental trip to the past. The pitch of sorrow that had fallen over me when I was informed of Lacey's death returned in full force with each mile I traveled. I wanted satisfaction for the vengeance that had once consumed me. I sought one thing now. Retribution.

I waited in a room to see my wife's killer. It had been some time since I'd been at the prison hospital. As Marisol rounded the corner, I was struck by how normal she looked. How ironic that someone's appearance could change so dramatically when they weren't clothed in the stench of pride and entitlement. A guard led her down the hall, and as he did so, she looked around the room for a familiar face. When her gaze fell on me, any semblance of civility she might have possessed disintegrated. It was apparent she'd been expecting someone else. She sat down in the seat across from me.

"Why are you here?" She wore her arrogance like a designer dress. I had to give her credit for getting straight to the point.

"To see that a rabid dog isn't let out of its cage." My reply was clipped. Marisol didn't react. Instead, she maintained her composure. "You didn't think they'd consider your release without notifying me, did you?"

Marisol shrugged, her chin tipped defiantly. "Frankly, I didn't consider you at all." She looked away from me to inspect her fingernails. "What my sister did to your wife was horrible. She should go to hell for taking the life of an innocent." She stopped looking at her fingers and turned her attention back to me. "Wouldn't you agree?"

She wore her sarcasm well. "You're a bitch and you know it. You should rot in hell." As I said the words, they left a bitter aftertaste.

Marisol again shrugged her indifference. "I'm sorry for what my sister did to your wife. All of this has left me traumatized, but I'm working with my doctors and counselors to get well." She leaned into me as if to tell me a secret. "Apparently, I had an undiagnosed emotional condition." She pulled away, and sat back into the chair with an evil smile on her lips. "My treatment has been a success."

I laughed. "You're so full of shit!"

"That's for the doctors and the State of Maryland to decide."

Her statement pissed me off. She was a cold-blooded psychopath. If she thought she could fool everyone by impersonating a human being, she was dead wrong. I leaned into her with a distance equal to the way she had approached me. Words cut the insides of my mouth like razor slices. "Marisol, I'm going to see to it you never get out of here. You might be able to spin that bullshit about your sister to everyone else, but you and I both know you're the one who mowed Lacey down. I might not be able to prove it, but I can prove you tried to kill Aria. If it's up to me, you'll be here forever."

"Then lucky for me it isn't up to you."

Anger boiled inside me. She was playing me. "You're a bitch."

She shrugged again. "My husband says otherwise."

Her husband. Manuel Vallega was a ruthless bastard who was rumored to be the head of a Colombian drug cartel. No one had known Marisol was married until recently. The ATF, the DEA, and the US Marshals had him on their radar. Unfortunately, nothing could be directly connected to him.

"Your husband isn't my concern, but if he manages to get you out of here, I'll put his life under a magnifying glass. Eventually he'll slip up and when he does, he will not be put in a place as nice as this." There was vengeance in my tone, and Marisol recognized it.

"If you think you have that kind of power, be my guest," she dared. "I will get out of here, and my life will be better than before. Everybody loves a comeback story, Mr. Sinclair. Even you should know that."

I wanted to send her and her smug attitude to hell. I countered immediately. "And even you should know you've been replaced."

"By who? Aimee Vincent? Don't make me laugh!" Her expression turned to one of satisfaction. "Besides, from what I hear, Aimee hasn't been working lately. I heard she had an accident. Seems such a shame."

"Go to hell."

My frigid tone elicited a sarcastic response from her. "I'll meet you there."

Chapter 56

Carter

The ride home served two purposes for me: enjoying the solitude and pondering ideas of something sweet to do for Aimee. It didn't take long before I was pulling into the driveway. As I entered the door, I was greeted by my furry girl and her little companion. Cody and Justice were becoming fast friends. I'd initially been concerned about how Cody would like sharing the spotlight but was pleased with their camaraderie. I bent to pet them both as Aimee approached.

"Hey, baby. How was your day?" She placed her arms around my waist and tipped up her chin.

There was something about holding her in my arms that soothed me and melted away the tension. We couldn't be more different, but when we were together, like icicles in the sun, our rough edges dissolved until all that was left was shine. After the day I'd had, the sparkle in her eyes and the smile on her face brightened my mood. "We're going out tonight." I kissed the tip of her nose and felt her tense in my arms. I knew the source of her angst: fear of an anxiety attack.

"I don't really want to," she replied. "I'd rather stay home if it's all the same to you."

"Sorry, babe, but we're going out," I insisted. "You need to get out of the house." I tried to calm her fears. "It's nowhere fancy, I promise."

Aimee rested her forehead against my chest as she hooked her thumbs in my belt loops. She inhaled a deep breath. "You're pushy, you know that, right?" She muttered under her breath in a chastising tone. "You never take no for an answer, do you?"

"I'm not pushy," I rebutted. Aimee looked up at me with skeptical eyes. "Well, maybe a little assertive. You can't fault a man for knowing what he wants." An unmistakable undertone of desire saturated my words. I pressed my lips to hers. The kiss was warm. Sweet.

Aimee pressed her chest against mine. "I'm better, you know."

Her statement carried a seductive implication that aroused me. My hands fell on her hips, and I pulled her against me. "Better than what?"

She defined her statement with a fervent kiss. Once she was finished with my mouth her lips traveled down toward my jaw and chin. She kissed each stop along the way. Once she reached my ear, she nipped playfully, tugging the lobe with her teeth. The sensations she aroused made me groan, but I was determined to wait, especially after all she'd been through. If I didn't stop this, I'd have her laid out and naked on the table in sixty seconds. Taking her hand, I pulled it to my lips. I gently kissed and teased her fingertips, silently promising myself we'd continue this later. Then I playfully swatted her butt. "You're deflecting. Go clean up." A dusting of desire coated my words. "We're going to be late."

She wrinkled up her nose, defying me. "You think you're so smart."

My eyebrows rose at her rebellion. "I'm brilliant." I winked at her, feeling mischievous. Sliding my hand down around her waist to her lower back, I pulled her to me. "I got a supermodel to fall in love with me."

Aimee rolled her eyes at me and sauntered into the bedroom. Thirty minutes later, she emerged, wearing a blue cable-knit sweater and jeans.

"You look beautiful."

My compliment pleased her. Although most people were struck by Aimee's looks, I was well aware of how painfully insecure she was. The marks from her assault were fading, but her self-consciousness had not.

"Where are we going?"

"You'll see," I answered. "Get your coat."

Aimee complied and slipped into her jacket. I had put mine on while she was in the bedroom. Taking her hand in mine, I guided her toward the kitchen. She pulled against my side. Confusion accompanied her frown.

"Why are we going this way?"

Her breathing had ramped up. I could tell she was uncomfortable. "You told me whenever you get close to this door, you feel anxious. I don't think it's the door; I think it's because of what happened when you went out the door." I squeezed her hand. "I want to try something. Do you trust me?"

She bit her bottom lip, and I patiently waited as she warred with herself. It broke my heart to see her inner struggle, but for our relationship to move forward, it was imperative that Aimee relinquish the tight leash of fear. She needed to trust I would do anything to keep her safe. After a moment, her shoulders relaxed. A look of resignation appeared in her eyes, and she nodded.

Chapter 57

Aimee

Fear fades beneath a loving heart. I deduced this as Carter led me out the door and across the back of the property. He took me to a place just inside a thicket of evergreens, a clearing I hadn't seen before. He sat me down on an Adirondack that was recently dusted free of snow. I shivered. I couldn't tell if it was from the cold I felt on the inside or the outside of my body. Carter draped a blanket across my lap and over my legs, tucking it in on both sides. Then he kissed me. It was sweet and quick. He turned his attention toward a firepit constructed with stacked stones. It didn't take long for a fire to blaze. As he turned back to me, he handed me a stick, the end of which was honed to a point. Taking a seat beside me, he reached into a cooler beside his chair and took out a hot dog, which he put on the end of my stick with a gloved hand.

"Dinner," he said with a smile.

I shook my head in disbelief and followed his lead as he placed his own stick over the fire. He then slid the cooler between the two of us. As he lifted the lid, I saw a bottle of wine and two glasses.

"You thought of everything."

"I tried." He returned my smile with one of his own and leaned in my direction. "Are you okay?"

I wasn't sure. The woods behind the house didn't seem quite so sinister now that I was with him. I hadn't been back here since the terror, and certainly not in the dark. It was a conscious effort not to summon the terrible memory. Instead, I engaged my senses. The season lent itself to my task, as winter in the mountains held a different charm than that of the ocean. I immersed myself in the beauty, instead of the threatening blackness of recollection. The crisp air was thick with the scents of balsam and cedar. I detected the earthy smell of dirt that had become malleable beneath spots of melted snow. Soon spring would appear, but for now, there were still occasional snowfalls. No crickets chirped, no bullfrogs sang, and no cicadas hummed. Occasionally the sound of crunching could be heard as raccoons and squirrels broke through the thin, icy surface. I could even see little eyes reflected by the firelight.

"A penny for your thoughts." Carter interrupted them.

"I realize I'm not afraid, at least not as much, with you here."

My confession incited a satisfied smile. He retrieved our hot dogs from the fire and handed one to me. "First course. Eat up."

I took it from him, holding it away from my lips while I blew on it to cool the temperature. "I'm glad you did this, but I'm curious as to why."

Carter took a generous bite off the end of his. As the heat registered on his tongue, he blew in and out to ward off the burn. He took a sip of the cold wine and then turned his attention to me. "This is your home, Aimee. There's no room for fear to live here. I wanted to help you take ownership and evict anything that makes you afraid." He looked around. "This was a place of horror. I wanted to help it become a place of peace." His tone grew more serious. "How are you feeling right now?"

I took a moment for introspection as I weighed his words. I looked at the beauty all around me, knowing full well what had been stolen from me just a few hundred yards away. I wanted so badly to become a victor, not a victim. "I love all of this and being here with you makes me want to experience more of it so I can love it more. It's a start, Carter. I'm not sure I'm ready to be out here on my own, but one day I will be." Emotion threatened as I noticed his satisfaction. I turned my attention to my meal and took a bite of my hot dog. "*Mmm*. This is good."

"You like?"

"It's different than I've had before. I like the flavor."

"Does this mean that I can get a supermodel to go camping with me?" His brow arched as he gave me a mischievous grin.

"Maybe."

My answer seemed to please him, and we sat by the fire enjoying the rest of our meal. I loved the contrast of the crisp air and the warm flame. Once I was finished eating, I went to hand him the stick.

His forehead wrinkled. "I told you the hot dog was the first course. You'll need that for dessert."

"Dessert?"

"Seriously? You've never roasted a marshmallow?" He gave me an incredulous look.

I shook my head, indicating I hadn't.

"Really? You've never had a s'more?"

Again, I shook my head.

"Well, you're in for a treat, babe. Let me introduce you to some chocolate, gooey deliciousness."

Carter loaded my stick with a marshmallow and guided my hand a safe distance from the fire. Within minutes, he had the sticky sweetness between two graham crackers and Hershey's chocolate. He held it to my lips.

"Oh, my God!" I savored the first bite. "This is good!"

"Mm-hmm. I know how to show a girl a good time." He comedically raised and lowered his brows while a look of satisfaction shined on his face.

I laughed and coughed simultaneously while looking at him. "Stop! You're going to make me choke!"

He left me to finish the sweet treat while he walked the short distance to the back door. He never moved beyond my line of sight, pausing only long enough to allow Cody and Justice to join us. Having just taken the final mouthful, I scooped up the puppy and placed him on my lap. The playful boy licked my face to taste the remnants of my gooey s'more.

"It won't be long before he doesn't fit on your lap." Carter stroked the puppy's head as I wrapped my arms around Justice and held him close.

"I know. I want to hold him like this for as long as I can."

He sighed. "You'll have to train him, or you'll have a hundred-pound lap dog."

I hugged my puppy again. "I will. I promise."

Not convinced, he shook his head. "Sure, you will."

As the fire died down, the cold crept in. I took the used napkins and bottles to the house while the dogs stayed close on my heels. Once Carter had doused the flame thoroughly, he followed.

While Carter busied himself elsewhere, I fed the dogs and made a pot of decaf coffee. He met me in the living room just as I approached with two cups. Taking one from my hands, he took a seat on the sofa. A fire blazed in the fireplace, revealing what he'd done while I was in the kitchen. I sat beside him, tucking my toes beneath his thigh, while his hand rested on my knee.

"You're in a good mood. What's going on in that pretty little head of yours?"

I gave my shoulders a shrug. "I was thinking about what you said, about this being my home. While we were outside, I kept coming back to that."

"What do you mean?"

"I'm not sure if I can explain it, but every time my thoughts turn to fear or something threatening, I try to stay in the present and remind myself this is my home. At first, it was hard, but the second or third time a bad thought popped up, it got easier."

He smiled. "Good. Hopefully, we can build on that."

Chapter 58

Marisol

Marisol noted Manny's mood. If the scowl on his face was any indication, the information she'd just relayed to him would incite consequences.

"What the hell do you mean, he threatened you?"

Marisol tried her best to appear sullen and depressed, knowing it would compound Manny's ire. "It's exactly as I told you. Carter said no matter your efforts, he'll do everything he can to keep me in here." She smiled inwardly as her well-rehearsed victimization worked its magic. Even though Manny loved dictating orders to her, he didn't appreciate anyone else doing the same. As her husband, he believed it was his right alone. His aggravation was well controlled, discernable only to Marisol. She looked down at her hands, which she folded in bogus submission. "That wasn't all that he said. He also said I would rot in hell." She gave Manny a repentant look. "I told him I was sorry for what happened to his wife and apologized for Marchelle's actions. It was horrible. He said he didn't believe me and that I was a psychopath."

A burst of laughter escaped before the muscles in Manny's neck tightened. Indignation thickened his tone. "You, my dear, are no psychopath. Look at me."

Obediently, Marisol did as Manny commanded.

"Remember this: you answer to no one but me. *¿Comprende?*"

She nodded in response, all the while continuing to act the victim.

"You are getting out of here. I don't give a fuck what Sinclair says."

The forceful decree placated her. Manny would do whatever he could to have Marisol released and prove Carter Sinclair wrong. She bit her lower lip with such intensity it forced a tear. In response, Manny caressed her cheekbone with his thumb while the guard looked the other way.

"No worries, chica. No one threatens my wife. Clearly, this man has no idea who I am or what he's up against. You take heart, my pet. I'll have you out of here soon."

Marisol leaned into Manny's hand, her cheek now resting in his palm. To keep from smiling, she continued to bite her lip until a trickle of blood accompanied her tears. Everything was going according to plan. Touching wasn't permitted between visitors and patients, but Manny had paid the guard to ignore them. When the visit came to an end, he squeezed her hand.

"You listen only to what I say from now on, ¿comprende? I'll will be talking to the attorneys to see if we can expedite the process. In the meantime, you must be a good girl. No outbursts, understand?"

He kissed the back of her hand and then exited the room. As Marisol watched him depart down the hall, satisfaction inched through every cell in her body. Carter Sinclair wanted to play? She and Manny were more than willing. Let the games begin.

Chapter 59

Carter

After the successful dinner in the woods with Aimee, I approached her about venturing further away from the house. I thought it would be hard to convince her, that she would have reservations about going beyond her self-described safe zone, But I was wrong. It appeared Aimee was embracing her newfound confidence. She was a fighter, and I was proud of her.

Without hesitation, she got in the car for the ride into town. I went into the first few stores with her, but then she surprised me further by telling me she wanted to browse by herself. My reaction caused her to burst out laughing. She rolled her eyes as I reminded her I had my cell and it would only take me a minute to get to her if she needed me.

I left the store where Aimee was shopping and went into a little café across the street. Grabbing a Coke, I paid at the register then went outside to find a bench to sit on while waiting for her to call. From there I could keep an eye on Aimee and enjoy the weather. The seat was inconspicuous and at the edge of Main Street. As I looked around at traffic, I spotted the entrance to the cemetery. The one where I'd buried Lacey. It had been awhile since I'd visited her grave. Within a few minutes, I found myself staring down at her headstone.

"Hi Lace. It's been awhile." I ran my hand over the curve at the top of the stone and then down over the name chiseled on its face. "I hope you're somewhere peaceful. But if you aren't, because you feel like you need to stick around to watch over me, I want you to know I'm doing fine."

I looked over at the street. There was no sign of Aimee, so I sat down on top of the grave and leaned back against the stone. "Truth is, I found somebody who makes me want to live again. And another truth is she didn't fall in love with your husband. She fell in love with someone else; the man I became after you died." Emotion bubbled up from inside. My words were true. I was a different man, and I was living a different life than the one I'd had with Lacey. "You see, Lace, your husband died when you did, and I have to apologize to you. I don't think you ever knew the real me. You knew the man who tried to be what you wanted. Now don't get me wrong. I loved you. But you loved a man who tried to be perfect for you. The real me is far from perfect, and Aimee loves that man."

I stood, brushing crumpled leaves from my jeans. "Lace, I'm moving on, and if you've been hanging around for me, I want you to move on too. The only thing that I ask of you is to ask the big man up there to keep an eye on Aimee. She's fighting her way back from some terrible shit. She's getting stronger every day because she's learning to love herself in spite of what happened. Although she'd say otherwise, I don't think she's broken. She helped me to see that about myself, and I'm hoping I can return the favor." I turned, having said my piece. I didn't want to say goodbye, so I didn't. I'd just crossed back over from the cemetery to Main Street when Aimee called.

"What's up, babe? Ready to go home?"

"No, but I am hungry. Want to meet me at the deli?"

I watched her cross the street. "I see you. Grab a table.

I stuck my phone in my pocket and ran to catch up with her. It didn't take long before our food came, and while we ate, Aimee told me about her purchases. I nodded through each description, thrilled to hear her sound so happy, and more than content to let her ramble. When we finished our meal, I excused myself and told her I'd meet her up front.

When I returned, Aimee was nowhere to be found.

I looked out the window and watched, dumbfounded, as she stormed down the tree-lined street, oblivious to people in her way. Her blonde hair blew haphazardly as she raced further away from the deli. She crossed the street without checking for traffic, and a driver slammed on his brakes and honked his horn at her. I tried to make sense of what was happening as I followed her. I wasn't far behind when I saw her approach a tattooed man leaning against a car.

Without warning, Aimee cocked her arm back in an effort to punch him. He grabbed her wrist before she made contact. Not to be deterred, she kicked him. He stood up, still holding onto her wrist and pulling her until she was on tiptoe, nearly suspended in the air. "Let go of me!"

Her order went unexecuted as the man looked down and laughed at her. My feet felt like they were in quicksand as I ran toward them.

"I'll kill you!" As Aimee's voice graduated from a scream to a shriek, the man continued to hold her at bay. I noticed a knife sheathed on his belt. I increased my pace, reaching her just as she was about to kick him again.

"Get your fucking hands off her!" I grabbed her and pulled her behind me. She dodged under my arm and flew at him.

"He's the one. The guy who attacked me. Arrest him!" She pushed him back against the car, and he grinned.

"You're the one who needs arresting, chica. You attacked an unarmed man." He put both hands up in mock surrender.

"That knife on your belt says otherwise, asshole." This time I grabbed Aimee around her waist and held her.

"Why aren't you arresting him?" She glared at me with angry eyes.

I did not doubt the truth of Aimee's accusation, but I knew I couldn't arrest him without evidence. If this was the man who'd attacked her, I wanted to kill him. But first, I had to get Aimee out of there before she did something foolish. "Aimee, I need you to go back to the deli." She shot me a look of fury. "Now! Go!" Reluctantly, she obeyed. Turning on her heel, she stomped back across the street and inside the cafe. Curious onlookers watched her go and then looked to me as I turned my attention to confront the man. My jaw was clenched so tightly I could barely get out the words. "If it was you—if you're the one that hurt her—I'll make sure you never see daylight again."

The man opened his arms, gesturing for me to come at him. It was a silent dare for me to try and do something to him in front of a crowd of witnesses. "You got to prove it first, ése."

Conditioned training cemented me to the spot. If it weren't for that, I would have lunged at the bastard and ripped his throat out. Instead, I gave him a chance to face me man-to-man with no witnesses. "Swallow Falls. Two hours."

Chapter 60

Carter

Aimee didn't speak from the time I collected her at the deli and led her to the car. My mind was focused on Swallow Falls, but I couldn't tell her that. Instead, I attempted composure while she rained fire and brimstone on me like a well-worn preacher.

"What the hell was that, Carter?" Her voice boomed inside the vehicle.

"That was me protecting your ass!"

"I didn't need protecting, damn it! Don't you get it? It was my choice to fight back. I was in the middle of the street! What could he have done to me?"

"The better question is what were you going to do to him in front of all of those witnesses? You could have been arrested for assault. You weren't using common sense, Aimee."

Both of us were breathing like bulls. Indignation was our inhale, while rage was our exhale. As I tried to concentrate on the road, Aimee stared out the window. The air was thick as both of us struggled for composure. Finally, Aimee turned to me. My lips tightened into a thin line as I tried to reign in my fury. I glanced over at her as she spoke. "I don't get you. You tell me to take control of the fear, and then you get pissed off at me when I stand up for myself."

"That wasn't standing up for yourself. You were acting like a crazed lunatic—one with an audience. What the hell was I supposed to do?" My words were accusatory and caustic. Aimee didn't respond but fumed silently as she ruminated on my words. I shook my head in disbelief. "You could have gotten hurt. "That damn temper of yours is gonna get you killed."

"Not in the middle of the street with an audience. He wouldn't have dared." She shot back at me with a heavy dose of sarcasm.

"Bullshit!" My anger escalated, and she jumped. I couldn't believe how shortsighted she was being. "People get killed in the middle of the day and in the middle of the street every day. What makes you think you're immune?"

Her mouth opened in shock, but then she pressed her lips together. She fixed her eyes on the scene outside the window and stayed mute for the remainder of the ride. I took it as a sign I'd made my point. It was just as well. I needed time to prepare.

WE'D BEEN HOME for an hour and still weren't speaking. I went into my office and Aimee disappeared into the bedroom with the dogs. It would work to my advantage if she stayed pissed off at me. That way I wouldn't have to explain what I was doing and where I was going. I retrieved my gun from the safe. My mind was heavy with thoughts of retribution. If I played my cards right, I'd get this prick to admit to Aimee's assault. The only problem was when he did, I'd have to keep myself from killing him. I planned to tape his confession by using the recording function on my cell phone. If the sound quality was clear enough, I might be able to use it to take to the police. It could provide sufficient justification for him to be brought in for questioning or arrested. All I had to do was keep thinking straight and keep my plan on track.

I felt murderous when I recalled the condition she'd been in after her assault. I'd believed her when she said that was the guy who hurt her. The bastard's reaction had exposed him. I had been a cop long enough to know guilt when I saw it. I couldn't distance myself. The images of Aimee's battered and broken body at the hands of this man competed with my sense of right and wrong. I struggled to remain impartial. And for good reason. This was personal. I grabbed my jacket off the chair and flung open my office door.

"I'm going out!" The door slammed behind me.

Chapter 61

Carter

S wallow Falls had just recently begun to thaw. Although it hadn't frozen solid this year, the remnant of the Youghiogheny River that still flowed crashed over the waterfall's edge and echoed among the trees. The spring season was slow in coming. Instead of bright colors, the weather lent itself to a more wintery scene. My breath was visible in the cold, resembling white smoke. I'd gone through this park many times and was familiar with the trail, but even with my experience, the woods held secrets. I'd slipped on a few icy patches that had been puddles under the heat of the sun earlier. I wondered if my nemesis would show up, or if getting here would prove to be too much of a challenge for him.

I reached in my pocket for my flashlight. There

was no light pollution here. Usually the night sky, in combination with the forest, kept the area pitch black. If not for the full moon tonight there would have been total darkness. I leaned against a wooden platform. A tree had cracked and fallen, the victim of a lightning strike. It cast a shadow on the area where I stood and I used the blind spot to my advantage. It had been almost two hours since I'd issued my challenge.

I didn't have to wait long. The crunching sound of boots on the ground alerted me to the man's approach. As he came near, I stepped out of the shadows. My lip raised to a sneer as bitter words fell from my mouth. "So glad you accepted my invitation."

He tried to hide the fact he was startled. I had the hometown advantage tonight. Recovering quickly, he answered me with equal venom. "Wouldn't have missed it, Sinclair."

"Seems you have me at a disadvantage. I don't think I caught your name, friend."

The man revealed his knife, gave it a little twirl, and inclined his head toward me. "My name is the same as my weapon." He turned the knife upside down until the point rested on the tip of his index finger. It pricked the skin. A bubble of blood rose up to meet the steel. He looked at me with hollow, black eyes, void of emotion. When he smiled at me, I was reminded of a shark. "You can call me Blade." He tucked the knife back into its sheath.

"Blade," I spat. "How original."

"So, what do you want to do here, ése? Talk about your pretty little girlfriend? She's such a busybody. Getting into other people's business is going to come back to haunt her one day. You need to tone that bitch down. Teach her who's boss. You got the balls for that, ése?" He grabbed his crotch to emphasize his point.

One word resonated with me. Busybody. It was the same term Marisol had used to describe Aimee. It immediately confirmed for me there was a connection between them. "Leave my girlfriend out of it. This is between you and me." I'd pressed the record button on my phone and could only hope I could goad this punk-ass bastard into revealing himself.

"That's a shame. She's such a pretty thing. And feisty. I like them feisty."

"You're a fuckin' animal. I know it was you who attacked her."

Blade shrugged. "Her skin is like porcelain. She was a piece of art when I finished with her." He winked at me. "You've seen the scars. Tell me they aren't pretty."

"Why her? Did Marisol tell you to do this?" My hand flexed of its own accord, the muscles cramping from the tight fist. If I lost it now, I'd kill the bastard and would never learn the truth.

"If you have a problem with Marisol, maybe you should talk to her."

"I did."

The words seemed to please him. His eyes crinkled

at the corners, the scar above his cheekbone blending with the expression. He pushed himself up from the railing. "Good for you, ése. Good for you. I'm sure her husband will love that. Who knows? He may ask me to pay a visit to both you and your girlfriend. You know? To clear the air." Blade walked toward the platform steps. There was no way I was letting him go.

"You're not leaving here until I get answers."

I blinked, and Blade had the knife in his grip. He gave me an evil look. "You're not getting shit."

I didn't have time to play around. My fist connected with his jaw. It surprised him, and he stumbled. It only took a moment for him to recover. He turned to me, wiping the blood from his mouth with his hand. He glared at me, flicking his tongue out to taste his blood. His smile was malevolent as more blood crept through the crevices between his teeth. He lunged at me. I turned quickly, and all the blade caught was my jacket. I spun back around and grabbed the man's wrist. Applying pressure, I twisted his hand into a reverse and grotesque position. Now his knife was pointed back at him. He crunched the sole of his boot against my knee, and I went down. He lunged at me but slipped on an icy patch on the wood. I never took my eyes off of him.

"You're a dead man, Sinclair." The threat came as he regained his balance.

"Funny, asshole," I raged. "I was going to say the same to you." I took my flashlight and slammed it down onto the back of Blade's hand, dislodging the knife. The platform we were standing on was now coated with a thin sheet of ice. The mist from the falls combined with the night air created a surface slick enough that the knife skittered across the wood and slipped through the railing. Blade's eyes followed it as it fell into the water below. With his attention diverted, I took charge of the moment and bashed the flashlight against his throat. The impact made him fall back onto the railing. He grabbed his throat as he looked up at me, his voice now hoarse from strained vocal cords.

"You won't kill me. You're a cop."

It was a dare. I no longer saw a man; I saw the source of Aimee's nightmares. As he struggled to stand upright, my hands pressed in around his throat. All I had to do was apply the right amount of pressure, and the fragile cartilage would shatter from the force. Blade's eyes bulged as he struggled for air, and the blood leaving his face gave it an ashy hue.

"I *was* a cop, but not anymore!" All the pent-up frustration, anger, and thirst for vengeance inside of me screamed for release. As Blade struggled to dislodge my grip, he managed to remove one of my hands. Undaunted, I slammed my fist into his face, feeling the fragile bones collapse as they broke. Images of Aimee's broken body ran rampant through my mind. My blood heated. An animalistic thirst for vengeance pushed me beyond the boiling point until the life source burned like molten lava in my veins. My vision blurred from the heat, leaving me with a crimson rage. The force of the impact sent both Blade and I spinning. Our feet lost traction as we slid on a coating of icy blood. The drops and sprays that fell to the wooden platform were instantly freezing beneath our feet. As I regained my balance, Blade lost his and reached out to grab me. My law enforcement training compelled me to offer aid, while a desire for retribution taunted me. The opportunity for street justice was at my fingertips.

Chapter 62

Manuel

Blade's phone call had caught Manny by surprise. He'd been about to board his private plane, but the impending confrontation between Blade and Carter Sinclair piqued his interest. He'd changed his plans.

Manny had found the perfect spot. He patted his torso, assuring himself his weapon was secure in the holster across his chest. Confident he was prepared for any scenario, he crossed his arms and leaned against a tree. As the two men fought, Manny had a front row seat for the bloodshed.

Chapter 63

Aimee

I was worried about Carter. He hadn't come home all night. I wasn't afraid for myself, because I knew Cody and Justice would alert me if anyone came near the house. But I'd decided to call Marcus, who now sat, not-so-hidden, in the driveway.

This had been our first fight. I thought about the events of the day and, in retrospect, I knew I'd been foolish to jeopardize my safety. I should never have confronted my attacker. I could only hope Carter hadn't been equally as reckless. My thoughts were scattered and fear filled because I had no idea where he was.

My attempt at sleep was useless. Instead, I sat on the floor at the foot of the bed. The puppy sat in my lap while Cody lay by my side. The warmth of the fire had lulled them to sleep. I wasn't so lucky. Overwrought and overtired, I leaned my head back. *Where is he?*

Tears began to flow, accompanied by torturing thoughts. *What if something happened to him? What if he never comes back?* I fought an impending panic attack like a keg of dynamite waiting for a match. The disturbing thoughts multiplied. They stacked up in my mind like dry tinder. Finally, they were interrupted by the barking of the dogs alerting me to someone coming through the front door. I opened the bedroom door a fraction and found Carter standing just outside of it. I pulled the door open the remainder of the way and flung myself into his arms.

"I'm so sorry. I wasn't thinking. I should never have gone after that guy." He didn't respond. Instead, he remained stiff. I held onto his jacket, burying my face in his chest. "I really am sorry." Tears flowed, a wet mix of regret and relief. As if on cue, both dogs began barking while they ran around us in circles. Carter's arms enveloped me.

"I think they're trying to plead your case."

I leaned back to look up into the face of the man who'd become my anchor. I rubbed my hand against his cheek and sucked in a breath. Tension filled my flesh. He was bloody and bruised—and I knew it was because of me. I mustered every ounce of my composure. "Please tell me you're okay. That you didn't do anything stupid."

Carter didn't answer. Instead he looked at me with

eyes full of love. He pushed my hair back from my shoulder, then tightened his hold on me. "What you did was foolish, Aimee. You risked your safety."

I pulled back. "But you—"

"Stop. Promise me that you'll never be that careless again."

Nervously, I bit my lip and licked the wounds of my pride. "I didn't mean to act like that. I don't know what happened to me. When I saw him, something went off inside of me. It was a knee-jerk reaction."

"One that could have gotten you killed!" Carter took my hand and led me to the sofa. His battered face posed more questions than answers.

"I'll make a complaint. We can have him arrested. I can identify him."

"We may never find him, Aimee."

Discouragement and defeat slumped my shoulders. I tried to look away, but Carter caught my chin with his fingers and forced me to look into his eyes. "I can promise you I'll never let anything happen to you again." His voice thickened with emotion. "I can't lose you. Do you understand that?"

Desperation commanded contact and we crashed into a kiss. Passion birthed from fear and longing connected us. I craved his touch. Carter pulled me to him with such force we melded into one. Lust erupted, filling the air with need. His erection dug into my hip. I wanted him as much as he wanted me. I surrendered.

"I don't want to hurt you." Carter's voice was thick

and low, sending pulses of pleasure through my mind and body.

"Make love to me." My voice was breathy, needy.

Using his lips, his tongue, and his fingers, he touched me. Each connection made me moan with pleasure. We coexisted within a world of our own, sensitive only to our need. We gave and took, sought and found. Nothing mattered but the two of us. Our lovemaking wasn't soft. It was a claiming. We pleasured and punished, pushing our bodies until they bent beneath our will. Passion, more powerful than I could have imagined, erupted between us. Time no longer existed. Carter guided me, moved me, and took me to places I'd never been. I followed willingly like Icarus to the sun. As we drove each other higher and higher, we splintered until all that was left was a million stars. The explosion rocked the universe and made the cosmos burn bright with the evidence of our love for one another.

Chapter 64

Aimee

I'd fallen into a hard sleep. When I woke up, I found Carter in the living room watching television. I leaned over the sofa and planted a kiss on his cheek. He barely moved. I followed his gaze to a live news report from the Clifton T. Perkins Hospital Center. The reporter, a perky brunette, stood at the edge of the crowd. She rested a finger against the bud in her ear as she struggled to hear over the noise, yet she looked directly into the camera to deliver the news.

"We're live here as fashion model Marisol Franzi, who now goes by her married name, Marisol Vallega, is being released from the Perkins facility. Officials report that Mrs. Vallega was wrongfully charged with the attempted murder of Aria Cole-Sinclair. This error resulted in an extended stay at the hospital…"

Anger rose within me. "They're letting her go?"

Carter said nothing. The camera pivoted away from the reporter in time to focus on Marisol. She was holding the hand of a handsome Latino man as they walked down the steps of the building. Reporters swarmed like bees. They were lost in a sea of microphones and cameras. Marisol was barely a step behind the man, shielding her face against the onslaught of hundreds of flashes. The reporters clamored for their attention until the man stopped to answer a question.

"Mr. Vallega, could you please tell us how you feel about your wife's release?"

The man on the screen stood tall and leisurely reached to a button on his suit jacket.

"I feel justice has been served. My wife was wrongfully accused of a crime she didn't commit. I commend the judicial system for discovering that fact."

"Sir, this question is for Ms. Franzi. How do you respond to those who are convinced of your guilt?"

"I would tell them they're wrong."

As Marisol responded, Carter snorted and muttered something obscene under his breath. Marisol maintained her composure, smiling for the cameras.

"It is my hope I'll be an example for those that suffer from mental illness. With the right medication and treatment, one can live a normal life. That's what I hope to do with my husband. I'm grateful to the doctors and counselors who discovered the imbalance that caused the fluctuations in my behavior. I would urge those who suffer as I did to seek help."

The paparazzi shouted a myriad of questions as Marisol and her husband made their way to a waiting car. They were almost there when one of the questions halted their steps.

"Mr. Vallega, how do you respond to the rumors of your criminal connections, and that you used your influence to have your wife released?"

Manny scanned the crowd. "Who asked that question?"

His demand silenced the throng. I was spellbound but heard a growl from under Carter's breath. I flicked my gaze from him to the television screen. As the camera zeroed in on a reporter, Manny glared at him. The man was short, partially bald, and wore a crooked tie. Manny motioned with his hand for the man to come closer. As he made his way through the sea of people, Marisol exchanged a look with her husband. Manny then zeroed in on his face.

"I'd like to respond to your question. My wife's release was secured by the legal system of the United States. However, if there was ever a reason for me to entertain illegal methods to secure the release of an innocent woman, I'm certain I wouldn't be the first husband wanting to protect his wife. As far as criminal ties, I can assure you I have none."

Dismissing the crowd, Manny took Marisol's hand and helped her into the car. The camera panned back to the woman reporter, who adjusted her grip on the microphone. "As you've just seen..."

"That's bullshit!" Carter yelled at the screen.

I couldn't have agreed more. I placed a comforting hand on his shoulder. "What are you going to do?" We were both rooted in quiet thought as the next news segment began. I felt my eyes widen. "Oh my God, Carter. Look!"

The TV showed a picture of the man who'd attacked me. A view of Swallow Falls rested above the caption "Unidentified Man Found Dead in Swallow Falls State Park." Carter's expression revealed nothing. I looked at the bruises on his face and knuckles. Questions began to form in my mind. *What happened last night? Was Carter involved in the man's death?* As I searched his face for answers, all I saw was the face of the man who loved me.

Chapter 65

Aimee

To some, it wouldn't seem like a lofty goal, but to anyone who's suffered from anxiety attacks, it was a high aspiration. Every day, I moved closer to the kitchen door. That door was my Goliath. Every day, I worked to overcome the fear. I had to get the message to my mind and body that I would survive if I walked through that door to the outside on my own.

My lilac bush. I imagined what it would be like to breathe in its fragrance on my own terms. I wanted to hold the lavender flowers in my hands and sink my nose deep into the petals. The only thing stopping me was me. I didn't take my eyes off that bush. If I did, the courage that was slowly bubbling to the surface would run dry. I looked down at Cody. "It's now or never."

The door rendered a familiar squeak as I opened it

wide. I flew down the steps. The act proved to be both exhilarating and terrifying. I had to keep going. If I stopped for one instant, I'd retreat in despair. I could feel, taste, and smell freedom. I tried to force myself to concentrate on the beauty of the mountains instead of my fear. I inhaled the mixture of scents and listened to the crush of needles and pinecones beneath my feet. Although anxiety rushed up and adrenaline crushed my chest, I pushed them down and refused to become their victim. I continued to take brave steps, while basking in the sunlight as it sliced through the trees. I didn't stop until I reached the river bank. The muscles in my legs burned from the strain of my excursion. I climbed onto a huge rock and stood tall as I soaked in my victory. It might have been only a first step, but it was a big one. I would live a happy life. I would overcome.

This was *my* moment.

Keep reading for a preview of the next title in the Imperfection Series.

No Perfect Secret (Book Four)

Preview

No Perfect Secret

An Imperfection Series Novel

Book 3

DD Lorenzo

Chapter 1

Paige

The heat is visible as it rises from the Vegas strip. It wiggles like a black-tar genie from a lamp. I stand in one of my favorite spots—the overpass between the New York-New York and the MGM Grand hotels. It embraces me where I am, nestling me in its warmth like a long, lost lover. Each time I come to Vegas I find myself in the same place. It's become as much a habit as breathing. Here is where I decompress. Like most people, my life is filled with stress from work and home. Good stress, but stress nonetheless. The hot embrace of the city caresses my skin and strokes me day by day until my body responds and the tension releases. Most people think it's hot here; I prefer to believe the energy makes me glow as the pulsing beat deepens our affair.

To most people, it seems I have it all together. I'm financially independent and have all the material things everyone hopes for. The truth is, it's all an illusion. I've always fancied myself a mistress of deception, and Vegas and I are the same in that, we are imposters. Each presents an alluring outer shell while disguising our true intent—we both want to sell you something.

I look out at hotels—concrete behemoths. They surround me with their architectural magnificence. The distinction of the respective properties pours itself into my senses until I'm esthetically drunk. With their open arms they break my resistance, and I'm no longer alone.

Each building is unique, and their careful alignment makes them stand as sentries in the world in which I languish. I've been coming here for so long I've witnessed many of their births. Masculine steel mates with feminine glass, and, together, they deliver the most sensuous bodies of architecture. This is a city dedicated to self-indulgence and it invites me to be one of its disappearing souls. Vegas and I are kindred spirits, sharing a cliché, appearances can be deceiving.

Anything can happen in Las Vegas, and I embrace its unpredictability. This place is my mecca; my holy ground. I left the church of due diligence behind to find peaceful obscurity in the land of smoke and mirrors. Vegas is the temptress that floods my soul, and I am happy to be in her arms again. Somewhere between the east coast and the dessert, at thirty-five thousand feet in the air, I left behind my constant introspection and relentless self-examination and traded it for sinful anonymity. With each complimentary and carefully measured airline cocktail, I left behind the woman inside of me who guards and approves everything I do. On any normal day I check myself from appetite to asshole, but not here in Sin City. As my desires remain incognito amongst hundreds of tourists, Vegas and I share another trait, we were both opportunists.

I take in a deep breath, inhaling toxic fumes of car exhaust mixed with particles of dust carried on the hot dessert breeze. This trip is both business and pleasure. If I focus on the business, the pleasure will be a sweet indulgence. A balance of the two. That's my purpose.

Chapter 2

Paige

The Realtors Conference and Expo were being held in Vegas, and I had to dedicate a portion of my time toward business in order to write off the trip. Necessary but boring. Most times the networking required was tolerable, but lately I'd been working my ass off and I needed the break. That's where my friend Elizabeth came in.

Elizabeth Santiago was my second best friend. The number one spot belonged to my lifelong friend, Aria Sinclair. By choice, I didn't have many. I'm private. Most people read me as shy. Though I was an introvert by nature, in my professional life I was a masterful extrovert. I could sell you anything. I kept company with a small circle of people, but, because of the social aspect of my business, there were some who believed themselves to be my friends, but, in reality, I was still deciding if they'd make the cut. Aria and Elizabeth were the two people who'd proven their friendship and loyalty to me. I trusted them with anything.

I'd known Aria since childhood. We'd met at the beach during our families' respective vacations. Elizabeth was a more recent friend. We'd met several years ago. She was much more an extrovert than me. A gorgeous Latina who I would've described as a serious party person. She's seen me at my worst! But, then, Vegas was known for bringing that trait out in people.

It was during a night of partying, while I was puking my guts out in a nightclub bathroom, that Elizabeth handed me cool, wet paper towels under the stall door. Though I didn't know her, it was a true bonding moment. She stayed with me in the bathroom, talking to me while I emptied the contents of my stomach. She resided in Vegas and had nowhere special to be that night. She took care of me, nursed me with a big glass of ginger ale and Angostura, insisting the concoction would settle my stomach. As she walked me back to my hotel room, she handed me her business card, all the while making me swear to call her the next day. The next morning I was terribly hung-over but I respected her request and called her. She insisted we meet for lunch, and somewhere between our iced teas and salads, my gut told me her sincerity was genuine. We've been friends ever since.

Today I was late. I hurried down the Strip to the

Hard Rock Hotel to meet Liz for lunch in a quirky little restaurant there called the Pink Taco. As I approached the hostess I gave her a quick description of Elizabeth. After telling me she hadn't yet arrived she led me to a table. I wasted no time getting into my Sin City frame of mind. The waitress came over to my table a moment later.

"Mojito." I paused, then smiled at her. "Actually, make that two."

"Sure thing."

As she went to get my drinks, I positioned myself so I could see Liz when she came through the door. Of course, while I waited I couldn't help but eavesdrop. It was a talent of mine that had proven to be most beneficial. I'd honed the skill over time. Bits and pieces of conversations wafted through the air and traveled to my ears. I dissected information as I enjoyed my drink. I'd learned much about people over the years by breaking down tone and verbiage, and had learned most people had an agenda, and most were opportunists—just like me. This ability drove my success while showing homes to prospective buyers. I'd peel away their kind words to reveal what they really loved or hated about a property. But, now, I needed a vacation.

My head was filled with many loads of bullshit, and I needed a place to dump the old information so my mind would be fresh when I returned. The best cure for what ailed me was alcohol. I rarely indulged at home because I was always working but had more than my fill while on vacation. I was just about ready to order my third drink when Liz came rushing toward our table.

"Where have you been?" I held up my empty glass. "I'm two ahead of you!"

"Sorry, chica! The traffic was terrible!" She seemed a bit frazzled but wasted no time launching herself at me to give me a big hug. "I missed you, Paige!"

"Yeah, yeah." My tone was very blasé. "I haven't been here *too* long," I said, rolling my eyes at her.

Our waitress returned to the table. "Whatever she's having? I'll have the same." Elizabeth pointed to my empty glass, a smartass smirk on her lips. "And she'll have another."

"You're going to get me drunk, Liz. I haven't eaten yet."

"So, we'll fix that! As soon as she comes back with the drinks, we'll order food." Her bossy but animated expression matched the excitement in her voice. Elizabeth had a way of infecting people with delight. I liked her carefree personality more than I cared to admit.

"I am happy to see you!" I said, placing my elbows on the table and leaning in so she could hear me above the chatter. "What've you been up to?"

"You're very chipper!" She grinned, avoiding my question, and circled her finger over the top of my two empty glasses. "My guess is this is why you're in such a good mood." Sarcasm dripped off the words as she playfully winked at me.

"I needed something to take the edge off." I shrugged and straightened my spine. "All I've been doing is working." I inhaled dramatically and then let out a sigh. "You know all that shit in the paper about Marisol and her husband?" Liz nodded in reply, and I continued.

"Well, all of her real estate transactions were done through me and my company. It was a real mess. We bought properties for her company—which I didn't know was her company—and then as soon as her husband came into the picture he wanted them all sold, immediately. Those two are evil. Pure evil."

A twinge of anger sparkled in her eyes. "When I saw that on the news I just knew it had something to do with your company!" She leaned in and lowered her voice. "Was this connected with Marisol's attack on Aria? When Marisol's sister was killed?"

"Yes." Though I spoke in a low tone there was a hard edge in my voice. "It's all connected."

"That's what I thought! The paper didn't give all the details, but I remembered you saying that's how you wound up in the hospital. I still can't believe you look as good as you do! Shit! You went through a glass window! It's a wonder you didn't need some plastic work." Her eyes widened, and her head bobbed up and down, as she looked me over.

I laughed at her. "Now, how do you know I didn't have work done?"

"Did you?"

I laughed at her question, holding my glass high to toast that statement. "I'll never tell."

She grew more serious. "How is Aria? You said she was coming along really well."

Her concern touched me, considerably lightening my mood. "She's great. Wonderful as a matter of fact. She and Declan are expecting a baby. I'm going to be an aunt!"

"No! Really?" She squealed. Her excitement nearly matched my own.

"Really. She also asked me to be godmother." I recalled the day Aria asked me to stand for her daughter. "She's been my best friend forever—more like a sister really."

"You two have known each other a long time, haven't you?" Her eyes softened, as did my heart.

"Yes. Since we were kids. Aria's family and mine vacationed in Ocean City every summer for two weeks. Her family owned two apartments, the Skipjack and the Rosemont. We always stayed in the same building—her family in the upper apartment and ours in the lower one. I was shy, but Aria was very outgoing. I guess we were so opposite we attracted." I took a sip of my drink. "Looking back, I'm sure Aria's parents worried about her. We'd be playing on the beach while our parents caught up. She'd walk up and talk to anyone and everyone. She offered hugs to complete strangers without reservation. Scary." I shook my head. "There's no way she'll let her child do that. It's too crazy these days." I paused for a moment. "I think that if it weren't for Aria I might not have had any friends growing up." I reached over, patting Liz's hand. "Now, I'm lucky enough to have two of them."

The melancholy moment passed quickly. I didn't want to dwell on the past. Monsters lived there.

To keep reading, purchase a copy from your favorite online retailer today!
No Perfect Secret (Book Four)

Note from the Author

Like what you've read? Please consider leaving a
review!

You are cordially invited to be a part of my close circle
of friends. You will be privy to exclusive excerpts,
deleted scenes, and did I mention gifts and prizes? Join
my mailing list at www.ddlorenzo.net

I want to thank you for purchasing and reading my
stories, and I value your opinion. I depend on your
review. Without them I have no way of knowing if you
would like to meet more of my characters and delve
deeper into my world. If you would be so kind, please
leave your thoughts with the retailer of your purchase
and at bit.ly/GoodreadsDDLorenzo.com

DD Lorenzo is an award-winning author of Women's Fiction and Romantic Suspense novels. She loves coffee, long lunches with good friends, and fresh flowers to balance her obsession with anti-heroes. You can find her most days plotting and planning her character's lives from her beach house on the Delaware shore.

To stay updated with DD's books, please visit her website at www.ddlorenzo.com and sign up for her newsletter. Want the inside scoop? Join DD's reader group, DDs Diamonds, at www.facebook.com/groups/ddsdiamonds

Stay connected with DD

Website:
www.ddlorenzo.net

facebook.com/ddlorenzo.author

x.com/ddlorenzobooks

instagram.com/ddlorenzobooks

pinterest.com/ddlorenzo

bookbub.com/authors/d-d-lorenzo

amazon.com/DD-Lorenzo/e/B00GA5ARJ8

goodreads.com/D_D_Lorenzo

Other Titles by DD Lorenzo

The IMPERFECTION Series

No Perfect Man

No Perfect Time

No Perfect Couple

No Perfect Secret

No Perfect Woman

No Perfect Beginning: An IMPERFECTION Series Prequel

The ROCK HILLS Series

Boundless Hearts: A ROCK HILLS Origin Story

Bone Dust: Rock Hills Book 1

Standalones

Indiscretion

(An Aleatha Romig's Infidelity World Novella)

Heels, Rhymes, & Nursery Crimes

(A multi-author series)

Twinkle, Twinkle Little Star: Fragile Flower to Femme Fatale

www.ingramcontent.com/pod-product-compliance
Lightning Source LLC
Chambersburg PA
CBHW031740180726
48283CB00005B/1592